Catching Feelings

JOANNE ROSE

*To my husband, Alex. Thank you for being with me through
it all and cheering me on when I wanted to give up.
I couldn't have done it without you.*

Disclaimers/ Trigger Warnings / Content Warning:

This story has been written with a mature audience in mind and therefore contains adult and sexual themes. Readers should exercise personal discretion and prioritize their well-being when deciding whether this content is right for them.

Chapter One

Tahlia

HONESTLY, I WOULD DIE happy if I never had to hear the screech of packing tape again.

As I squatted down to pick up the box filled with all the random pieces from my home, I decided I needed to start going to the gym. My back was sorer than it should be from moving a few boxes.

I stretched my arms above my head, pretending that would fix it.

"This place looks strange." Claire waved a hand around as she walked out of the bathroom with cleaning supplies. "I haven't seen it this empty since ... well, since you moved in." Claire was one of my closest friends in Boston. We met in English class in middle school and had been friends ever since.

Even though she had just been scrubbing the shower, Claire still somehow looked so pulled together. Her dark brown hair was clipped up at the back of her head, her cheeks rosy, and somehow, she was still smiling—I never smiled after cleaning the bathroom. She also managed not to get anything on her black leggings and crop-top set. Again, I wouldn't be so lucky.

Sighing, I forced a smile, too many emotions running through me to know how I was feeling. "I've been here a long time." I still remembered how it felt to move in here, on my own for the first time at only eighteen.

Living alone had been an adjustment—but in a good way. After my parents made it impossible to keep living with them, I'd been desperately applying for places, and this was the only one I was accepted for. The water pressure never held, the temperature in the shower would change suddenly from hot to ice-cold, the doors got stuck and wouldn't open. It wasn't flashy, but it was perfect for me—an apartment not too far out of the city, one bedroom, but with a larger living area and bathroom. There was even a gym in the building, not that I'd ever used it.

Nothing in my life up to that point compared to the utter freedom I felt. I could decorate however I liked, do whatever I wanted with my time, just exist peacefully without interference. There was nothing like it.

Claire helped me move back then as well, unpacking the small amount of stuff I had into a practically empty apartment. I didn't have a lot of money saved at that point, so she even helped me buy the shittest couch—the only one I could afford, even with her help.

It was small, and not very comfortable, but I refused to get a second-hand couch; there were always questionable stains I couldn't stop myself imagining gross origin stories for. So, I had to get my couch new, and as much as I hated it, I was so proud of myself. In the end, I found it so hard to sell when Tim and I bought a new one.

"I still remember that painting you bought when you first moved in. What was it even supposed to be?" Claire laughed.

"It was an interpretive piece!" I shook my head, mock-offended, as a small laugh bubbled out. It was a lovely example of representationalism, if you appreciated that kind of thing, which Claire readily admitted she didn't.

"I don't know about that. Thank God Tim had better taste than you." She bumped her shoulder into mine, taking her bottle of water from her bag and having a big sip.

I ended up getting rid of the piece when Tim moved in, but I kind of wished I had kept it. It was strange when all of a sudden the apartment wasn't just mine. I'd been living there for years on my own, and then he lived there too—which I loved, don't get me wrong. But it was another adjustment, including compromising on the decor.

But I really didn't mind; it meant I got to be around Tim more. And I'd loved it.

As I looked around at the empty walls, the rooms with no furniture once again, my emotions were hard to interpret. Six years. I'd lived here for six years. I would miss this place, but I couldn't stay. As much as it held so many special memories, the first taste of my independence, my freedom ... he was everywhere. I couldn't grab a snack from the kitchen without being reminded of him. It hurt so bad, like my heart was breaking all over again every time. I didn't need that.

Claire waved her hand in front of my face. "Hello, Major Tom. Are you excited to meet Jeremy?"

I looked up, confused, until I realized what she was talking about. "Oh, yeah, a bit nervous."

"It would be a bit odd if you weren't nervous." She laughed. "He's great, though. I think you'll love living with him."

"I hope so." I tried to sound positive, feeling emotional at the prospect of leaving, living with someone else, starting my life over. I was excited to do something different. Making such a big change was not something I'd really ever thought I would do.

Florida was the last place I had expected to move. But a job opportunity came up that I thought sounded alright, and it was near an art program I had been wanting to do. It just felt right.

The intercom buzzed, pulling me from my thoughts.

"Oh, I forgot to tell you." Claire beat me to the intercom, buzzing up whoever it was. "I ordered some takeout. I'm starving, surely you are too, after all this." Claire gestured to the empty apartment.

My stomach chose that moment to growl, like it was agreeing with Claire. We both laughed as we waited for the delivery person to bring the food up.

There was no table, so we would either eat standing at the kitchen bench or sitting somewhere on the floor. Just like we did the first night

I moved in. Claire and I had sat on the floor in the living room eating crappy pizza, debating how I should decorate.

When Claire opened the door following a knock, it wasn't a delivery driver on the other side. Instead, I was caught off guard by two familiar faces.

At the door, holding bags of takeout that made my stomach audibly growl again, were Owen, Tim's best friend, and his girlfriend, Nat.

"What are you two doing here?" I reached past Claire and pulled them each into a hug.

Owen gave a boyish smile, clearly pleased they'd managed to surprise me, and returned my hug before making his way to the living room and sitting on the floor. His curly blond hair formed a halo around his head in the stark light bouncing off the white walls as he lowered himself down with a groan. "You didn't think you were going to leave town and not say goodbye, did you?" he joked. At least I thought it was a joke.

Nat gave me a tight squeeze then followed suit, sitting cross-legged and unpacking the food.

I was planning on saying goodbye to them, but life had been so hectic since I got the job and only had a few weeks to move my life across the country.

"I invited them," Claire whispered as she attempted to close the front door.

It got slightly stuck, so I waved her off and shoved my shoulder against it to get it to close. I wouldn't miss that. My landlord didn't care to have it fixed, and we'd given up trying. The rent was cheap, and Tim and I were planning to buy a house once we got married anyway.

That obviously wasn't going to happen now.

"I thought it would be nice to have one last get together before you leave," Claire said as I turned back to her. Nodding, I pulled her under my arm. The fact I wouldn't be living in the same city as her made my heart squeeze. What would I do without her?

Claire cared a lot about other people. She was always there for me when I needed her— like today, helping me pack up instead of enjoying her weekend. And now she'd organized this little dinner for me.

"Come eat before it gets cold," Owen called as he popped the lids off containers.

"Oh, yum." The smell of the Indian food had my mouth watering. There was a ridiculously large pile of naan bread along with butter chicken, palak paneer, lamb korma, and so much rice. I didn't know what to have first, but eventually piled the deliciousness in a plastic bowl Owen and Nat had brought.

We chatted about a lot of nothing while we ate, but something felt off. We never hung out as the four of us; there was a fifth person missing. It just didn't feel right.

"Tell us a bit more about this job you're starting." Nat smiled, tearing off some of the buttery naan bread and dipping it into her bowl.

"I'm going to be working at an airline, as a personal assistant in the office." That was the extent that I really knew about the job. It seemed like a pretty generic assistant job, but it was with a big company with good opportunities, so would be a good place to start. Nat's face screwed up a little bit before she covered it with a smile. "I know it's not the most glamorous sounding job, but it pays well enough, the work they do sounds interesting. I should get to meet lots of people, which will help in a new city."

"Will you get free flights? 'Cause fuck, that would be good," Owen said in between mouthfuls of food. I had no idea how he wasn't choking.

"Owen." Nat shoved his shoulder, giving him a pointed look.

He shrugged. "What?"

I chuckled, shaking my head. "I don't think I'll get free flights."

"Man, that sucks." The room went silent as we all finished the food, the heaviness I felt earlier hanging around.

I would miss this city—the people in this room most of all. Was I making the right move? I couldn't help but keep second-guessing myself.

Maybe this wasn't the right path. Maybe I was supposed to stay in Boston, start a new life here?

"What's going on in there?" I looked up to find Claire looking at me, her eyes narrowed. She could read me like a book.

"I um ..." My throat felt like it had closed up, the emotion taking over. I cleared my throat, trying to hide my sadness with a small smile. "I'm going to miss this." My voice was quiet, so quiet I wasn't sure if I had said it in my head or actually voiced it. But everyone in the room looked at me, their expressions matching my own.

"Trust me, I wish you weren't leaving." Claire scooted in closer to me, pulling me into her side. "But you have to do this." She lowered her voice, so that only I could hear her. "You need to go. This isn't the place for you anymore."

"But what if I regret it?"

Claire's soft smile and eyes that looked a bit watery made me feel a bit calmer, my mind a bit clearer. "I don't think you will, but if you do, you can always come back." Her voice matched mine from only a few moments earlier, croaky and coated with emotion. "It's going to be hard—for you, for me—but I know you, and you have to do this. When you told me you were going, the excitement in your eyes confirmed for me that this was what you were supposed to do."

"I am excited, it's just ... such a big change."

"You've got this, girl. You know I'm just a phone call away." She pulled me in for a tighter hug. I couldn't help but let a tear roll down my cheek and drop onto her shoulder. "Tim would want you to move on, do something you want to do, something you'll love and be happy."

More tears dropped involuntarily at that. I had no idea how she basically read my mind and knew exactly what needed to be said. I guess good friends just know.

We pulled away, our faces streaked with tears. Nat and Owen were chatting away as they cleaned up the food, giving us the space we needed. The room didn't feel as heavy after that.

Chapter Two

Orion

THE WAY THE LIGHT was pouring in through the balcony doors onto the marble countertops was a beautiful sight I wasn't used to. By this time of day I was usually at work. I sipped my coffee, appreciating my apartment, all that it had to offer, but it didn't work for a dad. It was in the city, near my office, with lots of open space. But it also had a small wine cellar which was too easily accessible for a kid, and stunning views from the balcony—which was definitely not easy to childproof. It was the sort of apartment you expected a high-level executive to live in, not a single dad.

Sophia: Be there soon.

Speaking of. I was so excited to spend the day with my daughter, Grace, but as I surveyed the view of the rest of the apartment from my kitchen, I knew we would be going somewhere else. I washed my coffee mug and made my way to the bathroom to get ready for the day.

The bathroom was massive, designed for a couple, with its double shower, a double basin, and a toilet hidden behind a wall. That could be good if you had a partner and didn't want to go to the bathroom in front of them. I didn't have that issue.

After tossing my clothes and missing the basket, I turned on the shower and stepped under the spray. It only took about two seconds to heat up, being instant electric hot water. Some perks never got old.

What would my life have been like had I not started as a baggage handler at Florida Airlines all those years ago? I knew where I wanted to be, what I wanted to do, so it was hard starting at the bottom. But fifteen years later, and I was almost at the top—almost.

But then Grace came along. Now, all I thought about was if it was really worth the long-as-fuck days, missing her dance performances, reading to her at nighttime. She was only five years old, and I already felt like I had missed so much of her life.

Thankfully, Sophia and I were good friends before we got together, so we were able to make it work after we broke up. I could see Grace as much as I wanted—well, more like when I could. My job made that hard sometimes. I had been at Florida Airlines for a long time, worked my way up the ladder and made a difference. I couldn't just walk away. I'd sacrificed everything: a relationship with Sophia, and maybe even my relationship with Grace. But if I left, it would be a slap in the face to them. Knowing that I had let them down time and time again, not been there for them when they needed me, working for the career I wanted, to suddenly just give it all up like it was nothing. I couldn't fathom it.

As I dressed, there was a knock at my door. I quickly buttoned my shirt as I ran down and opened it.

"Daddy!" Grace exclaimed as she rushed at me for a hug. The strawberry shampoo smell of her hair overtook my senses as I pulled her in tight.

Even though I had been looking forward to this day for weeks, I wasn't sure what to do. I always felt like I needed to do something over the top, take her to the best places in the world. But those days were fun and all, but also exhausting. Sometimes I just wanted to spend time with her doing normal kid stuff, like going to the park or ... fuck, I don't know, taking her shopping? Grace never seemed to care what we did, as long as she was with me. She was a Daddy's girl—it killed Sophia, but I lapped it up.

"My princess, how are you?" I pulled back from the hug and gave Grace a big kiss.

"Good." Grace ran off into the house, putting her things in her room. I had baby-proofed my place as much as I could, but Grace was five now. Baby-proofing really couldn't do much when this was, as Sophia called it, my 'bachelor pad'.

I needed to find a way to make it better or move somewhere so I could have Grace stay with me more. She didn't stay here much, but I still made sure she had her own space, decorated how she wanted. The theme was *Frozen*—her absolute favorite.

But I was also at work a lot, so a new house wouldn't be the big fix I'd want it to be. More like a shitty Band-Aid.

"Thanks for dropping her off today." I smiled at Sophia. "Do you want to come in for a coffee?"

"No, I've got to get going. You two have fun." Sophia headed back to her car with a wave.

"What do you want to do, Gracie?" I called out, knowing it would cause her to leave her room and come back to me. She jumped into my arms for a hug, snuggling her head to my chest.

"Mmm." Grace pulled back from the cuddle and rubbed her chin like she was deep in thought. "The park!" I held back my sigh of relief.

"Oh, that will be fun!" I didn't know what I would have done if she had suggested Disney World or something.

"Frozen!" she added. I should have expected she would want to watch *Frozen*. I was so sick of that movie, but I would watch it with her if that's what she wanted.

"Let's go then, princess!" I took Grace's hand as we headed off to the park.

We ended up driving to her favorite park, closer to Sophia's place. There weren't any good ones near my place. There was also conveniently an ice cream shop right around the corner from this one.

As soon as Grace was out of her car seat, she bolted to the playground.

Typical.

I quickly grabbed the snack bag, which I made sure to always bring after an incident one time where I'd forgotten. She'd thrown a tantrum because she wanted carrot sticks. *Carrot sticks?* It still boggled me, but I didn't risk it anymore.

I followed Grace, who had already positioned herself on a swing and was now waiting for me to push it. She didn't have a care in the world for the other kids who were running around. I didn't mind them, the careless fun they had was enviable. I wished I could be like that now.

The other parents bothered me, though, particularly the moms. It was like I was a magnet for unwanted attention. As soon as they found out I was single, they became even more interested, some offering to set me up with a friend or even shooting their shot themselves. Sometimes I wondered if they forgot they were in a park with their kids, not trying to pick up at a bar.

A couple of moms looked at me, smiling, their eyes showing interest in talking to me. I smiled back to be polite but turned completely away from them, concentrating on Grace.

"You ready?"

Grace nodded excitedly in her swing. "Daddy?" Grace asked as I started to push her.

"Yes, princess?"

"Can we get ice cream after this?"

I chuckled. I'd known full well she was going to ask this at some point. "What about *Frozen*?" I joked.

"You know we can do both." She giggled. There was no tricking this kid into ice cream or *Frozen*. It was always both.

Eventually, Grace was bored of the swing and took off to the slide and soon started playing with another kid. It wasn't super common for her to start talking to other random kids, but this particular kid came here often enough that I sort of recognized them. Maybe they went to the same daycare as Grace, but I couldn't be sure.

I quickly checked my phone, confident Grace was fine.

Henry: Drinks tonight? I think I have someone you would like. I could set you up.

I shook my head, laughing at his persistence. Henry had been my best friend since I was a little kid. He knew me well enough to know that I didn't want a relationship. When would I have the time for that?

Me: Fuck off.

Henry: So no drinks?

Me: Can't. It's a Grace day. And it's a definite fuck no to you setting me up.

Henry: You're no fun. I just want to live through you, the single, hot bachelor. Rich bachelor, I should say.

Me: I am none of those things.

Henry: Sure. Ry, sure.

"Daddy, I'm tired." Grace's pigtails drooped as she dragged her booted toes across the ground with each step toward me. The sound of her sparkly boots bumping over the rubber tiles set my teeth on edge. We had barely been here thirty minutes, but I wasn't surprised. She hadn't stopped moving in all the time we had been here.

"Want to go home?" I passed her some water to drink and she nodded. "Too tired for ice cream?"

Grace's face perked up. "No, I am awake. Ice cream!" I laughed, knowing I could never say no to this kid.

My phone had started ringing in my pocket.

"Oh, one second, Gracie." I assumed it would be Henry, calling to talk more about this woman he wanted to set me up with.

It wasn't.

It was work.

I was tempted not to answer. It was my day off, for fuck's sake. I was with my daughter.

But what if it's urgent?

Fuck.

"John." I really shouldn't have answered. This was the first day I'd booked off during the week all year. But he was my boss. It had to be important.

"Hello, Orion," John, the CEO of Florida Airlines, responded casually.

"What's going on?" I looked at Gracie, sitting patiently next to me swinging her legs back and forth, waiting to get ice cream. "I'm with my daughter, is everything alright?"

"I need you in the office."

My heart sank, even though I'd known that was likely where this conversation was going.

"Do you really need me to come in? I'm only out for today." As much as I liked my job and was proud of what I accomplished, I really just wanted one day to spend with Gracie. Just one day. She smiled up at me, somehow not tired of waiting for me to get off the phone. The thought of disappointing her broke my heart.

There was muffled noise in the background of the call. Probably Rachel telling John he was late for another meeting. He was never on time—not a great look for the CEO, but it wasn't really my business to say anything. "Yes, it's urgent."

I wanted to argue, fight, scream, but I knew it would get me nowhere. "And it definitely can't wait until tomorrow?"

"Orion." It was like I could feel him shaking his head at me, popping mints in his mouth, rolling his eyes. "Missing one day with your kid really isn't a big deal."

He wouldn't know. He didn't care about family, not like I did.

There was a niggling thought at the back of my mind that I tried but failed to ignore. What could be so urgent? It was early morning, I was about to treat my daughter to ice cream at an hour I was sure Sophia wouldn't be the biggest fan of, but it would score me some points. Shit came up all the time. It was the life I lived as Chief Operating Officer, putting out fire after fire. But the workday really had barely started.

"Daddy." Grace pulled on my sleeve. "Can we get ice cream now?"

I pulled the phone away from my ear. "Sorry, princess. Just give me a few more minutes." I ruffled her hair before going back to the call.

"I'll come in." I hated myself the second those word came out of my mouth. I'd picked work. Again. "I will be taking this time off in the coming weeks, though."

"Sure, whatever." He'd already lost interest, paying attention to something that wasn't our conversation. "See you soon, Orion."

Fuck, he pissed me off sometimes. He just didn't get what he was doing to my personal life.

Or maybe he did.

I tried to ignore that thought, wishing I had left my phone at home, or not noticed it ringing. John knew that I'd come in because I always did. It had better be worth it.

This job was seriously making me worry about my relationship with my daughter. I was struggling bad to find a balance, and I desperately needed to. She may have only been five, but there was only so many chances she would give me. Sophia, too.

I didn't know what to do, but I had to figure it out soon.

My head started to pound, the thought of going into work and ditching my day with Grace, like I had done many times in the past, made me feel sick. My new assistant was starting today, which I had been glad to avoid. The assistant I didn't have the time to deal with. Sure, people got PAs to help them manage their diary and emails, but the thought of someone being in my space was not something I was interested in. I'd told John I didn't need one, but I'm fairly sure he put pressure on HR until they told me it wasn't my choice.

Grace acted like it was okay that I had to go, but the look in her eyes felt like a punch to my stomach. Sophia was understanding too, disappointed, but also it looked like she pitied me.

I was just lucky she was able to take Grace to work with her. Sometimes it was too busy at her bakery for Grace, but she was overstaffed that day, so she would be able to watch her in the office.

Walking out of there, Grace with her mom, me feeling like the biggest asshole, made me wonder once again if all of this really worth it. I'd gotten where I'd wanted to be my whole life, but was it really any sweeter at the top?

My thoughts continued to spiral as I got ready to go into the office, not sure exactly what I was going to be stepping into.

Chapter Three

Tahlia

MY EARS BURNED, AND I cringed at the horrible scraping noise my broken suitcase made on the polished concrete of the internal staircase as I dragged my bags up the three flights to my new apartment. Hopefully, it wasn't loud enough that everyone in the building could hear it. A 3 A.M. wake-up call was certainly not an ideal way to meet my new neighbors. At least I didn't need to worry about scraping the stairs up with my broken bag because they were already completely scratched up, with some jagged chips that would definitely hurt if I fell on them. Even though I was out of breath, it also didn't smell great in the stairwell—I wasn't sure what it was, but it was musty and smelled like armpits—so I tried to keep my breathing as shallow as possible.

What had Claire gotten me into? If this was what the apartment was like, there was no way I could live here.

I tried to brush it off. It didn't matter. I'd get another bag eventually; this was just for now. As much as I tried to convince myself it didn't, it really did. It had been a terrible trip. My flights were delayed, so I'd landed in Florida in the middle of the night instead of mid-morning yesterday. Now, all I could see were red flags walking up the stairs, and I was probably making enemies with my stupidly heavy suitcase I couldn't afford to replace before I'd even met anyone.

Bit dramatic there, Tahls.

Nerves flooded my body as I reached the door to my new apartment, my new roommate somewhere on the other side of the door. My heart beat rapidly and sweat formed on my brow as my breathing became shallow for a whole different reason.

Just breathe. It will all be fine.

Before I could knock, I found a folded note taped to the door with my name on it.

Tahlia, I'm sorry I wasn't able to greet you as I'd hoped. Stupid flight delays. I texted you the door code, and your key is on the dining table. Make yourself comfortable, your room is down the hall on the left. There is some leftover food in the fridge if you're hungry (which I totally would be. Airplane food = gross). I'll see you after your first day tomorrow! Can't wait to meet you in person.

Tucking the note into my pocket, trying not to knock my suitcase over, I pulled my phone out of my pocket to check the code.

The red battery icon caught my attention as I quickly made my way to my messages: one unread from Jeremy. There was four percent left on my battery because, of course, I'd forgotten to bring my charger cable in my carry-on. Knowing my luck, I wouldn't have long until my phone completely gave out altogether. I could add that to the list of new things I couldn't afford.

I typed in the door code, glad to hear the whir of the locking mechanism just as my phone screen went black. Whatever, it didn't matter. The main thing was that I got the door open before it died. I'm not sure what I would have done if my phone had run out of charge. Slept on the floor in the armpit-smelling hallway with a broken suitcase for a pillow?

Brushing the thoughts off before I cried, I lifted my bag into the apartment, shutting and locking the door behind me.

You're just overtired, Tahlia. You've had a shitty day, that's all.

It was dark, but the first green flag was that it didn't smell anything like the hallway I had to come through to get here. I found a light switch to my right, hoping that if Jeremy was home it wouldn't wake him up. But I figured turning on a light would be less disruptive than me fumbling my way through the apartment, running into things and probably knocking my suitcase over.

Once my eyes adjusted to the brightness, I saw the kitchen to my left, overwhelmed with appliances and knick-knacks. But it somehow managed not to look overcrowded, just homey. Probably because of how big it was. It looked bigger than it did in all the photos I had seen—I probably could have fit my whole old apartment just in this kitchen/dining area.

There was a kitchen island that had one side connected to the wall, and another bench top across from it where the sink and stove were, as well as the dishwasher and fridge. Among the appliances on the countertop were ceramic cats, candles in the shapes of bodies, and jars of candy on shelves that were above the stove and sink. I loved it.

But it was the Nespresso coffee machine and the pod stand that caught my eye. I was probably way more excited about it than any normal person would be, but I'd never had a pod machine before. Or even just a regular coffee maker. Immediately, I imagined making my way to the kitchen first thing every morning, unconsciously picking a pod from the assortment, then listening meditatively to the machine make the perfect cup of hot coffee, the smell filling the whole apartment ...

I was tempted to make one now, just for fun, but I actually had no idea how to use it. Plus, Jeremy was probably asleep—like I should have been. I had work in only a handful of hours. Shit.

Grabbing my suitcase, I was about to try and find my room when the lounge room caught my eye.

There were mismatched couches, more knick-knacks everywhere, books all over the place. I was surprised it didn't make me want to clean it up, but it still felt cozy and welcoming.

I was tempted to go see how comfortable those couches were, but if I sat down I would probably instantly fall asleep. Which I needed to do, but not in the lounge room, preferably in bed. I'd have to wait to find out which couch was going to be my "unassigned-assigned" seat later.

I turned the lights off as I made my way down the hall and found my room easily enough. Jeremy had left the door open and another right across from it, which was the bathroom.

Dragging my bag into the room, I looked around at the furniture. It had a queen-sized bed, one side table with a lamp, and there was a built-in wardrobe—more luxury. The room wasn't exactly big, but it didn't matter, this would be fine for me. It looked like no one had lived here before, though Jeremy had told me his old house-mate left about three months ago.

The thought of having to unpack my bags made me want to crawl under the bed and hide. Especially since it wasn't just that one duffel bag that I took on holidays with me where the clothes would get shoved straight into the washing machine, eventually folded and put away at a later date. I had everything I owned in my suitcases—which was honestly not much, anymore—but I still had no interest in unpacking.

I did, however, quickly open my bag to grab my phone charger, plugging it in before kicking my shoes off, unclasping my bra, and pulling on the pair of pajamas I'd thankfully left at the top of my suitcase.

I was under the sheets just as my phone awoke from the dead. Did I need to wash these before I slept in the bed? Surely, they were clean.

Who cares, Tahlia? Just sleep.

I quickly typed a text to Claire to let her know I landed and was at the apartment. I was barely able to hit send before my head hit the pillow; my eyes drooped shut and I was out.

I was late.

Somehow, I slept through my alarms.

Wait, did I even set alarms?

It was hard to remember. I knew I fell asleep as soon as I was in bed, but maybe I set some before the plane.

Oh, what did it matter? I was still running late. They'd asked me to come in at ten for my first day, and it was already nine. Considering I had no idea how to get to the office or how long it took, I was sure I wasn't going to make it on time.

I jumped off the bed, straight into action, cursing myself that I hadn't left an outfit on the top of my suitcase like I did with my pajamas. But I hadn't expected the flight to get in so late.

When I finally managed to find something I quickly got changed, wishing I had time for a shower. I didn't smell too bad somehow, but I felt disgusting. I sprayed myself liberally in deodorant and ran a brush through my hair, hoping to hide how tired and not ready for my first day I was.

A notification popped up on my phone letting me know the Uber I had booked was approaching. As I quickly shoved my feet into my new court heels, I saw something shining on the floor—my engagement ring. My heart dropped into my stomach. It must have fallen out when I was trying to find something to wear. The oval-cut diamond stared at me.

When Tim gave me that ring, I was so excited, now I wasn't sure what to feel when wearing it. Sad? Happy? Like my future had been ripped away from me?

I knelt on the ground and pulled the ring into my hand. I couldn't just leave it on the floor never to be worn, could I?

Slipping the ring on to my left hand, on my ring finger, I couldn't stop staring at it.

Maybe I should wear it on the other hand. I couldn't bring myself to do that, though. Maybe I should take it off? I didn't need people thinking I was engaged. But did that really matter? If people asked, I could just explain it to them. Oh no, people were going to ask if I had a boyfriend or husband, and I was going to have to tell them. Or I could lie? It probably wasn't the best idea to lie at this job. But maybe no one would ask. Sure, people were curious, but we were all adults and it was a workplace. People wouldn't care that much.

The ring stayed on my finger as I grabbed my bag and left the apartment. As much as looking at it brought a wave of different emotions, I wanted it with me. It was a reminder of him, of everything, but it also gave me courage. It gave me the push to go to work, leave the house, start my life again. Almost like he was here with me, even though he never would be again.

My Uber driver gave me a confused smile as I sat in the back seat. I was guessing it was the outfit I had quickly thrown together. It was probably not the best idea.

I was wearing a tight-knit, three-quarter sleeve dress with court heels. I found this in the back of my closet with the tag still on when I was packing. I only packed it because I had made the decision to try and step out of my comfort zone and wear different clothes. In hindsight, it probably wasn't the smartest move; I'd already changed my entire life by moving to Florida. But one more change wouldn't make that much of a difference, right?

Wrong.

One, I now lived in Florida, which was significantly warmer in January than it was in Boston. Two, rushing around in a tight dress and heels was also not ideal. And three, it was gray and really showed off my sweat marks. I just hoped the air conditioning kept the office at a nice temperature. I'd rather not drip with sweat and get heat stroke on my first day.

After arriving at the office with little to no time to spare, I made my way to the security desk to let them know I was here. It had been such a long time since I had been a brand-new employee that I wasn't exactly sure what to do.

The security guard at the desk called upstairs to check everything was in order, and then got me to fill out a form for a security pass.

A security pass—so fancy!

I had never worked somewhere where I had a lanyard and a pass; it made me feel like a real adult knowing I would be getting one.

I smiled for my picture and waited for the card to print.

"Sign here, please." The security guard pointed to the form where I had forgotten to sign.

"Oh." I grabbed the pen and went to write my name, seeing the engagement ring flash up at me. I signed my name, Tahlia Walters, wishing instead it was Tahlia Green.

My eyes stung.

"Here you go, ma'am." The guard passed over my card with a smile. "Have a wonderful first day." I smiled woodenly as I accepted the pass—it suddenly felt like a good day might not be possible.

Swallowing the lump in my throat, I forced out a thank you when they advised me where I needed to go and sent me on my way.

I tried to shake the feeling of misery that had taken over, but it seemed impossible.

Walking over to the elevators, I saw a cute coffee shop and the aroma of the coffee somehow made my body ache. The yawn that escaped my mouth confirmed my thoughts. I needed a coffee. I hadn't seen Jeremy that morning or had time to mess around and make one. There wasn't much of a line, just a few people waiting, so I figured I had time.

After ordering, I waited near the counter, my mind buzzing. My chest started to feel tight, and my breathing quickened as my anxiety decided to kick in for my first day at this job. I had no idea if I was going to be able to do it. Well, I could do it, but would they believe I could?

They hired you. They want you. Believe in yourself.

"Tahlia," the barista called. I thanked them as they called another name and turned to head to the elevators.

And bumped right into the next customer. Our coffee's collided, spilling burning liquid all over my dress and his suit. I'm not even sure what happened.

Oh, fuck.

"Fucking hell," the guy snarled.

"I wish people would watch where they are going," I mumbled, fairly certain it wasn't my fault we ended up this way. There had been no one there when I'd turned to head to the elevator. Now my dress was covered in burning coffee for my first day. Great.

My breath caught in my throat as I finally got a look at the person I'd bumped into. He was a wall of muscle, six foot five, tanned, and very attractive. Mortifyingly, I almost swooned. His hair was dark, almost black, which matched his glaring eyes. Coffee was all over his previously pristine, pressed white shirt and gray suit, which looked much more expensive than the dress I was wearing. At least it seemed to not get on his black tie, which looked like silk. That was one positive. I went to apologize when he interrupted, his tone the opposite of friendly.

"You're aware that you are not the only person in this coffee shop? Maybe have some consideration for those around you."

Wow, really? I was about to apologize, but what an arrogant asshole. This was not my fault. Getting coffee spilled on you was not the end of the world, especially when it was definitely—I think—his fault. Mr. Grumpy-expensive-suit-guy needed to calm down and not take out whatever was really pissing him off at me.

It was just coffee.

"You ran into me, not the other way around," I responded. I walked off to the elevator, not interested in continuing this conversation or bothering to get another coffee. That ship had sailed, and I was extra late. I was sure my boss or supervisor or whoever was going to be wondering where the hell I was.

He followed me to the elevator. A coincidence, I assumed. I reached to press for level three at the same time as the grumpy guy. He raised his eyebrows at me.

"What?" My anger started to rise back up.

He shrugged his shoulders, trying to wipe his shirt with a napkin from the coffee shop. "Haven't seen you around before." He looked like he was assessing me.

"It's my first day." A look that seemed like realization plastered his face for a second before he schooled his features.

As we got to the floor, he gestured for me to exit. "Good luck, I guess."

I nodded, exiting the elevator, not sure where to go after that. I wasn't interested in talking to him any longer. He hadn't smiled or even tried to apologize for how he spoke to me. What an asshole.

Pulling his wet jacket off, he stormed past, not looking back in my direction. Seemed he felt the same about me as I did about him. As he walked through the cubicles, it was like everyone avoided looking at him. Somehow it felt like they were all staring at me instead, a massive coffee stain down my front sticking my clothes to my skin. I had no idea how I was going to survive the day in this dress—or just at all.

"Tahlia?" I pulled my eyes away from the grumpy but attractive man to find someone approaching me. "I'm Rachel, I'll be helping you out today. You're late, which isn't ideal for your onboarding, but I will sort it." Rachel was about my height, with beautiful strawberry-blonde hair. She seemed super friendly until that last comment. But I was late, she wasn't wrong.

Plastering a smile on my face, I followed her. "It's nice to meet you. Sorry about that. It's been a hectic day of moving."

"Happens to the best of us." The office was packed with cubicles like the ones you see on TV shows. All the desks were decorated with different personal belongings. The thought of getting to decorate my desk made me more excited than I'd expected to be. I was definitely getting curious looks from everyone, which made those nerves pipe back up. "What happened to your dress?"

The feel of my ring as I twirled it around made me think of Tim and reminded me to take a few breaths.

"Someone spilled coffee on me." I was tempted to say more, but I didn't know Rachel. She might know the guy who spilled it, or maybe not. She'd seemed friendly at first, but the way she said I was late and even just then, about my dress, just felt a bit off.

Rachel stopped at a desk, one of the only ones next to an office that wasn't among the other cubicles. I assumed it was hers by the way she rummaged through the drawer. "Lucky for you, I always have a spare; I would definitely recommend you get one."

She handed me the emerald-green dress, that had a pleated skirt and belt. How was her backup dress the kind of dress I wished I owned but had never found? I wanted to keep this dress so badly. I needed to ask her where she got it. No more tight-knit clothes for me. Not while living in Florida anyway.

Pulling the coffee-soaked dress off was the best feeling in the world. Rachel had thankfully brought me to the bathrooms to get changed. I'd kind of expected her to hand me the dress and wait outside, but she insisted on holding the dress while I got the other one off. She didn't want any coffee getting onto her dress, not that I was sure how it would do that.

"What's your role here, Rachel?" I asked as I dried my skin with the clean parts of my dress before she passed her dress over the stall door. It seemed a bit odd she hadn't told me what she did. Did she work in HR? I doubted that would make sense, since she was sitting next to a big office. She was probably an assistant too.

"I'm assistant to the CEO, John. After doing my business administration degree, I got a role here in admin and was promoted not long after." She seemed so proud of that. I guessed she should be. It sounded like a big accomplishment. "You'll be assistant to the COO, so we will work closely together, I'm sure." What was a COO? It sounded like a well-known acronym, but for some reason I had no idea what it was. I was definitely going to Google it later, preferably before I met them.

Was I supposed to have a degree to work there? Well, probably not since they hired me, but I was sure I was a bit out of my depth. I had admin experience, but not as an assistant. I honestly wasn't sure I would have got this job if Claire hadn't helped me with my resume and cover letter. She was good at that stuff.

"How do you like working here?" I was a bit worried the dress wouldn't fit, but I slipped it on with no issue.

"It's great." I could hear the smile in her voice as I zipped the dress up and buckled the belt. "Everyone's lovely, John is a great boss, really knows how to run a company, and has created a very flexible workplace." Oh wow, flexibility was great to hear. I initially wasn't sure if I was going to have issues completing my art course, but this news was relieving.

"How long have you been here?" I questioned as I left the stall, my dress strewn over my arm.

"A few years. Being John's assistant, I basically run the place." What a weird comment to make. I nodded back, though, making sure my confusion at her answer didn't show.

"I just need to check my emails to see if John needs anything, but then I will introduce you to Orion. You're going to love it here—everyone is so lovely." Something about her tone seemed off … I wasn't sure if I believed her.

"Orion is the COO?"

Rachel nodded as we made our way back to her desk.

"Great."

As Rachel sat at her desk, I looked around again, feeling less eyes on me. The big office next to her I now guessed was John's. Would I have a similar setup with Orion? What would it be like to work with the COO, Orion? Was he a nice guy? God, I hoped he was. I couldn't work for an asshole.

I looked back at Rachel to find her scrolling on her phone, not even slightly pretending to work. Why was she making me stand there awkwardly when she just wanted to scroll? Surely, she could have just introduced me to Orion and then come back and done this?

She was giving off weird vibes that I wasn't sure I liked, having experienced people like that before. She seemed friendly-ish at first, but now I wasn't so sure. I kind of wanted to give back her dress and wear my coffee-stained one anyway. Maybe I needed to get the dress dry-cleaned, just to make sure she wouldn't say I damaged it or something.

"Alright, let's go." Rachel got up from her desk and gestured for me to follow. I took a deep breath, letting the thoughts of this morning leave my mind, and reminded myself they'd hired me because they wanted me here. It would all be fine.

Chapter Four

Orion

THE GLASS DOOR OF my office rattled in its frame as I slammed it behind me. I was trying to remind myself that it didn't matter, it was just coffee, it was nothing to be so upset about. After taking a few breaths to calm myself, I wished I hadn't spoken to her that way. It really wasn't called for—just the icing on the cake of my day, it seemed. Well, maybe. Something told me there was another surprise in store.

It was a relief to strip the now cold and wet shirt off. The squeak of my door had me turning to find John had let himself into my office. I was hoping for a few minutes to myself—and maybe to be dressed—before someone walked in. But that's what I got for getting changed in my fishbowl of an office everyone could see into, rather than the bathroom. Throwing my dirty shirt over my chair, my closet door screeched as I opened it to grab a spare shirt. It was wrinkled, but it would do. This was my day off, for one, and I hadn't planned on someone spilling their coffee on me.

"Morning," I said.

"You finally came in, I see." He sat down in front of my desk and helped himself to a mint. The harsh crunch of John chewing the mint—like that was how you ate them—filled the quiet room.

The tips of my ears were burning, irritation at him rising. But it's what I signed up for. I was COO, after all; he had a right to have me come in. It must have been important. I made myself take a few breaths before responding. "How can I help you?"

"You have by just being here." My face scrunched up at his response as I slid an arm into my sleeve. What was going on?

"How? What's this urgent matter?"

"Your assistant starts today. I thought it best that you are here on her first day, since you were so sad to see Mr. Abernathy leave." John crossed his arms across his chest, awaiting my response.

"Oh, right." Did he seriously call me in on my *one* day off to welcome my new assistant? The only day I had requested off in almost a year.

When my last assistant left, I was a bit upset; he had found a better job, though. How could I blame him? It didn't mean I needed to be at work for my new assistant's first day. They'd surely be getting their computer and completing training—all the stuff I didn't need to be around for. And if I did need to be here, why they were scheduled to start on my one day off made no sense, but John had to be part of the reason. I just knew it.

"What happened to your shirt?" John deflected. "Did you spill something on it? Is that why you were late? Hooking up with someone?"

I couldn't hold back the eye roll at his comment. "Come on, that's inappropriate, this is a workplace." In my role I dealt with managing people, including workplace relationships, and this sort of stuff just irked me—even if he was just trying to make a joke. "You know that I was spending the day with my daughter." The look on his face made me wonder if he really even cared that I was with her, making my anger bubble back up.

"Oh fine." John stood and buttoned his jacket as I realized my shirt was inside out and cursed under my breath, pulling it off again a little aggressively. John, by comparison, still looked as smug as he did when he came in here. His blond hair was freshly styled, his suit pristine—and probably worth an obscene amount of money—his face devoid of any beard, and he held that irritating look of victory, even as he got ready to leave my office. "Let me know how you go with your new assistant."

"Sure," I mumbled, once again attempting to slide my shirt on, hoping agreeing with him would get him to fuck off a bit quicker.

John laughed just as the door opened and Rachel walked into my office.

God fucking help me, more people wanted to speak to me now.

The clumsy girl who spilled coffee all over me followed behind Rachel hesitantly, and I groaned internally. I had suspected this but had held out hope that something would go right today. I quickly finished throwing on the shirt, buttoning it as fast as I could.

"Orion, this is Tahlia, your new assistant," Rachel said.

Tahlia held her hand out for me to shake just as I finished the last button, before retreating and standing awkwardly near the door.

"And this is John, the CEO." Rachel slid her hand down John's arm as she said it.

He nodded, holding Tahlia's hand a bit too long before letting go. "Rachel, is that your dress? Looks much better on you."

Rachel laughed, but the silence that followed was deafening. Eventually, John and Rachel made their leave, closing the door behind them. Just Tahlia and I remained.

She was young, maybe mid-twenties, and had soft looking blonde hair that framed her freckled face. She was short in comparison to me, and when she smiled—even though she was clearly nervous—she had these dimples on both cheeks.

"Sorry about that." I moved to sit in my chair, feeling incredibly awkward. I didn't remember the last time I had to welcome a new staff member and train them up. I was tired just thinking about it.

Tahlia shrugged as she looked around my office, her eyes wide. It was big, with glass windows. A corner office, too. It was easy to forget that this wasn't what everyone had. I had worked my ass off to get this and when I was offered this specific office, I recalled having to hide my jaw almost hitting the ground. I'd been shocked at the sheer size of it. The massive oak desk that sat in the middle of the room with two chairs on the other side, bookshelves that matched the desk lined one wall, and there was a lockable closet on the other that had hanging space. There was also a sitting area with a two-seater couch and two other lounge chairs that were separated by a glass table. Near the door was also a high desk with two chairs that was less formal than the oak one.

It seemed like overkill at the time—I still thought it was some days, but I'd earned it, this office, this position. Honestly, I was surprised when John didn't try and get me moved to a shittier office when he was promoted.

"Oh, um, please sit." I gestured for her to take one of the chairs in front of my desk. She nodded and slipped into one, waiting for me to continue the conversation. "So, why don't you tell me a bit about yourself?"

"Oh, sure." She looked like I had asked her to present to a full boardroom. I forced a smile, to hopefully try and ease her worry, but her face still got redder with every second. "I just moved here from Boston, got in this morning."

"This morning?" I interrupted, surprised she was even here. "Why did you pick a flight that got in the day you started here?"

"It wasn't supposed to be like that. There were some major delays."

"I hope it wasn't Florida Airlines." I couldn't help but chuckle. She smiled, but it seemed forced. I gestured for her to continue.

"Other than that, there's not really much to tell. I like to draw, I'm a hard worker." As she spoke, she gestured with her hands, an engagement ring sparkling in the light. I nodded in response, unsure of what else to say. Was I supposed to say something about myself now? Fuck. I hated this shit.

"Is that your daughter?" I followed her gaze to the photo of Grace on my desk from about six months ago. She was running towards me, and I'd snapped a pic right before she launched into my arms. It was my favorite photo of her. I loved that kid so much.

"Yeah, Grace." I smiled.

"How old is she?" Tahlia seemed genuine, which was unheard of here.

"She's five." I loved talking about Grace, but no one here really cared, so I didn't share.

Memories of earlier that morning at the park surfaced, my shoulders slumping at how I had to leave her and the brave face she put on. That face broke my heart. It was likely it would happen again, though.

"You should probably go find Rachel and finish your induction." I wanted to be alone—I wasn't even supposed to be here, I was meant to be with my daughter. I didn't want to talk about her, I wanted to talk to her, spend time with her, play with her, watch movies with her.

"Oh, sure." Tahlia rushed to get up and to the door, like she wanted to get out of my office as quickly as possible. She sounded kind of relieved, which I wasn't sure how I felt about. "It was nice to meet you." Tahlia rushed out of the room, closing the door quietly behind her. My stomach twisted with a twinge of guilt, but it quickly passed when I realized why I was at work and not with my daughter. Then I found I couldn't find it in myself to care.

I finally had some peace and quiet to think, thoughts rushing through my head, but the one that stood out was what a shitty Dad I was.

I had a missed call and text from Henry when I got down to my car after work.

Henry: Need a drink. Now.

Me: On my way.

I left quickly, heading to Teddy's Bar. We had been going there for years, particularly when one of us was having a rough time—though it had mostly been me in recent years. When I found out Sophia was pregnant, when she told me we wanted to split up, and when it was no longer an option for me to become a pilot with Henry because of my partial color blindness. That threw our friendship through a bit of a loop, but we got back to where we were in the end.

Henry was already nursing a drink at the bar when I finally arrived. I clapped my hand on his shoulder as I sat next to him and signaled for a drink from the bartender.

"Hey." Henry smiled, but it didn't meet his eyes.

"What's up?" The bartender slid my drink over, and I took a sip as I waited for Henry to tell me what the fuck was going on. I couldn't remember the last time he did this. It had to be something bad.

It was loud in the bar, the metal bar stools scraping on the concrete floor as people dragged them around, the clack of the pool balls against the cues, the constant slosh of drinks being poured, and the cracking sound of ice being dumped into an empty glass. I was oddly comfortable around it all, the people yelling, people crying sometimes, even with the grossly sticky floors. It felt weirdly like home.

"Charlotte's sleeping with someone else."

I choked on my drink. "Since when?"

Henry looked defeated, bags under his eyes, his face colorless. Shit. "Not sure. I think at least a year. It makes sense looking back. I can't believe I didn't notice it."

This was the last thing I expected to hear. Charlotte and Henry had been together since college. I honestly didn't think I'd seen either of them with anyone else. There was a brief time after college where they'd split, but it wasn't really a breakup. They'd said they were "on a break"—like that *Friends* couple, they always told me. I had no idea what they were talking about, but they were still texting each other and meeting up in secret the whole time. Then they got married and had seemed solid since.

"Shit, man." I wasn't sure what to say, having not gone through anything like this before. Sophia and I split, but not under those sorts of conditions. It had to fucking hurt.

"She was constantly hiding things from me, and anytime I was away working, she would barely respond to me or take calls. If she did, it was always super rushed. I feel like an idiot. Here I thought we were trying to start a family—instead she's gone and done that with someone else." Henry downed the rest of his drink and took mine.

My jaw almost hit the laminate bar top. "Wait, what the fuck does that mean? Is she pregnant?" Henry nodded and my stomach sank. No fucking way.

"Yep. She told me today—then packed a bag and left."

I gripped his shoulder. "Fuck. I'm sorry, man."

Henry laughed humorlessly. "I should have seen it coming—we haven't had sex in months. We were supposed to be trying to have a baby, but she wouldn't fuck me? And I didn't think anything of it." He scrubbed his face with a sigh. "God, I'm a fucking idiot."

I had never seen Henry like this—fuck, it was not right. He was the fun, happy one in this friendship, and I was the grumpy asshole.

"You're not an idiot," I said eventually. "We're not supposed to expect the person we swear to spend the rest of our lives with would pull this shit."

Henry made a non-committal noise.

We drank in silence for a bit, the noise of the bar humming around us, before Henry groaned and pressed the heels of his palms into his eye sockets. "I just can't bear the thought of going back to that empty fucking house, filled with our shit."

"Then don't—you're staying at my place 'til you figure something else out, end of story," I said without hesitation. There was no way I was leaving him alone in the state he was in, anyway; I could finally return the favor from when Sophia ended things with me.

Henry looked at me gratefully.

I nodded. No words needed.

"Enough about me," he said, sitting up a bit straighter and signaling the bartender, "tell me something good." Henry's eyes were glossed over as he ordered another drink, his words starting to slosh, and his skin was flushed. He didn't have long left until he was gone for the night. How long had he been at the bar before I arrived?

"I've got nothing new to tell you. Grace is great, Sophia is fine, work is driving me up the wall. I've got a new assistant."

"New assistant?" Curiosity beamed in Henry's eyes, and a smile grew on his face as he seemed to forget all about Charlotte.

"Yeah, Tahlia." I wished Henry hadn't downed my drink—I could use it now. But it wasn't a good idea for me to drink any more. I needed to get Henry home and I had work tomorrow.

"A chick. Shit! Is she hot?" If Henry was speaking like that, it was time to go.

"Hen, no." I shook my head, trying to get the thought of Tahlia out of my head. She was … well, I wasn't blind. She was attractive, beautiful even, but I wouldn't let myself think about her like that. I was her boss and that was so fucked up.

"So, she's not?" Henry teased, knowing from my face that this wasn't the truth.

"It doesn't matter whether she's hot or not. I can't go there. I'm her boss, she's engaged."

"That doesn't matter." Henry shook his head as he slurped the remainder of his whiskey, almost breaking the glass when he dropped it onto the counter.

"Time to go home, Hen." He frowned, but obliged, leaving some cash on the bar and trailing after me.

I bundled Henry into the passenger seat of my car, the sound of the city buzzing around us.

"I don't believe you," Henry muttered in my ear as we put our seat belts on.

I raised my eyebrow at him, not sure what he was talking about.

"You like her," he insisted, "or if you don't already, you will."

I huffed. There was no way that would happen.

Challenge lit up in Henry's eyes. "Hundred bucks says you sleep with her, five hundred you fall in love."

Chapter Five

Tahlia

IT KEPT PLAYING THROUGH my mind. The grumpy-coffee-guy was shirtless. And he looked good.

Oh—and he was my boss. Orion was the grumpy man who spilled his coffee all over me, the guy who had a stained shirt and was obviously in the middle of changing when Rachel took me into his office.

He didn't seem too impressed to have me as his assistant, but I shook it off. It was my first day, I hadn't really even started yet. He just was still pissed at the coffee thing, which I wasn't too thrilled about, either. But he would get over it. He'd have to.

I found Rachel at her desk, on her phone again. She either didn't see me approach or was ignoring me. I wasn't too sure about her. It was like she was trying to give off this super likeable, "nice girl" vibe, but there was something hidden underneath.

I'd have to keep my guard up around her.

"Hey." I smiled, feeling awkward as Rachel finally looked up at me, her brows furrowed.

Placing her phone on the desk, she crossed her arms over her chest. "What can I do for you?"

I blinked rapidly, surprised by her demeanor. "Orion asked I find you to finish my induction."

"Alright," she huffed before pushing back from her desk and leading me around the office. "I'll take you on a tour, but we have to be quick. Lunch is being delivered soon."

Her bubblier personality seemed to come back as she showed me to the copy room, mail room, the meeting rooms, break rooms and the main kitchen where everyone was going to be having lunch.

Eating lunch with a bunch of people I didn't know on my first day was the last thing I expected or wanted to do. It was probably a great way to meet everyone, but I needed some time to myself to recoup and reset before whatever we were doing in the afternoon.

Thankfully, I had a few minutes to myself while Rachel went and grabbed the catering.

Was this something they did all the time? It was an interesting dynamic. Catered team lunches weren't really something we would do at my old jobs unless there was an event or someone's birthday or something.

I joined everyone in the kitchen, twisting my engagement ring. Rachel and someone I hadn't met yet came in with platters of sandwiches, wraps, and some sweets.

My stomach grumbled at the sight of the food. I didn't remember having anything for breakfast that morning, I'd been in such a rush.

It didn't take long for everyone to make their way into the kitchen and fill up their plates. I wasn't sure what was going on, but maybe it was just something they did. I wasn't going to question it—I was starving and hadn't brought any food to eat.

Rachel introduced me to a few people who were seated around the same table. "This is Tahlia, she just moved here from New York."

"Oh, from Boston, actually," I said. Did I mention where I moved from to Rachel? Maybe she had seen it on my resume or something and just got mixed up. Not a big deal.

"Cool. Nice to meet you, Tahlia," said one of the people whose name had already slipped my mind, along with a few others.

I was inhaling a bite of the roast beef sandwich I had picked and caught Rachel's eye. She was staring daggers at me. My brows drew together as she quickly looked away. Had I done something to offend her? I had barely said anything at this lunch, only where I'd moved from. If that had upset her, she needed to do some work—go to therapy, or something.

The room filled with chatter as everyone ate. My stomach was more than thankful I'd finally fueled it. I couldn't believe how long I didn't eat for.

"Tahlia," the woman across from me caught my attention. She had short brown hair, matching eyes and was wearing a standard black pencil skirt. "What role are you stepping into?"

Swallowing my bite of food, I smiled at her. "I'll be Orion's assistant, I just started today."

Suddenly, it was like everyone's eyes were on me. "How has that been?"

"Well, I haven't really worked with him yet. I only just met him." I took a sip of water, feeling hot from all the attention.

"I'm surprised he got a new assistant," someone else chimed in. "Him and Charles worked really well together."

John had mentioned this Mr. Abernathy earlier. That must have been Charles, Orion's old assistant. "He was somehow able to get him to not be such an asshole."

"Yeah, I don't envy you Tahlia," someone else piped in. I was surprised at how openly they were talking about Orion. What if he were to walk in mid-conversation? Surely, he wouldn't be too happy about being the center of gossip. "He's not the most approachable guy."

"Hopefully, I can figure out how to work with him." I sat up a bit straighter, trying to come off more confident than I was feeling. They were worrying me a bit. Maybe the first impression I got from him was truly what he was like: a dick.

I really hoped he wasn't actually like that.

"He is good at what he does, though." Everyone nodded their heads in agreement—except for Rachel. Curious.

The conversation eventually changed to random work things I couldn't keep up with. It was kind of nice to sit and eat with everyone, even though I didn't know them.

But their comments on Orion did worry me a bit. But it would be fine. He couldn't be that bad. He had an assistant before, and they made it work.

I just had to do the same; figure out how I'd work with Orion, and we'd be sweet.

It didn't take too long to get home, thankfully. Walking up the steps in my court heels wouldn't have been fun on a good day, let alone today, as completely exhausted as I was. I changed dresses before leaving the office, though, stopping at a dry cleaner for Rachel's dress. I'd pick it up and give it to her tomorrow.

Catching my breath at the top of the stairs, I was already dreading having to figure out what to have for dinner. I was starving, but also way too tired to bother cooking or doing groceries.

"Tahlia?" Attempting to make it look like I wasn't huffing and puffing from the stairs, I turned to see Jeremy walking up the stairs—I recognized him from our couple of video calls before the move. He had brown skin, hair buzzed to his scalp that was dyed a bright purple, and was carrying bags that emanated some delicious smells as he drew closer.

My stomach growled.

"Hey." I waved awkwardly. I had chatted with him multiple times and Claire knew Jeremy, but it was always a bit weird meeting new people in person—especially since we were roommates.

"It's nice to finally meet you," Jeremy said as he fumbled with the door and the takeaway bags. It wasn't until he'd already got the door open that my brain caught up, and I realized I could have opened it for us.

I followed him inside. He dumped all his bags on the counter, while I quickly threw my bag and shoes in my room.

"Let's eat!" Jeremy said.

"Oh, I don't have anything for dinner."

"Don't be silly, I got enough for the both of us—hope you like Mexican food." He pulled me after him into the living room, gesturing for me to sit. "I had a long day, and after the night you had, I'm sure the last thing you want to do is decide what to eat."

I sat on the three-seater couch that I could see now was emerald green. "Holy shit," I mumbled as I sat down. "This is even more comfortable than it looks."

"I only buy things for comfort." Jeremy sat across from me in a single brown leather chair. "I also love the furniture all being different. It really gives the space some character."

He emptied the bags onto the coffee table, pulling out more food than we could possibly eat for one meal—tacos, nachos, and burrito bowls that made my mouth water even more than it already was.

"I wasn't sure what you liked. But if you're cool, you'll like something I bought." He winked, and I chuckled as I reached for a burrito bowl.

"How was your first day of work?" he asked.

"It was okay." I must have sounded more fake than I thought because Jeremy's expression said I wasn't fooling anyone. "Okay, it wasn't amazing."

"Tell me all the drama," he said, tucking his feet under himself as he pulled the blanket that was draped over the couch over his knees. Curled under the fluffy blanket with his crochet sweater-vest, he looked like a little grandpa. It was a bit adorable.

He gasped when I told him about the coffee incident, and groaned when I revealed grumpy-coffee-guy was actually my new boss. "Hopefully, Orion is actually a nice guy when he hasn't just had coffee spilled all over him and you guys will get along fine," he said when I'd finished.

"I hope so," I said. "I'm supposed to start my art program soon, so I have that to look forward to—I'd ideally like to be settled in when classes start." I couldn't help but laugh. I just had a feeling it was going to take me a while to get used to living in Florida and really be settled in.

"Oh, what kind of art?" Jeremy seemed genuinely interested, which surprised me for some reason. He only gave off good vibes, but it was strange to talk to someone other than Claire about my art.

"I think it's going to cover a few different mediums, but I'm most excited to do some more focused classes on drawing. I love it."

"It's going to be great! You already seem so excited—that's half of what you need to make it through a course like that."

"I hope so." I finished off my burrito bowl, feeling much better now that I'd eaten. It was honestly some of the best Mexican food I'd ever had. I was going to need to find all the good takeout places now. I just had a feeling I wouldn't end up cooking much. Would I be able to afford that? The move had eaten through most of my savings, and my salary wasn't the best. Maybe once I was more settled, I could look at getting a service job on the side—tips might help.

"It's just across the road," Jeremy said when I asked him where the restaurant was. "I have a drawer filled with the menus for the best places. Feel free to help yourself."

We cleaned up together, the smell of the delicious Mexican food lingering in the apartment.

It wasn't long after that we went our separate ways. I was so ready for bed. But I made myself have a quick shower, brushed my teeth, and slipped on my pajamas before sliding under the sheets. My still unpacked bags stared at me, but they could wait. It had been a long day and I just needed some sleep.

I grabbed my phone, planning to turn on five thousand alarms, when I noticed I had a message.

> **Claire:** How was your first day? Miss you already!

> **Me:** It was … interesting.

I sent her a voice note with the main points. Describing the day was weirdly hard, even after talking to Jeremy already. I hadn't done much after lunch, just set up access to the systems and clicked through some online trainings—but it was draining. I could feel eyes on me the whole day, and I was sure it was Rachel. Whatever I had said had really pissed her off. But Claire's response to my vague message was typical.

> **Claire:** OMG! I need to know more. Call me?

> **Me:** Maybe tmrw? I'm exhausted, got no sleep last night. Got in at 3am.

> **Claire:** FINE. Tell me something though. Anything.

> **Me:** My boss may be the grumpiest man on the planet, but omg he is hot.

> **Claire:** How hot???

> **Me:** 6 pack

> **Claire:** OMG

> **Claire:** You work in an office right??

Claire: How do you know he has a 6 pack???????

Claire: Also I want a pic thx.

Me: Good night, Claire.

Claire: I am gonna need WAY more than that.

Me: Tomorrow 😴

Claire: You better call me. I NEED ALL THE DETAILS.

Me: You got it. Night.

Claire: Night Tahls.

I laughed quietly as I put my phone on charge and snuggled in under the blanket.

Falling asleep was a lot harder than I thought it would be. I really hoped this job went well, but I was nervous. All I could think about was the day. It replayed in my head—the sound of the coffee splashing on the floor, how my face had burned as I was introduced to Orion, those abs …

Shit, I couldn't be thinking that. I needed to get it out of my mind.

But apparently that was impossible.

The last thing I saw before I fell asleep was Orion standing in his office, looking irritated but undeniably sexy with no shirt on.

I was screwed.

Chapter Six

Orion

THE ELEVATOR FINALLY DINGED after I'd been waiting for what felt like ages. Coming to work after yesterday was not easy. I couldn't stop thinking about how I missed the day with Grace. Just adding another disappointment to the pile. Another reason why I'm a shitty dad.

There was a muffled "wait!" as I pressed the close door button in the elevator. I stuck my arm out, even though I was tempted to keep pushing it and make whoever it was wait like I had to. But that wasn't who I was—no matter what people in this office thought.

"Thank you," she said, puffing as she stepped into the elevator with a coffee. I blinked, realizing it was Tahlia. She had on a black pencil skirt with a cream blouse and matching heels—and there were no coffee stains on it, unlike yesterday. It also looked like she had picked up dry cleaning on her way in.

"Morning," I sighed. A moment to myself in the elevator would have been nice before the chaos of the day began.

"How are you today?" Her eyes were locked on mine as she took a sip of her coffee, leaving a red lipstick mark on the plastic lid.

I tucked myself into the corner of the elevator, not wanting to have to visit the dry cleaner again myself. "Fine." Was it the norm to have small talk in elevators? No one usually spoke to me, but maybe that was because they thought I was an asshole.

I was very aware of what everyone in the office thought of me. It wasn't the best to be known as the office jerk, but I didn't have the time or energy to try and fix it—plus, if I started being too nice, they'd stop avoiding me. Then I'd have to actually talk to them.

Gesturing for Tahlia to exit the elevator ahead of me, I trailed behind her until she reached her desk, then passed her and headed straight into my office, closing the door.

I really did love my office. The glass windows were great for me to see what was going on out in the main space. I hated that everyone could see into it, even though I was just always working at my computer. Would one-way glass have been too much to ask?

Shrugging my jacket off, I looked out the window at the view of the city. I didn't do this enough—appreciate where I was and how far I'd come.

John, sauntering into his office, caught my eye.

Becoming CEO had been my next goal, but I'd missed that boat at Florida Airlines. John wasn't going anywhere fast—literally. You'd think being CEO was a leisure activity from the way he'd been acting since being promoted.

My laptop was pinging in my bag already. Groaning, I plugged it into my monitor, not ready for whatever was going to be thrown at me.

New emails: 117

Unread chat messages: 35

Missed voice calls: 44

Fuck.

A knock at the door caught my attention.

Tahlia.

I gestured for her to come in, chugging half of my coffee down. If I didn't drink it now, I'd get too busy and then it'd be stone-cold.

"Sorry for interrupting. I was just hoping you had a minute." She hovered in the doorway, looking more nervous than she had in the elevator.

Nodding, I pointed to one of the chairs across from me. "Sure, how can I help?"

"I was hoping we could discuss how you would like to be supported. I completed my training yesterday, and I'm ready to start helping you out." Her can-do attitude threw me slightly. I should have expected it. People were often like that when they started a new job—before they decided they hated the place.

"Oh, um … you've done all the training?" I had no idea how much there was, but maybe she had missed some, and it would give me more time not to have to worry about this. But she nodded confidently.

My last assistant was good because we worked together for so long. The thought of now having to train someone new was exhausting. It just felt pointless. If I had to train someone to help me, how would I get any actual work done? How long was it going to take her to get up to speed?

Nothing against her, but this just was not a great time for this shit. I had so much to do.

My notifications kept going off, more new emails, messages, and people trying to call me coming in.

One email specifically caught my eye from Andre Garcia, the COO of Air Mexicana. Curiosity piqued, I opened it on my phone. He was trying to set up a meeting with John regarding Florida Airlines' merger offer and having no luck. Typical.

Maybe Rachel should do her job instead of—nope, not going there.

Instead, I mentally added smoothing relations with Air Mexicana to my pile to deal with.

"Sounds like you're getting lots of emails and calls. I can help with that—I have done this sort of work before, but just need to know your preferences and get used to the content."

Maybe it wasn't a bad idea. But shit, what if something went wrong?

"I think there are a few meeting requests you can sort through."

That should be easy enough not to screw up, right?

"Sure, I can give that a go. Anything else?"

She was eager. My phone started ringing again, a random number. I ignored it, rubbing my eyes. I was so behind already. They could email me.

"I can screen your calls, see if they can wait or really need to talk to you. I'll set them up to go to me—if I don't answer, then they'll come to you."

Fuck it. "Sure." That would keep her busy at least. I swore my phone never fucking stopped ringing. It would be nice to not have to listen to it all day.

She made her way over to my side of the desk. "May I?" After I rolled out of the way, Tahlia leaned down and fiddled with some settings that I was sure I could have figured out without her. "Can I give myself access to your diary now, too? So I can schedule meetings."

"Be my guest." The sound of people stomping around outside my office distracted me. It was probably the time most people went downstairs to get a coffee. That's why I typically brought one up first thing—I had no interest in waiting twenty minutes to get a coffee.

"Done." Tahlia stood up straight, a satisfied smile on her face, revealing those damn dimples. "I'll get started on those meeting requests. But if you want anything else, let me know."

"Will do." She left my office, shutting the door and not looking back. I watched her sit at her desk, looking super determined as she instantly answered a call that came through. Curious, I waited to see if she would try and transfer them to me or not. To my surprise, she hung up the phone.

Hmm. Maybe having a new assistant wouldn't be so bad after all.

I downed the rest of my now lukewarm coffee before getting stuck into my backlog of messages. I had a meeting in forty-five minutes, so I had to power through as much as I could before then—even though I felt like doing the absolute opposite.

Scrolling through my messages, I was baffled to see they were almost all meeting requests. Why couldn't people just send an email? I copied and pasted a generic message telling them to contact Tahlia. The poor girl was going to be overwhelmed with requests.

The thought of tackling my emails made me groan out loud, but I didn't have a choice. When I finally worked myself up to opening my inbox, I found there was a new color. Tahlia had made herself a category and was already assigning any emails asking for a meeting to herself. She was quick.

Dealing with things chronologically made the most sense, so I methodically worked through from the oldest to the newest emails, but it was a slog. I just didn't want to be there. Nothing was interesting for me to work on. I had so much to do on top of shit John was supposed to do that he obviously wasn't doing, so people were coming to me for help. Like they thought I had time to do it all. Well, I'd have to make time.

I had ten minutes until my first meeting. At least it was online, so I didn't have to spend time finding the meeting room. Grabbing my phone from my pocket, I opened Instagram to hopefully distract myself.

The first story was Sophia's: a drawing Grace did at Preschool of our family, Grace in the middle holding mine and Soph's hands.

I shouldn't be in that drawing. I was barely there, and yet she still wanted me around. I was a shit dad and needed to fix it, but didn't know how. How was my little girl going to rely on me to be there for her when she needed me, when I couldn't even spend one day with her?

I needed to prioritize her. Come up with a plan and be better.

Another knock at my door interrupted my thoughts.

"Sorry, Orion." Tahlia popped her head in. "I have a really quick question before you jump into your meeting."

I nodded, my emotions feeling a bit all over the place.

"I have Stacey on the phone from HR, she said she needs to speak with you urgently. I know you have a meeting, but she kept insisting it's urgent."

"I have a meeting, so I obviously can't take it." I snapped. "Figure it out. That's what you're here for."

No emotion showed on her face as she shut the door and scurried back to her desk.

Fuck, I shouldn't have spoken to her like that. She was a human, and it wasn't her fault I was having a shit day. God, maybe I was the asshole everyone thought I was.

Just as I was joining my meeting, a message popped up.

Tahlia: I scheduled a meeting with Stacey for after this meeting, she said it's related to an urgent employee complaint. Let me know if you want me to move it.

Great. Another thing to add to my list.

Chapter Seven

Tahlia

THE BARISTA, CHLOE, FROM the café downstairs knew my order by heart now. It was to be expected; I was coming up on my two weeks working at Florida Airlines and had stopped at the café every morning. She smiled as she handed me my caramel latte and Orion's oat cappuccino.

It was strange to think I had been here for two weeks and done nothing more than get coffee, manage Orion's calendar, answer his phone and kind of manage his inbox, but not really.

I made my way up to the third floor, luxuriating in having the elevator all to myself. A lot of mornings, I ran into Orion in the elevator; memories of our first encounter always bubbled up when we did. But there was no Orion today. He was either already in his office or coming in later.

I honestly had no idea—he didn't tell me anything. I wasn't sure if that was strange or not. It felt kind of weird, but what did I know? I'd worked in similar roles to this before but never at an airline. Maybe it was normal?

I dropped my bag into my desk drawer, which was broken, and it was being particularly stubborn today. Something was wrong with the runners, so I had to jiggle the drawer to open and close it. I slammed it shut, locked the drawer, and logged into my laptop with a huff. At least the lock worked. When I'd mentioned it to Rachel, she'd brushed it off and changed the subject. I figured it wasn't worth bringing it up again—it was clear she wasn't interested in helping.

The office was eerily quiet for nine o'clock, but I thought nothing of it as I started prepping for the day.

I opened my notebook, checking my to-do list as I did every morning. And, like most mornings, it was basically empty. I did the same things every day. Brought us both coffees, not that Orion had asked me to do that. I had just noticed after a couple of days he would get upstairs and swear when he realized he forgot his coffee, so I just started getting it for him when I got mine. He was surprised the first time, but he now expected it—which I considered a win.

Usually, my laptop finished loading by the time I'd reviewed my to-do list. Once it was up, I would open Orion's emails and calendar, check those. Then when that was done, I would print out any papers for his meetings, and then basically start all over again. There had been a couple of occasions where he'd asked me to do something, like set up a meeting room for him or order lunch, but nothing else. I was starting to go crazy with boredom. I needed something else to do.

Just as I had finished looking at Orion's calendar and inbox, the elevator dinged and he stepped out, looking like he just got out of the shower. His hair was wet, his face freshly shaven, the bags under his eyes even more prominent today.

"Morning, Orion." I grabbed his coffee and followed him into his office.

"Tahlia." He nodded as he shook his suit jacket off, leaving him in a baby blue, button-down shirt. I was pretty sure the shirt was too small for him with the way it was showing off his chest. Not that I was complaining.

I shook the thoughts away as I handed him his coffee.

"How's my day looking?" he asked as he sat down and took a long sip of coffee. My eyes caught on the way he pursed his lips on the cup. When he looked at me as he placed his cup on his desk, his brow quirked, I realized I was taking too long to answer.

"Um ..." A rush of heat flooded my body, but I tried to ignore it. "Busy as always."

Orion pulled part of his bottom lip between his teeth, like he was suppressing a smile. "Of course. Anything in particular?" My mind blanked. What did he have on today?

A tight and sexy baby blue shirt.

I gave myself a second to regroup, running out to grab my laptop off my desk. I'd noticed he was hot on my first day—how could I not?—so why was he making me feel all flustered this morning? It was fucking annoying. I must have been close to ovulation or something.

"You have a board meeting in ten minutes, then your weekly team leaders meeting, a call with some airline, and another meeting where the team is presenting to you about the updated policies they are working on—I think. The invite was fairly vague." I sounded like a babbling idiot. Could I just curl up and die? I was trying so hard to be good at this job, but with no guidance, I was floundering.

"So, an easy casual Friday, then," Orion deadpanned. Was he making a joke? I wasn't sure.

"I can order your lunch today if there's something specific you want?" I offered, hoping it might ease how shitty his day would be.

Orion nodded. "I'll let you know. I better get to this board meeting." He sighed, loud. He didn't want to be here today. I didn't blame him. I swear, from nine to five he was in back-to-back in meetings almost every day. When he actually got any work done, I had no idea.

I followed him out of his office, closing the door behind me. The desks were finally starting to fill up, everyone chatting with baked goods and coffees. Like they all went out together, or something.

"I'm surprised you didn't go to that," Orion said.

"To what?"

"There was a team breakfast or some shit like that, I think. I declined it weeks ago."

"Oh." I had no idea what to say. Was I purposely left out of the team breakfast, or was it an honest mistake because the invites had gone out before I started?

"Rachel set it up. I assumed you would be there this morning, I was surprised to see you at your desk when I got in."

"Oh yeah, um, didn't feel like it." I was unconvincing. Orion's features drew together, a look of disbelief on his face. "Anyway, I was wondering if there was other work I could help you with? I have time."

Instead of brushing me off like he had previously, Orion actually seemed to consider it. "Like what?"

I shrugged, a bubble of frustration rising in my chest. It wasn't my job to come up with ways to help him—only he knew what he needed. Yes, he was overwhelmed, but I could only guess so much before I needed his input. "I'm not sure, but I would like to help you more."

"I'll think about it. I have to go." Orion turned and headed to his meeting, leaving me with the hope that I might actually get something else to do.

I headed back to my desk and pulled out my sketchbook, ignoring the gnawing feeling in my gut about this breakfast, and drew.

The trip home felt like it took hours. I was exhausted, ready to order takeout, have a long shower, and go to bed. My energy had continued to deplete all day. I barely saw Orion again, only when he was ducking in and out of his office for meetings and then when I handed him his lunch. He'd mumbled a thank you and I'd got out of there. He'd looked frustrated, almost ready to throw something through the window. I didn't push any further on the more work thing. It wasn't the day for it.

When I finally let myself into the apartment, the smell of wine hung in the air. Loud voices and laughter filled the space.

"Tahlia?" Jeremy called. I wandered towards his voice in the living room, finding it full of people I didn't know. A couple was cuddled up in the single brown leather chair—I wasn't sure how it could be comfortable, but they were making it work. Another person sat on one end of the emerald-green couch, Jeremy on the other side, and another sat on the floor at the end of the coffee table that was covered in books.

"Hey." I waved to the group, unsure what to do or say. This was the last thing I'd expected to walk into.

"Grab a glass and come sit!" Jeremy swirled his red wine in his glass, a bit tipping over the edge and onto the couch. Jeremy either didn't care or didn't notice.

"Oh, no, that's alright. I'm pretty tired—it's been a long day. Sorry for interrupting." I turned and headed to my room, dumping my bags on the bed. Footsteps followed me down the hall, and I looked up to see Jeremy at my door.

"You don't need to hide in here, come meet my friends, join our book club!" Ah, that made the books on the coffee table make more sense.

"I don't want to intrude." I shrugged off my jacket and flats, shoving my feet into my fuzzy slippers.

"You couldn't even if you wanted to." Jeremy grabbed my hand and dragged me after him into the living room. "Everyone, this is Tahlia," he said, taking the middle seat on the couch and pulling me down to sit where he was before. A glass was filled with wine and placed in my hand.

I smiled and took a sip of the wine. "Oh, that's good."

"Ashton works at a winery, so he always brings the good stuff." Jeremy gestured to the guy on his left. He was not much taller than me by the looks of it, with fair skin, raven black hair that was pulled into a bun on his head. Rectangle glasses sat on his nose, and a beard covered his face.

"That's September on the floor. They don't like chairs."

"I like chairs, Jer, just not your lumpy-ass couch." Jeremy tossed a bookmark at them and I laughed. I liked them already. They had auburn hair down to their shoulders, a patchwork pair of overalls on, and a big smile on their face.

"I'm Suzie, and this leech is Liam, my other half." Suzie was draped across Liam's lap, wrapped in Jeremy's fuzzy blanket. Her face was covered in colorful makeup, her hair in space-buns. Liam had long blond hair, a face covered in freckles, and a smile that looked like it was only meant for Suzie. All of Jeremy's friends seemed so genuine and fun, the way they joked with each other.

"It's nice to meet you all. Jeremy invited me to join your book club, but I don't really read much."

"No need to read." Suzie gestured to Liam. "I don't think this one has ever read a book in his life."

"Hey!" Liam pretended to push her off his lap, and we all laughed.

"So, what book did you guys choose?" I took a long sip from my glass as Ashton explained.

"We aren't like a regular book club. We sometimes pick a theme and read to that, or we just bring whatever we have been reading. But there have been times where none of us could bother to read at all, so then we just play games, watch TV, talk shit."

"You sound like my people—the part where you couldn't be bothered to read, anyway." Jeremy pulled me in for a side hug as the others laughed.

They all fell back into their discussion of their books. Ashton had brought a book called *Red, White and Royal Blue* by Casey McQuiston; September said they were reading *Yellowface* by Rebecca F. Kuang; Jeremy was halfway through *A Court of Thorns and Roses* by Sarah J Maas; and Suzie had just finished *We Should All Be Feminists* by Chimamanda Ngozi Adichie. I had nothing to add to the conversation, so I sat silently listening and watching them interact while I drank my wine and ate cheese and crackers from the charcuterie board Jeremy had made.

Ashton was talking about his book, about the relationship that grew between Alex and Henry. Everyone listened intently, but not as much as Jeremy was. He was hanging on to every last word that came out of Ashton's mouth.

When there was a moment of silence, I asked, "So, how do you all know each other?"

"We met in college," Ashton responded. "We were all in the same psych course, except Liam. He didn't go to our college but has been with Suzie forever." Suzie and Liam smiled at each other before they kissed.

"Get a room!" September laughed, throwing a pillow at the couple when the kiss didn't stop at a peck. Liam caught the pillow and used it to cover their faces, giving the room the finger with the hand holding the cushion. September and I shared a look, and they rolled their eyes dramatically.

"It was really Jeremy and me that started this group, though," Ashton continued. "We were partners for an assignment and grew really close—as friends." Jeremy's expression faltered, but he recovered almost instantly. "But once that ended, we created a study group because we both kind of sucked at the class, and these clowns joined."

"What about you?" Liam piped up, Suzie now holding their "cushion-shield" in her lap. "How'd you meet old man Jer, here?"

"I don't know who you are calling old, Liam, but it better not be me." Jeremy shook his head at him—he was clearly trying to keep his tone playful, but his smile barely stretched his lips.

"It's all those sweater-vests—did you raid your grandpa's closet?" Suzie teased.

"I believe," September interjected, "it's called 'grandpa-chic'. I think it suits him!"

"Oh my God. Tahlia, save me." Jeremy slid down on the couch, lifting his sweater-vest to cover his face, much to everyone's amusement. I couldn't remember the last time I'd laughed this much.

"My friend Claire knows Jeremy from a while back, and I needed a place to stay, so she introduced us."

"How do you like my old room?" Ashton wiggled his eyebrows at me.

And the plot thickened. I'd been wondering a little bit about Jeremy's previous roommate—it was interesting to know it was Ashton. "It's great," I replied. "I did find some toys in there you might want back, though." I clapped my hand over my mouth as the room erupted with laughter. I had no idea where that had come from. I never made jokes like that, especially with people I barely knew. My face was turning red, embarrassment seeping in.

"You picked a good roommate replacement, Jer." Ashton ruffled Jeremy's hair. "I honestly thought you wouldn't have the heart to replace me."

It was clear something was happening between Ashton and Jeremy, but I could have been reading too much into it. "Why did you move out?"

"I moved into my boyfriend Steve's place."

Jeremy deflated slightly next to me. I don't know how I knew, but I could tell he didn't want to have anything to do with this conversation.

"So, was there anything else you left behind I should be worried about?" I joked, trying to steer the conversation away, hoping to make Jeremy feel more comfortable again. The conversation eventually turned back to the books and then to ordering pizza.

When everyone was distracted, I caught Jeremy's eyes and he nodded at me, mouthing "thank you". I smiled back, wondering what had happened between the two of them.

Chapter Eight

Orion

THE NUMBER OF MEETINGS in my calendar was growing and growing, with John now openly giving me his work to do on top of mine. Great, just great.

But I was impressed by Tahlia. She had somehow caught up to speed on most of the things that were going on, without me or anyone that I could see helping her. As much as I hadn't wanted the hassle of a new assistant, I could admit I needed her. My workload was fucked, and even just not having to answer my phone or worry about my calendar helped more than I'd anticipated.

It was Monday, and there were a lot of messages coming through from her today. I could tell she was bored out of her mind, but I didn't have the time to teach her, mentor her. I wished there was someone here who could, but there was no way I would suggest she ask Rachel. She was almost as bad as John.

Tahlia: Morning, that email that just came in, I think it's important. Just thought I'd let you know.

Tahlia: Did you have a chance to review that meeting agenda I sent you?

Tahlia: I'll take that as a no.

I had a missed call from Sophia and a text inviting me to dinner tonight. Grace had asked if I could come over.

Me: I'll be there. Need me to bring anything?

A knock at my office door interrupted me.

"Yeah?" I called out in response.

"Sorry." Tahlia's head popped in, looking concerned.

"What do you need?" I muttered as she closed the door behind her. She was wearing a black pencil skirt again, with a white buttoned blouse.

"I just had a question." Tahlia chewed on her bottom lip, avoiding eye contact with me.

I raised my eyebrows, waiting for her to respond. She looked worried, I wasn't sure why. I didn't think I had given her any reason to be nervous around me.

"An email came through from another airline. It looked like it was a high-priority one, but I wasn't sure about that, so thought I'd bring it to your attention while you are between meetings." I opened my emails and found my way to the one she was talking about, a request for a meeting with Leslie Becerra, CEO of Air Mexicana. Even though Leslie and I go way back, I would technically be overreaching if I stepped in. This was something our CEO should handle ... but I had a sinking feeling that wouldn't be the case.

"I did find in your emails previous correspondence forwarded to you by an Andre Garcia that might help with context. They've been working with John, some kind of merger bid."

My eyebrow raised involuntarily at her looking in my emails to help understand what was going on—her initiative continued to impress me. Her tone suggested that she had deduced John had dropped the ball, but it wasn't my place to badmouth the CEO.

"They've asked for a meeting with John, but due to my experience and friendly connections with Air Mexicana, I'll help with this one." I tried to ignore the feeling in my chest that was rising, telling me to leave it and let John deal with this—whatever the consequences. But I couldn't. I typed a response to the email and sent it, including her in the cc field. "I just responded. Thanks for bringing that one to my attention. If you could liaise with them and organize a time for the meeting."

"Of course." Tahlia smiled, the tension easing from her shoulders. Something, I wasn't sure what, came across her face, but it gave me the impression that she wanted to ask me something but wasn't sure she should.

"Just ask whatever it is you're thinking."

Tahlia seemed taken aback, her eyes widening slightly. "Oh, um," she stalled. I crossed my arms over my chest and waited, so she relented. "Why do you take on so much?"

I had no idea what I had expected her to ask, but I hadn't thought it was going to be that. "What do you mean?"

"I see your emails, your meetings. Does John do any work, or are you really both the CEO and COO?" Her voice quietened as she finished her question, probably worried people could hear her outside my office.

"He's my boss, I have to do what he tells me to." It sounded weak even coming out of my mouth. I didn't do it because he told me to—well, not entirely. It was like me and this company were one and the same. I had been there for a long time, and without it, who was I?

Maybe a good and present dad.

Tahlia made a face that said she could tell I wasn't being fully truthful, but she didn't push it and I didn't offer anything further, instead shifting the conversation. "How are you going with everything else?" Guilt that I hadn't given her any time rose in my body. She had asked about me, my daughter, my workload, but I had barely thought about her. Fuck, I was an ass.

"It's going fine." She looked like she wanted to say more, but again held back.

"The look on your face says otherwise." I closed my laptop, giving her my full attention. Tahlia was thinking about her response, avoiding eye contact. Her breathing quickened, the rise and fall of her chest more noticeable.

"Do you want my honest answer?" she said at last.

I gestured for her to continue. What did she have going on in that brain of hers?

"I'm so bored. I have nothing to do and just feel like you don't think I'm capable."

The breath whooshed out of my lungs. Shit, I hadn't meant to make her feel like that.

"I don't think that."

"Then what is it?" She crossed her arms over her chest, frustration evident from her pointed look and stern posture.

I struggled to think of something to say. Taking a deep breath and rubbing my hand over my face, I noticed my five o'clock shadow was making an early appearance. "I just have a lot on."

"That's a terrible excuse. That's why you have an assistant—to help you."

"I know." I didn't like where this conversation was headed. She obviously thought I was an asshole, and it was my own doing.

"So let me help. Use me." I visibly cringed at her choice of words, especially because she said them so sweetly, so earnestly.

"I'm not going to 'use you', that's language I would like to avoid. However, I will start looping you in on more things. I have a feeling I'm going to have a big project coming up soon that I'll need your help with. If you want to, that is."

She rolled her eyes at me. "Yes, I will help. Is that not what I've been saying?" She was sassy, and it made me smile—almost laugh. I couldn't remember the last time I'd laughed at work.

"Alright then. I will work on giving you more tasks." I reopened my laptop. I was a few minutes late for my next meeting. "Shit."

"It's online, so at least you don't have to run to a meeting room," Tahlia said as she left my office without being asked, her stride a whole lot more confident than when she came in. It suited her—the confidence, being sure of herself. Maybe I could help her be more like that, make her question herself less, help coach her.

Even though she left the way she did, I still felt like the biggest asshole after her admission that she was bored and had nothing to do. She showed great drive and initiative, but it wasn't her job to figure out how I needed to be supported—it was mine. And I'd let her down.

Another disappointment to add to the list.

Dinner with Grace and Sophia slowly made me start to feel better about the day. I considered confiding in Sophia about my issues with Tahlia, but wasn't sure if it was the right move.

Grace's face scrunched up, her arms stretching wide as a yawn took over.

"Time for bed, princess?" I started collecting the plates from the table as she nodded. "Okay, you head to your room and grab your pajamas. I'll come get you ready for bed in a minute."

She walked like a zombie from the table. I wouldn't be surprised if I found her asleep by the time I finished cleaning up.

I was finishing loading the plates into the dishwasher when Sophia padded into the kitchen, more dirty dishes from the table in tow.

"I've got this." She smiled. "You go read her a bedtime story or something. She's missed you."

"You sure?" I hoped she was. I loved having the chance to put Grace to bed and read her a story. It was such a special time.

"Go already." Sophia laughed as she pushed me out of the kitchen towards Grace's room.

Grace was already changed and in bed, underneath *Frozen* sheets. I wondered when she was going to be sick of that movie. My guess was a few years, if Sophia and I were lucky. Her room was filled with toys, and she also had a chalk wall where she could draw.

I turned her night light on as I walked over to her bookshelf that was filled with a variety of picture books. "Do you think you are too tired for a story?" I looked over to see her shaking her head aggressively. She slyly pulled her favorite book, *Where is the Green Sheep?*, out from under her pillow.

I chuckled and slid onto her bed, taking the book as she nestled in next to me.

"I've missed you," I said when we got to the end of the book, patting the top of her head softly.

"Me too. I always miss you," Grace murmured as I tucked the sheets around her sleepy form. Once she fell asleep, I kissed her forehead and exited the room, shutting the door quietly.

I found Sophia on the couch watching some trashy reality TV—our favorite.

"Did she fall asleep?" She gestured for me to sit next to her, pausing her show.

"Yeah, it didn't take much." I poured myself a small glass of wine from the bottle of red that was sitting on the coffee table.

"You alright, Ry? How's work?" Worry lines and her concerned eyes caught my attention. Even after everything we had been through, she was worried for me and wanted to make sure I was okay. I was so lucky to have found her. Besides Henry, she was my best friend.

"It's not great." I huffed, taking a sip of my drink. "John's being John, Rachel's being Rachel, and I'm being me—an asshole."

Sophia rolled her eyes—the second person to do that today—and hit me with one of her many couch cushions. "You're not an asshole, you idiot."

"How kind of you," I joked, swirling my wine. The silence felt heavy as Sophia waited for me to continue, her feet tucked under her, a cushion on her lap. "I have a new assistant, who I've completely neglected and consequently made her think she's not good at or capable of doing her job."

"I doubt that's true." Sophia shook her head at me as she placed her empty glass on the table.

"It is."

"Fix it then," she said matter-of-factly as she shrugged.

"How?" The most I could think to do was try and train her, get her to help more, but would that be enough?

"You make her the best damn assistant that Florida Airlines has ever seen."

Chapter Nine

Tahlia

I KEPT REPLAYING HOW I spoke to Orion earlier that day. Guilt was eating me up, but there wasn't anything I could do about it now. At least I might actually get some work to do.

"Hey, Tahls," Jeremy called as he walked in the door, carrying what looked to be a whole lot of takeaway. It was our new tradition—when we had long days at work, we took turns buying takeout and leaving it in the fridge for the other person. We had a lot of long days. I hadn't seen Jeremy except in passing since book club with his friends. "How was your day?"

"It was okay." I didn't know how else to explain it. I hadn't actually spoken to Jeremy about my job much at all since my first day. He was always working or out, so we hadn't been able to spend much time together.

"Let's talk about it over dinner." I followed Jeremy into the kitchen. He unpacked the bag filled with delicious smelling Chinese food. I was opening the lids of the different dishes when my phone started ringing with a video call. The smells from the Mongolian lamb and fried rice made me salivate as I reached for my phone.

"Claire!"

"Oh my God, is that Chinese?" She had her hair tied in a knot on the top of her head, and it looked like she was sitting in her living room. I missed her more than I thought possible.

"You know it!" Jeremy jumped into frame, waving. A part of our new takeout tradition was a video chat with Claire when we could actually eat together. It made it easier for both Jeremy and I to catch up with her.

"What were we talking about? I want to know EVERYTHING!" Claire raised her brows through the camera. Jeremy and I started dishing our food out. I had Claire balanced against a drink bottle on the kitchen counter.

"Tahlia was about to tell us about her day." Jeremy nudged me aside to take over dishing up the food. I kind of was hoping he would forget he'd asked, and we wouldn't have to talk about it. I just couldn't be bothered to relive it all, honestly.

"Today was ... different. I spoke to my boss, Orion, um ... maybe a bit rudely? I'm not entirely sure." They kept quiet, waiting for me to continue. But I could see Jeremy was curious as he stopped dishing the food into our bowls. "I maybe told him how bored I've been, and also asked why he is doing two jobs worth of work. It wasn't really my place—for the second bit. The first he asked, so I answered honestly."

"You have to give me more context than that, Tahls." Jeremy popped open more lids, little droplets of liquid from the condensation spraying onto the bench.

"Yeah, this sounds a bit juicy. I need more," Claire added.

"Orion hasn't been the best boss since I started. I know it's because he's overwhelmed. But he's barely given me anything to do. I just sit around and draw, really, except for the few things he lets me do for him. He asked how I was going today—which was unlike him—but I was honest, even though I wasn't really sure how he'd take it. He looked like he maybe felt bad, but I'm just not sure."

Jeremy dished out some honey chicken from the last container, trying not to spill it everywhere as it tumbled to the edges of the over-filled plates. "I would have assumed he would be trying to palm all his work off to you—isn't that what old men do to their assistants?"

Jeremy closed the container and licked some honey off his fingers before washing his hands properly.

"I wouldn't say he is an old man." I wouldn't think an old man was hot.

Jeremy quirked his eyebrow at me. "So, how young are we talking?"

"I'm not sure, I think he's maybe in his mid-thirties? He has a kid in preschool." I hadn't really thought too much into it. I usually tried not to make assumptions about people's ages—it would always come back and bite me in the ass.

Claire shaking her head drew my attention to my phone. "You haven't told me any of this! You've been holding back, you bitch."

I finished closing the containers for Jeremy, clicking the lids into place and moving them to the side before peering into the bag. "Did you get spring rolls?"

"Don't try and change the subject!" Jeremy and Claire shouted in unison.

Jeremy reached into the takeaway bag and pulled out a smaller paper bag that had me salivating. "But obviously. Who eats Chinese without spring rolls?"

I grabbed the bag and placed two spring rolls on each of our plates. My stomach growled. It looked delicious.

"Is this boss of yours hot?" he asked. I dropped the serving spoon I was holding, and it clanked on the bench top, spilling rice everywhere.

"He is!" Claire crowed. "She told me he has a six-pack!"

"Oh my God, how do you know he has a six-pack, Tahlia?" Jeremy's voice rose a couple of octaves in excitement. Claire was a straight shooter and Jeremy loved the tea, so I wasn't sure why I was surprised at the turn this conversation had taken.

"It was after the coffee incident—nothing untoward."

"But he's age appropriate enough that something untoward could happen." Claire wiggled her eyebrows.

"C'mon, he's my boss!" I said as I rounded the island.

"Office romances are a thing!" Claire insisted. I opened the cutlery drawer and paused, looking blankly at the mismatched silverware as Tim crossed my mind—I felt guilty thinking any of this at all, even if we were just joking.

Jeremy seemed to know without asking that I was looking for chopsticks and reached past me to grab two pairs from the jar on the counter and waved them in front of my eyes. "Earth to Tahlia."

"Sorry," I said, taking a set and picking up my plate. "So how are you two, anyway?" Jeremy narrowed his eyes at me as he pulled a bottle of wine from the fridge, grabbing two mismatched wine glasses from the cabinet.

"I'm fine," Jeremy answered, but his eyes said, *We will be coming back to this later, but I'll let it slide for now.*

"I'm boring." Claire shrugged. "Nothing new. Everything's the same in Boston."

"Well, boring, you're going in my armpit for some excitement," I said, wedging my phone under my arm so I could carry the wine Jeremy had just poured me and my plate into the living room in one trip.

We took our "unassigned-assigned" seats, and I balanced Claire upright on the arm of my chair so she could see the screen as Jeremy pulled up the Real Housewives. We had bonded over this show when I came out one night and found him watching, and now we had a pact to not watch it without the other. I knew that Claire loved Real Housewives, too, and would probably watch it with us.

"How's Ashton?" I wiggled my eyebrows at him in my best imitation of Claire, dying to know more about what was going on with the two of them.

"Ashton? What about him?" Jeremy acted suspiciously nonchalant. I knew he was lying. There was something he wasn't telling me.

I dipped one of my spring rolls into the plum sauce as I asked, "How is he? When are you going to tell him you're into him?"

Jeremy's hand flew to his chest, his mouth forming a telltale 'o'. "I don't know what you are talking about, let's just watch the show."

"Nuh-uh." I grabbed the remote off him and pressed pause. I wouldn't force him to tell me what had happened—or was happening—between him and Ashton, but I was enjoying not being the only one with an easy-to-tease target. "You've made me tell you about Orion—"

"Barely," he interrupted.

"So, it's your turn to share." I bit into the spring roll; the crunch of the pastry filled the silence.

"I am also quite interested in this gossip. Well, all gossip, really." Claire chuckled, shoving whatever she was eating in her mouth.

Jeremy puffed out a breath before picking up a piece of honey chicken with his chopsticks and shoving it in his mouth. He chewed slowly, obviously delaying having to answer. I followed suit, shoving fried rice and Mongolian lamb in my mouth. Fuck, it was so good. Jeremy's menu drawer had struck again.

We were in a stare-down, neither of us budging, but I could be patient. I continued eating, acting like it didn't bother me even though it totally did—I was really nosy. But didn't want to push.

"You two are putting me to sleep. Entertain me with your lives! I have none of that here in freezing Boston," Claire whined.

I had almost finished my food, licking the sticky honey from my fingers when Jeremy finally spoke up.

"There isn't anything to tell with Ashton, we're friends." I narrowed my eyes at him, not buying his blatant lie. "Not to mention he has a boyfriend, as you're well aware."

"Come on, Jer." I mock-pouted. "If you really don't want to talk about it, that's okay, but we're here to listen." I took my empty plate to the kitchen, leaving it in the sink before heading back in. I was about to press play on the show when he grabbed the remote off me.

"Okay, fine."

"Yesss." Claire did a little fist pump.

Jeremy rolled his eyes and placed his plate on the table before turning to face us, hugging a cushion to his chest. "I may have a ... small thing for Ashton." I felt giddy at that. Claire mouthed an exaggerated "I knew it", which I think only I saw.

I wasn't so subtle. "I knew it!"

"But it doesn't matter because he doesn't feel the same." Jeremy looked sad, defeated at his admission.

"Did something happen?" Claire's earlier sarcasm dissipated. My heart hurt—I could tell this situation made him really sad, and I hated it for him.

"No, not really. We were friends, and we grew close, but I guess my feelings took a different turn to his. We had a close call, but flirting comes second nature to him, so I guess he thought nothing of it because the next week he introduced me to his new boyfriend, Steve. Ever since, I've kept those feelings on lockdown. It's hard because I spend so much time with him. I don't think he ever realized how I felt ... *feel* for him."

I pulled Jeremy in for a tight hug. "I'm sorry, Jer, that sucks."

"I wish I could squeeze you, too," Claire said. "Boys suck."

"It does, they do," Jeremy said as he pulled back, his lips quirked at the edges. "But you know what would make me feel better?"

"What?" I said.

He smiled mischievously. "Tell me more about this mysterious Orion."

Claire and I laughed. I was not at all surprised that he brought the conversation back to me.

"You walked right into that one, Tahls!" Claire said.

"He isn't mysterious," I protested.

"I beg to differ," Jeremy said as Claire scoffed.

"He is mysterious when you won't tell us a single thing about him," she said.

My gaze fell into the distance as I struggled with what to say. I honestly hadn't thought about him much.

Liar.

I had barely had anything to do with him, really, beyond getting him coffee or small talk in the elevator. Today was the first time he'd asked me how I was going. "There really isn't anything to tell," I said eventually. "I don't know the guy."

Jeremy steepled his fingers under his chin in mock-contemplation. "Let me rephrase my question from earlier." I groaned, knowing exactly where he was going with this. "Would you sleep with him?"

"Jeremy!" I pushed his shoulder, shocked he would ask such a thing. Claire's cackling filled the room, making me laugh as well. "He's my boss, there's no way."

"If he wasn't though?" He shrugged like it was normal for me to think about sleeping with my boss.

"I haven't thought about it. Sure, he's attractive, but he has a kid so is probably married or something." I couldn't deny that he was hot—he was *so* hot—but it didn't matter.

"Do you know that for sure? Single parents exist, Tahlia." Claire sipped her wine, which made me reach for my glass. I needed it for this conversation.

"Well, no but—"

"Exactly, don't go making assumptions about the man. Now, describe him to us."

"What?" I could barely keep the confused look from my face. Why would they want me to describe him?

"Just tell us what he looks like." I didn't get why, but I did. I told them about his bushy eyebrows, dark hair, tall stature, muscly arms.

"But seriously, though"—I thought back to earlier in our conversation—"I was rude to him, and I'm worried I'm going to get into trouble. The last thing I should be doing is thinking about how hot he is!"

I'd never really gotten in trouble at work before. "Tahls, I'm sure it's fine!" Jeremy took my hand in his and gave it a squeeze. "You are smart, kind, and I am sure amazing at your job. You moved across the country to work for him."

"Well, not for him specifically ..." I retreated when Jeremy's eyes narrowed so much I wasn't sure if he had just closed them.

He sighed before continuing. "Maybe you came across rude, but it probably needed to happen. To work well with him, he has got to appreciate you, understand what you are capable of, and let you in."

I was skeptical, but maybe he was right. Maybe I needed to make him appreciate me. Make him see how good I was. I was tired of thinking about it for the night, though. I just wanted to watch TV, stuff my face with Chinese and forget it happened. "Can we watch the show now?"

"Tell me when you start so I can press play at the same time," Claire jumped in. Jeremy grabbed the remote and played the show, leaving whatever questions he still had for a later date.

Chapter Ten

Orion

Henry was rummaging around in the kitchen as I got dressed for the day, and it occurred to me that the sounds of someone else living in the house were oddly comforting: the clanking of mugs, the sound of his spoon scraping on the bottom of the cereal bowl, the whir of the coffee grinder. It was the kind of domesticity I hadn't realized I'd missed living alone, but it certainly made my mornings feel less … echoey. Buttoning up my white dress shirt and shrugging my black suit jacket on, I checked my hair wasn't all over the place from sleeping before heading into the kitchen.

Henry's back was to me, frothing the milk for his coffee. There was a box of Frosted Flakes and the milk carton on the counter next to his now empty bowl. Constantly having Frosted Flakes stocked in my apartment was the last thing I'd expected when he moved in, but he was obsessed with them. He ate them every day for breakfast, and for dinner half of the time. But I didn't mind—as long as he was happy staying here and not at his place wallowing, I didn't give a fuck what he ate. As long as he was eating.

Of course, when I was home to cook dinner, I always offered up some more nutritious options. I was no doctor, but I was sure that eating a balanced meal would help him feel better—even if it was just a fraction.

"You want some?" Henry looked over his shoulder at me, pointing at the open box of Frosted Flakes. This had become our morning routine. He was usually up before me, would be eating, having just eaten, or be pouring himself a bowl of cereal and always offered me one, knowing full well my answer would be no.

But I played along every morning, pretending to consider it before declining. "Thanks, but I'll stick with the muesli."

This had become familiar over the last couple of weeks. I was honestly surprised at how much I enjoyed him staying here. We had lived together in the past, but this was different. We were both grown adults; I had a kid. To be fair, I don't think it would have gone as smoothly if Grace was here more often.

Henry chuckled, shaking his head at me. "Suit yourself. One day you will say yes, and you will not regret it." He poured himself a second bowl while I grabbed the Greek yogurt and fruit from the fridge and my toasted muesli from the pantry.

"What's your plans for the day?" I sat with him at the table and dug into my breakfast.

Henry looked as if he sat in thought, deciding what to tell me. "Not a whole lot," he said in between bites. "Have a couple of meetings and appointments."

"Anything interesting?" I kept my voice as nonchalant as I could. I wasn't generally a nosy person, but I was worried about Henry. I'd never seen him like this, so down. I wanted to make sure he wasn't lying and then just going to do nothing.

"Since I'm off roster for a few more days, just sorting some shit out." Henry took a long drink from his mug. "I have an appointment with my divorce lawyer."

"Shit, really?" I had no idea he was planning on speaking to anyone so soon. "How's that been going?"

He shrugged. "This is the first in-person meeting. I've only spoken with them over the phone." Henry's chair scraped against the floorboards as he got up to rinse his plate in the sink. "I just ... I've been thinking about how things have been and what I want going forward. I've been, um ..." He trailed off as he put his dishes in the dishwasher and started tidying the kitchen like he was on autopilot, his brow knitted in thought.

"Hen?" I nudged. "If you don't want to talk about it, that's fine."

"No, I do. It's good to talk about it—well, my therapist said so anyway."

I raised my eyebrows in surprise, but kept quiet.

"My future looks so bleak right now, and that's not what I want," he continued. "I want it to be fun and exciting, but also fulfilling. With the way things are going right now—sitting around on my ass and wallowing—that's just not possible. So, I am hoping to get the wheels in motion, see what the process is with the lawyer and what I can do to move forward. I don't think I'll be able to move on until my ties to Charlotte are broken."

I nodded, making a thoughtful sound in the back of my throat as I picked up my empty bowl and put my dishes in the dishwasher before turning to him. "I don't think I've ever said this to you"—I placed a hand on his shoulder—"but I'm proud of you."

Henry's face screwed up in mock disgust. "Don't go getting all mushy on me now."

I laughed and continued getting ready for work, packing my laptop and some snacks into my bag to tide me over until I eventually ordered lunch. I needed to stop wasting so much money on ordering takeout for lunch and start meal prepping.

"Do you think Charlotte ever actually liked me?" Henry asked just as I slung my bag over my shoulder and grabbed my keys.

I faltered, feeling a bit at sea. How do you answer something like that? "What do you mean? You were in love, right?"

Henry paced back and forth like he needed to move to have this conversation. "I honestly don't know anymore. Like, she was never how you are with me—she was always so negative. Saying things like being happy just as a pilot meant I had no ambition, or that I was just 'okay' in bed—she used to compare me to you a lot because you're a hot-shot exec, and I was 'just' a pilot. Stuff like that."

I opened my mouth to say something—anything—but I was lost for words at that last point. Charlotte had known us when I'd found out I couldn't be a pilot, had known how devastated Henry and I both were. Not to mention, Henry loved flying.

"I've started to realize that maybe our relationship wasn't what I thought it was since I started seeing this therapist."

Letting my bag slip off my shoulder again, I sifted through my memories from when we were younger, when Charlotte and Henry started dating, their "break", when they decided to get married, right up to recently. Now that Henry mentioned it, everything did seem very Charlotte led—what they did, where they ate, who they hung out with. But I thought that was normal in a relationship, someone usually took the lead on that sort of thing, and Henry hadn't seemed to mind at the time.

I wasn't sure what to say, but I tried anyway. "I'm sure she liked you—loved you—but you guys met in college, we were all just kids. Sometimes shit just doesn't work out. It sucks."

Henry nodded, rubbing the back of his neck. "Yeah ... I want to put that all behind me, though. Just starting this lawyer process has helped—I feel lighter already, like a weight has been lifted off my shoulders." I smiled at Henry, amazed at how he was about all this. I'm not sure if I was in the same situation that I would have gone the same route as him.

"Maybe we should celebrate?" I offered.

"Yes! Go to work, you're going to be late, but we can talk about it later." I nodded and headed to the door. "Did you want a coffee for the drive? I'm going to make myself another."

He needed to calm down on the coffee, but I wasn't going to say anything after that conversation. He was doing great, and if having an extra coffee was going to help him, then so be it. "No, thanks, I'll get one at work."

The whole drive to work, all I could think about was who was going to greet me with a coffee when I arrived.

The smell of my burrito was making my mouth water as I returned to my office after collecting my lunch delivery. I passed everyone who worked on my floor on my way back, forcing out a polite "hi" as I went, but was ignored. They had to have been going out for lunch together, which happened regularly enough. Everyone thinking I was an asshole meant I didn't get invited to team lunches or whatever. It wasn't my favorite thing, but there wasn't much I could do about it. They'd already made their minds up about me.

Tahlia was hunched over at her desk when I got back to my office. Was she not going to lunch with everyone else? What was she doing?

"Too busy for lunch?" I nodded at what she was doing.

She looked up at me, surprised. "What do you mean?" As I walked closer, I noticed she was drawing—her desk was covered with other drawings she had done. How had I not noticed these before? The one she was working on was a landscape with mountains, a lake, and trees covering the page. It was amazing. They were all just in regular pen, too, and she'd somehow managed to still add beautiful shading and texture to them—they were stunning.

A blush crept onto Tahlia's face as I studied all the drawings. She seemed a bit worried. I wasn't sure why. Grace would love these—maybe I could ask Tahlia to draw her something.

"You didn't go out for lunch with everyone else?"

Tahlia packed up her sketchbook and stuffed it into her desk drawer. She tried to shut the drawer quickly, but it got stuck.

"Obviously not," she snipped, struggling with the drawer. Had I hit a nerve? Why didn't she go? Did they invite her?

"Why not? A person's gotta eat," I asked, squatting down next to her to examine the drawer. She made a small sound of protest, but I waved her off. I couldn't say I blamed her for not wanting to eat with them, but something about her just sitting on her own, drawing, seemed ... wasteful.

"Why are you not eating your lunch and leaving me alone?"

I held back the chuckle that formed from her sharp response. Well played. "Fair enough—this drawer is broken. Have you sent a repair request?"

"No ..."

Of course, she probably didn't know who to email. "I'll message you the email of the maintenance team." I picked up my burrito and headed into my office when she called out.

"If I had work to do, I wouldn't resort to drawing. Sure, I love to draw, but I'd rather work when I'm at work." She crossed her arms with a pointed look in my direction.

Dropping my takeout bag on my desk, I stepped back to the doorway and leaned on the frame, arms crossed over my chest. I had given her more to do after our conversation the other day, but she'd just taken it all in her stride. "I don't want to give you too much while you're still learning."

Tahlia huffed, her eyes narrowing. It was kind of cute, if I was honest. "You're full of shit, Orion."

I laughed, caught off guard by her candor. Some execs might not like their assistant to be so forward, but I liked that she was quick to respond, called me out on this shit and kept me on my toes. I liked having her around.

Shrugging, I left my door open and turned back to grab my lunch before sitting on the couch, ready to eat my now sad and definitely cold burrito. After a moment, Tahlia followed me, sitting opposite me but not saying anything. This woman was too smart for her own good. It was time I gave her work meaning.

"So, what would you have me get you to do?" I challenged, as I took a bite of my lunch.

She sat in thought for a bit, while I continued eating. She intrigued me, the way she stared into space, how she sat up straight and not slouched, one leg crossed over the other, her arms hanging in her lap; it was obvious that her mind was buzzing.

I had almost finished my burrito when she finally said simply, "Give me more work."

It was my turn to roll my eyes. "Obviously." I grabbed a napkin from the bag and wiped my mouth.

"It's not my job to tell you what to give me. You just need to give it to me." There was fire in her eyes, she was not backing down.

"Alright." I got up, throwing my rubbish in the trash can before standing next to the chair she was sitting in.

There was only one thing I instantly thought of that I could give her. I wasn't sure if it was too much, but if she could pull it off, it would definitely make an impression. She had more to offer than I was taking, and she could really help me succeed if I let her. I'd been such an asshole, not allowing her to show off her talents, make a name for herself, like I did when I started here. I needed to be what I wished I had when I started. A mentor. Maybe then the board would see what a mistake they'd made.

I looked at Tahlia, and she turned in her seat to look directly at me, her skirt snagging on the fabric couch. "To make sure we're both on the same page, you don't feel that your current workload is enough, and you want to do more?"

"Yes."

"You want to be challenged?"

She stood up, her heels making her taller but still not standing eye to eye with me. "Please."

The way she said "please" did something to me that I didn't expect, but I pushed it down.

"You remember the meeting with the Air Mexicana CEO?" Tahlia nodded eagerly. "The purpose of the meeting is to smooth relations with Air Mexicana following their rejection of our first offer to merge our operations and expand both of our businesses, and to present them with a more enticing offer. I'm putting you in charge of the preparations for the meeting, including my presentation of a refreshed merger offer." I turned and sat at my desk, opened my laptop and logged back in. "Have you worked on anything like this before?"

She shook her head, coming to stand behind me so she could see my screen. She leaned down slightly, placing her hand on my desk for balance. Her perfume wafted over me as her hair slipped off her shoulder.

I cleared my throat, looking at the engagement ring on her finger to help me snap out of it. "The pitch is the main focus," I said. "Think—how do we want to present our ideas? What are the key benefits to them and our projected outcomes of a merger? What do we want to leave them thinking about? The key is to not make them feel like this is just another corporate buyout where they'll be completely absorbed by us—it should feel more like a partnership proposal. I will also need you to take minutes during the meeting."

"The meeting's not that far away." Panic swarmed her eyes. Shit, it was too much, wasn't it?

Let her try, Ry. If she struggles, then help her, but give her the chance.

I listened to my inner voice and continued, hoping it wasn't too much for her. "You'll be fine. I can send you some examples from similar meetings if you'd like."

She shook her head. "Nope, I've got this." I smiled, glad to hear that. I was still unsure how she would go, but at least she had a chance to try.

"I will need to review the presentation a few days before to ensure it is appropriate, so ensure that's calculated into your timings for drafting."

"Okay, you got it, boss." She seemed genuinely excited as she almost jump-skipped out of my office.

I held back my smile, glad to see she was happy and ready to give it a crack.

"I won't let you down," she called out as she went who knows where.

I was nervous for her, but I was certain that she wouldn't let me down.

Chapter Eleven

Tahlia

> **Me:** Is it weird that I'm excited to make a presentation 😄
>
> **Claire:** LOL yes. Happy for you x

EVEN THOUGH I HAD wanted to start working almost immediately, I made myself grab a sandwich from the café downstairs, my stomach grumbling as I picked what I wanted, before rushing back to my desk and getting started.

Truthfully, I had no idea what to do—so I researched. I looked through Orion's emails and calendars for similar meetings, and what we provided. He did offer to send me some, but I wanted to do it myself. I wanted to show him I could do it. The last thing I wanted was to waste this opportunity by doing a shit job and then have Orion not give me projects in the future. I definitely wasn't built to sit around, watching his inbox and calendar all day. It was so boring. If I had started my art course, I could at least work on that during work, but I'd still rather do work.

Maybe Orion could help me figure out where I wanted to go.

Woah, jumping a bit ahead there.

I needed to focus instead of letting my mind race ahead. I had to do this presentation, do it well, and then look forward.

My eyes were stinging from spending the whole afternoon reviewing previous presentations of Orion's and making a new one for the meeting.

I fought the urge to add in the fancy transitions that my high school self couldn't resist, but there was no way that was appropriate for this sort of meeting.

Interestingly, it appeared the CEO of Air Mexicana, Leslie Becerra, had blind cc'd Orion into the majority of the emails between him and John, so I was able to access the full previous merger offer as well as read the exact issues Air Mexicana had with it, which allowed me to tailor the presentation to their concerns. It was clear they were interested in the merger if they could be assured their company values were respected—they were worried about losing their identity. But so far, neither John nor Rachel had offered any real opportunity for further collaboration or negotiation, leading to first Andre Garcia and then Leslie himself to reach out directly to Orion.

I had basically finished the slides for the presentation when I realized Orion would probably want some talking points added into the notes as well. He hadn't outlined what he wanted or needed to help him present when he put me in charge of preparations. This wouldn't be the first meeting I'd been to with him, so I was somewhat familiar with his presentation style, however all of this prep work was a bit of a guessing game. But I figured if I was going to present at such an important meeting, I would rather be over-prepared than be under-prepared.

I hadn't realized how long it had been since I'd had some water, so I grabbed a glass on my way to the printer. It was nice to step away from my desk. I could feel my eyes adjusting to having a break from the screen.

"Tahlia." I turned just as I hit print, and the whir of the machine took over the space. Rachel was behind me—I'd had surprisingly little to do with her since my first week, and after Orion confirmed that everyone going out to lunch together was indeed a pre-arranged thing, and not just a coincidence, I knew that she had a problem with me. Even when I gave her back the dress she'd lent me on my first day—dry-cleaned and, if I'm honest, cleaner than when she gave it to me—she inspected it and gave a tight-lipped 'thanks', obviously not impressed. People like her never sit well with me. I'd done nothing to make her feel whatever way it was about me, but I also knew she was probably like this with a lot of people. It seemed I was just the new, fun target of her hatred.

"Hi Rachel, how are you?" Plastering the friendliest smile on my face that I knew would annoy her, I moved out of the way, gesturing at the printer. "I'll hop out of your way."

"I'm great." She started printing whatever she had to and faced me with her arms, crossed and her face pinched. "Whatcha got there?"

"Just preparing for a meeting." I didn't want to give her any more information than she needed. My gut was telling me more and more not to trust her, and my research into the previous correspondence between Air Mexicana and John showed that both she and John had mishandled this merger bid so far. She narrowed her eyes at me.

"What meeting is it?" She looked over at the paper I was holding, seeing what it was. She shrugged, obviously not really caring. "Who wrote these?" A small chuckle escaped her lips. "I wouldn't be showing anyone these, let alone letting Orion present this." She turned on her heel and left without saying anything else, the smell of mint left in the air.

I was frozen as I watched her leave, the door slamming shut behind her. The click of her heels was slowly replaced by the humming of the printers. I could barely hear them over the blood rushing in my ears.

What just happened? I thought back on all of our interactions. She'd been harsh, rude, all the things, but not straight-up cruel. Rachel was obviously trying to hurt my feelings, and she finally had done it. But why was I the target of her cruelty? All I did was accept a job, come in for my first day, and do what I've been told. There was no reason for her to treat me like that. I wasn't sure if I could stand it for much longer. Going to work and being treated like shit by someone who is supposed to help me, train me, was one of the worst kinds of torture.

I took a few deep breaths.

"In, out, you're fine Tahlia."

I could feel my heart rate slowing, the sound of my blood rushing quietened. Tears threatened to spill out of my eyes. "Don't even think about it." The door opened and someone who I recognized but didn't know stopped in their tracks.

Don't cry, just breathe. Maybe they don't know what happened. Maybe they just ... realized they didn't need to come into the printer room?

They looked back, their gaze following Rachel's walk. An exaggerated look of pity crossed the woman's face as Rachel looked back at me and waved. I felt like a deer caught in headlights, I didn't know if I should say something or run.

They opened their mouth, their eyes filled with conflict. "Hey, are you ..."—they looked back again before continuing—"are you done with the printer?"

I smiled, and blinked the remaining tears from my eyes. I drew my shoulders back and took a breath. "Yes, all done." I grabbed my paperwork off the printer and walked past them with my head held high, even though I felt the opposite of confident.

The anxiety from that interaction lingered, and I needed to shake it off. I had to make sure everything was perfect for this meeting. Orion had to get this deal sorted. The board wanted this airline and John couldn't give a shit about it, having initially given them a lowball offer which they'd rejected. John had basically ignored them since—which was the reason for this meeting. Orion had to clean up the mess John made, which I was noticing was a pretty common occurrence.

Rachel's comments wouldn't leave my head and had me triple-checking my work, using more of a critical eye, which was hard considering I hadn't done this before. I was trying to convince myself it was the same as drawing. If I saw an imperfection, thinking how I could turn it into something else rather than erasing it, and knowing when it was better to erase and start again.

My neck and shoulders were tight from reviewing and editing all afternoon. Before hitting send on an email with the content to Orion to review, I checked on my presentation again to make sure everything was perfect. Rachel had achieved what I assumed she'd set out to do; she had me second-guessing everything. I was worried Orion would send the presentation back instantly with hundreds of notes, but he was radio silent for the remainder of the afternoon.

As I was about to log off and go home for the day, an email popped into my inbox from Orion.

Tahlia,
Good work, a few edits in the attached.
Thanks,
Orion Ariti
Chief Operating Officer | Florida Airlines

Holy shit. I didn't do terribly.
Leaving the office that day, I felt lighter and ready to take on what was next, despite Rachel.

My screen lit up when I plugged my laptop into my charger—my minutes' template was ready to go and the presentation was working. The CEO of the Air Mexicana would be joining online, but I thought the presentation would run smoother if we were in a meeting room; we'd be less likely to be interrupted.

The meeting room was spotless. I came in early to make sure it was in good condition, and it definitely wasn't. It had been left a mess from the last meeting, which I was pretty sure was Rachel and John. The whiteboard squeaked as I wiped off the writing, crumbs flew on the floor as I cleaned off the desks, tucked all the chairs in, and put the pens, markers, erasers—all the crap that was left out—away.

Even though Orion worked with digital copies, I printed out the talking points for him anyway, though I was sure he wouldn't need them. He really knew how to command a room and capture everyone's attention without looking at notes. Either he memorized them beforehand or just knew everything. I suspected the latter. There was something undeniably charismatic about a man who knew what he was talking about ... not that I should have been thinking about that.

The water jug shook in my hand as I poured water into the glasses I had brought into the room. My laptop dinged and distracted me, making the water slosh onto the table. I swore under my breath and was about to grab a paper towel from the kitchen when Orion walked into the room. I was still rattled from Rachel's comments, and knew it was outwardly affecting me.

"Ready to go?" He sat down opposite me, his suit freshly pressed. It looked like he also had just touched his hair up in the bathroom.

"You sure look ready. Your hair, wow, looks amazing." I chuckled, getting a small smile and an eye roll from him.

"I've got to impress Leslie somehow." Orion nodded at the water covering the table. "What happened there?"

My cheeks heated.

I can't even pour a glass of water without fucking it up.

"Tahlia?" I didn't hear Orion get up, but he was next to me, his hand on my shoulder, a concerned look on his face. "Are you okay?"

I nodded, swallowing back the anxiety trying to rise. "I just need to clean this up."

"I'll get it. You sit or go take a breath." He smiled at me, obviously trying to calm me down. "It will be fine, I promise. You don't have to do any talking. Leslie is nice, you'll love him." I nodded as Orion left to get a cloth.

I sat in my chair and took a few deep breaths, trying to calm myself. I had no idea why I had suddenly gotten all flustered. There wasn't a reason to be. Orion was right, he would do all the talking, I was here to take minutes and listen.

Orion came back in and wiped up the spill before sitting back down, not a trace of any judgment on his face. I thought maybe for a second that he would think I was acting childish. He had these sorts of meetings all the time, and I was sure he didn't even get nervous.

"Tahlia, are you ready? Leslie is in the meeting." I took another breath and nodded. "I get nervous too, so don't think it's just you that feels how you do right now."

Orion smiled at me reassuringly, his kindness throwing me off slightly. His smile wasn't something I had seen much, but it was something I needed to see more. Somehow, it made him more attractive than he already was.

Tahlia, not the time.

I quickly shook the thoughts from my head as Orion started the meeting and Leslie popped up on the big screen. I needed to focus on the meeting, listening and taking minutes.

"Leslie!" Orion smiled, waving at the camera. Oh my God, he just waved at the camera, it was kind of cute. He seemed genuinely happy to see Leslie. "How are you?"

"Great now that you're here." Leslie replied, the smile on his face mirrored Orion's. He was older than Orion, that much was obvious, with a graying beard that matched his hair and wrinkles under his eyes, but I already got the sense he was nothing like our CEO.

"This is Tahlia"—Orion surprised me by gesturing to me and tilting the camera slightly, so I was in full view—"my assistant. She's taking minutes for us today."

I quickly smiled and gave a small wave, hoping my nerves weren't super obvious.

"John finally made you get a replacement for Mr. Abernathy." Leslie chuckled. "Nice to meet you, Tahlia. Minutes seem so formal for our meeting, Orion." The sound crackled slightly; I guessed the connection was a bit poor considering Leslie was in a different country.

"I know, but after how things went with John, I thought it best to capture everything."

Leslie nodded in agreement. "Look, if I'm honest, the only reason I'm even considering anything is because of you. I don't want to work with John, he's ... a piece of shit—maybe keep that off the minutes, Tahlia." We all laughed. Leslie was clearly comfortable to speak his mind with Orion. "What John offered us was abysmal. I don't know if he did it in hopes we would agree, or because he didn't want us to."

"Honestly, Leslie, I have no idea. He didn't consult me on that, I found out after the fact. I'm still pretty furious about it."

"This is why I prefer working with you. You're straight to the point and honest. So, let's get to it."

Leslie including Orion in the emails with John was starting to make sense now. Maybe my initial view of Orion being an asshole wasn't right? Leslie seemed to have an immense amount of respect for him, he did so much of John's work on top of his own, and only moments ago he helped me when I was starting to panic—being sweet in a way I'd never expected.

"We want to merge," Orion said, "but we don't want to just dissolve everything you have. One, that is just a waste of resources, and two you've worked so hard to build your company, we don't want to tear it down. We want to rise up together."

I couldn't help but feel more respect for Orion; the way he spoke was professional and honest. It was easy to tell he meant what he was saying and wouldn't go back on his word.

Leslie adjusted in his seat. "You know, this all sounds great, Orion, but there is one thing that worries me." Orion's face turned serious. It looked like he knew what Leslie was going to say. "I'd happily jump on board to work with you again in a heartbeat. But I don't trust John to uphold anything you're proposing, given the lackluster nature of his lowball offer and subsequent unprofessional dealings with me and my team. We're a family business, we run on gut instincts—and I trust you, but not him."

Orion paused, seeming to consider Leslie's comments before continuing. "What if I could get John to sign off on delegating all decision-making rights regarding this merger to me? Then I would be able to absolutely ensure that the core tenets of Air Mexicana are not only preserved, but flourish due to the merger." He was so sincere.

Leslie nodded at Orion's proposal, rubbing his chin. "Look, I will only consider this if I can get that in writing. I want proof. I would prefer you were appointed CEO as part of the merger—if your board is as eager for this merger as you say, they would consider my suggestion—but I know the likelihood of that happening with John around." Leslie appeared to be aware of what was going on at Florida Airlines, his tone implying something more than he was saying. How did he know so much about John and Orion?

I focused back on my minutes as they continued to go back and forth, Orion winning him over with each word. He was convincing. I was enamored by what he was saying, and it definitely wasn't in the notes I prepared for him.

It wasn't long until Orion was wrapping up the meeting.

"I'll finalize my written proposal and get that over to you this week." He smiled at Leslie. "Thanks again for meeting with us, and I'm sorry about the whole John situation."

"Not your fault, Orion. It was nice to meet you, Tahlia. I'll chat to you both later."

Leslie left the call, and I had to remind myself to stop staring at Orion. The way he held himself in that meeting was mesmerizing and made me think more highly of him. I saved the minutes, planning to fix them up when I got back to my desk, and started packing up.

"I think that went well," Orion said to no one in particular.

"Are you and Leslie friends or something?" I asked as I unplugged my laptop charger and closed my laptop.

"Yeah, we're old friends. Feels weird having formal meetings with him." His earlier smile returned, widening as he laughed.

I couldn't help my curiosity. "Is it really that important to merge with them, when it would mean such a huge increase to your workload?" I spoke so softly I wasn't sure Orion heard. It felt like something I shouldn't ask.

"It's not ideal," he admitted with a sigh. "But being COO means making some hard decisions, and it's one way to keep expanding without having to start a whole new branch ourselves. This way we can absorb Air Mexicana's existing resources and customer base and build on it. The board wants us to be one of the most competitive airlines in the world—and it's my job to find the most efficient ways to make it happen."

"Seems like something a CEO should be doing," I said as I grabbed my stuff.

Orion smiled and held the door open for me. "You don't miss much."

Chapter Twelve

Orion

TAHLIA SURPRISED ME WITH her comments about John, my workload, and especially if taking on the merger was the best idea. It made me wonder why she was questioning those things, but I think she was just a go-getter, willing to get things done. Maybe she would be able to help me with this more than I originally thought, giving me back a tiny bit of time.

A loud laugh drew my attention as we passed the break room. The rest of the team from this floor were all huddled around the table—it looked like they were cutting cake. Was it someone's birthday? Rachel was in the center of it all, directing people to hand out the cake to others. It was subtle enough that I wasn't sure if I imagined it, but Tahlia's shoulders slumped forward slightly, and she seemed to deflate.

"You can go in if you want," I said, thinking maybe she was worried about missing out.

She shook her head, quickly straightening her posture and lengthening her steps.

She'd been nervous before the call, that much was obvious. But she'd definitely not been herself since lunch, and this wasn't the first time I'd noticed her on the outside of these team events. I'd worked with the people in this office long enough to have an inkling of what was going on. The cynical part of me said it was none of my business unless she raised a concern, but something pressed me to take an interest anyway.

Tahlia placed her stuff on her desk and murmured something about getting a drink, but I called after her, asking her to follow me into my office first. The way her smile didn't meet her eyes confirmed my suspicions that something had upset her.

I hadn't said something, had I?

"Take a seat." We sat at the table near my door. I didn't want this to seem like I was going to scold her, even though the look on her face said that's what she was expecting. "You did really well today. The presentation notes you prepped were great."

She forced the smile a bit wider. "Thanks."

The silence between us stretched; she fiddled anxiously with the ring on her left hand.

"Are you alright?" I asked.

"Yeah, why wouldn't I be?" Her voice was pitched a little too high to be convincing.

I leaned back in my chair and combed my fingers through my hair. "I've worked here a long time, Tahlia. I know what certain people are like." She dropped her eyes to the hem of her skirt. "If something is going on, you can trust me." I didn't want to make her feel like she had to tell me, but I hated seeing her like this. "I've noticed that you are on your own, not going to those team ... events they have. That lunch the other day, drinks after work, now that cake. Is that your choice? Are they inviting you?"

Tahlia took a deep breath before responding. "No, they don't invite me. It doesn't matter, I don't know them." She looked out of my office towards the kitchen where they were still gathered, finishing off their cake. Though her words were feisty, the sadness was written all over her.

"It does matter." She had every right to be invited to all of the team-bonding shit they did. I didn't care if I was, but she was their peer, she should be included.

"It's fine. Was that all?" Her heels snagged on the carpet as she shimmied off the chair, spoiling what I was sure was meant to be a cool, unaffected exit.

It was that moment that John walked by, hands in his pockets. He gave a two-fingered wave as he passed, that smile on his face that Sophia had always said reminded her of a snake about to eat a mouse.

"Ass-wipe," Tahlia said with a sweet smile as she waved back.

I burst out in shocked laughter and, after a moment, Tahlia joined in. I couldn't help but notice how the sadness left her face and a smile brighter than I'd ever seen in this office took over.

"Okay, fine, it upsets me that they don't invite me. I don't know what to do about it—or why they even do it." Tahlia moved to the much more comfortable couch, kicked her shoes off and tucked her feet under herself. The way her skirt hugged her thighs more tightly when she sat like that caught my eye, but I quickly looked away, knowing how inappropriate that was.

"I think it's me." There had been this nagging thought in the back of my mind ever since I saw she didn't go to that lunch. What would be any other reason for her not being included? Rachel. It had to be Rachel. She didn't like Tahlia because she didn't like me. Fuck, I hated office politics.

Tahlia's eyebrows drew together as she dropped further back into the soft couch. "Why would you be the reason? No offense, but not everything revolves around you." The smirk on her face told me that she was just joking. At least she was making jokes now.

"Oh no, it doesn't?" I feigned fainting onto the other end of the couch, which made Tahlia to laugh more. "What am I going to do now?"

"I don't know, Orion, how can you live knowing that not everyone is thinking about you all the time?" Her smile reached her eyes now as she teased me.

"At least I know you do." I winked and Tahlia rolled her eyes at me.

"You can go back to fainting now."

"But seriously, they all think I'm an asshole. Maybe they think it's contagious." Even though I was being facetious, an idea sparked in my mind on how I could fix this situation for her. When I was working my way up, the one thing that even John and I could bond over was a horrible boss. A tyrant who made us work late, start early, do all their dirty work, take all the credit. Maybe if people thought Tahlia was going through that, they'd give her a break.

"Contagious? Like bad boss cooties? What are we, children?" Tahlia dismissed my suggestion.

"Entertain my idea for a minute at least." Tahlia's eyebrows rose, but she didn't interrupt. "I'm going to pretend to be an asshole to you, a horrible boss—"

"Like the movie?" she said, half laughing.

"I haven't seen it," I admitted sheepishly. "But, if they back off, start talking to you, inviting you to places, then we know the world does, in fact, revolve around me, and we fix your problem."

She snorted, seeming unconvinced, but—eventually—she nodded. "Fine, we can try it." She pulled her lip in between her teeth, and my brain may have short-circuited. "But you won't actually be mean to me, will you?"

"Of course not." All the teasing left my mind. I didn't want her to think I was doing this because that was how I wanted to be. That was as far from the truth as we could get. "Just when the others can see, to get them to feel bad for you. Then maybe they'll start talking to you at least."

Tahlia hummed. "Feels super deceptive." She got up, and made her way to my desk, picking up the picture of Grace. "What would she think about this?"

"Don't bring Grace into this." I grabbed the picture from her, putting it back on my desk.

"Yeah, there's no way you can pull this off. You're too big of a softy." She chuckled.

"You were testing me?" I was genuinely shocked. This woman had kept me more on my toes in the last few weeks than anyone had in my life. Well, except maybe Grace.

She snorted again—I could get used to that sound—shaking her head at me. "Obviously. But fine, let's try it." I held my hand out for her to shake, but she continued. "On one condition."

My curiosity was piqued. "Depends," I said, one eyebrow raised.

"You let me help with the merger. I did the prep, I feel almost all across it, and want to continue helping." She stood so straight, her chin tipped up, confidence oozing from her. I was impressed. When John had said I was getting an assistant, someone wanting to help on projects was not what I expected, but I wasn't disappointed.

I pretended to think about it, before eventually agreeing. "Now get out of my office, I have lots of work to do."

"Is this you pretending to be a mean boss?" She seemed amused at my poor attempt.

"It was just a practice round."

"You need more practice. Maybe start with slamming the door after I leave." She laughed, then in an instant her expression changed stone-cold. She opened the door and walked to her desk. As I went to slam it, she turned back and winked at me.

I laughed as I walked back to my desk. The office was starting to become somewhat more enjoyable.

Strangely, Henry was cooking dinner when I got home. He didn't cook that often. I couldn't recall a time he had ever cooked for me, but then again, maybe he was just cooking for himself. That would be weird, though, wouldn't it? I was thinking too much into it, standing in my doorway.

Whatever was on the stove smelt amazing, steaks maybe. The oils were sizzling, while a pot almost boiled over. Typical Henry, doing too much at once.

"Need some help, Hen?" I set my stuff down, my stomach gurgling loudly when I saw the steak. Fuck, it looked good. I hadn't had a home-cooked steak in a long time.

"Nah, it's done." Henry pulled the last steak off the stove and left it to rest, mashing up the potatoes he was boiling. "Grab some beers, would ya?"

I grabbed two Coronas from the fridge, opening them on my way back to the table.

Henry joined me, bringing both of our plates, a dish filled with pepper sauce and some cutlery.

"What's the special occasion?"

Henry gestured for us to start eating. I cut into the juicy steak and devoured it. It was amazing.

"I have an idea." Henry said between bites. He wasn't usually someone to talk a lot while eating, usually too busy scoffing down his food.

"What kind?"

"Just give me a second to explain, don't interrupt. Enjoy your steak and beer." He had piqued my interest, but I complied and waited for him to continue. "I think it's time to leave Florida Airlines."

"Hen, what the fu—"

Henry pointed at my beer, a pointed look on his face. "What did I say?"

I sighed, took a long pull from my beer, and gestured for him to continue. I had to give him a chance to say whatever it was he wanted to, even if it sounded crazy from the first sentence.

"You've done great there, made change, but they fucked you over one too many times when they made that idiot, John, CEO over you. It's time for your fresh start, time for *our* fresh start. Something we can do together, like we always wanted."

"Wait, are you quitting being a pilot? I thought you loved it!" I took a swig of my beer, it tasted sour with the thought of Henry quitting the job he loved and worked so hard to get.

"I could never quit flying, I like it too much, but I want to do this with you. So I'll just do both." Henry looked amused that I even thought he would consider leaving his career. He was born to be a pilot, and I didn't ever want him to give that up, especially if it was for me.

"Thank fuck." I clinked my bottle against his.

"Will you let me finish now?" I nodded. "I know you like the work you do, so I've been thinking about this for a while. We can start up a consultancy firm. You could do everything you love about your job now. You would still review companies' policies, help with workplace culture, and suggest ways to expand business—except as a freelancer. You would get hired for specific projects and work your own hours and be paid a wage we set and agreed on in advance. I'm looking into potential clients."

When did he come up with this idea? "That's ... interesting." It honestly sounded ideal, being able to set my own hours, turn down projects with idiots I didn't like. "But wait, why do you want to do this? You have no interest in the shit I do."

"I want something that's my own. Well, our own." He shrugged. "I love being a pilot, but sometimes the hours and shifts are a bit much. I have no interest in getting some corporate job, but I also don't want to quit my job. I want something that I have a say in, I can choose my hours so I can still fly. It's the best of both worlds, as Hannah Montana would say."

I couldn't hold my chuckle back at his reference. The days of getting drunk and watching Hannah Montana reruns in our dorm felt like a lifetime ago now. "How often do you want to fly?"

"I still want to fly plenty. I'm about to start doing overseas flights, actually, so I will get to fly and get more time between the flights here at home—which is perfect for this."

"I guess that makes sense." It was similar to how I wanted more time with Grace, in a way.

"Just think about it, okay? I'm not expecting you to say yes right now, but think about what it could be. You could see Grace more, move to a house in the suburbs where she could spend the night. You could have a nice home office, work the hours you want and with the people you want. No more Johns. I really think this could change everything for you." Henry was smiling in a way I hadn't seen in a while. His eyes were lit up, his hands were flying around, commanding attention.

"You said we could start this, but you've only talked about what I would do." Henry hated the type of work I did. He had no interest in being some big shot executive who was stuck in meetings all day, which I didn't blame him. So how did he fit into this puzzle?

"I would obviously help you get it started, do research and find potential clients, do some more of that backend admin stuff, unless of course you wanted to get an assistant."

I froze at that. I had only just gotten used to Tahlia, just offered her my help, and was now considering leaving her in the lion's den. Not to mention Leslie and the merger. I couldn't do this. Henry was still talking, though.

"But it would depend on my flying schedule. We would need to nut a few things out."

"I don't know, Hen. It's a massive change, and what if it fails?"

"You're right, it could." We grabbed our dishes and headed to the kitchen to clean up. "But we won't know unless we try."

Henry loaded the dishwasher while I filled the sink to handwash the big-ticket items. The sound of the water gushing into the sink helped me to think more clearly.

There was a thought, like a devil on my shoulder, begging for attention. "I can't just leave Florida Airlines. After everything Sophia and I went through, the struggles with my work ... I practically gave up on us for this job, just to up and leave a few years later because it suits me now, when I wouldn't do that for her, for our child? Imagine what that would seem like to her. It would be like a kick in the gut. There's no way I could." Even considering leaving had the guilt eating me up.

"You could talk to her about it." Henry turned the dishwasher on and then took to drying the pots and pans on the drying rack.

It wasn't just Sophia that worried me. It was Henry. Was he actually all in this, or was he just trying to distract himself? He had been through so much lately, I wouldn't blame him if he clutched onto something to keep his mind occupied and off Charlotte. How would he help run a business while also being a full-time pilot as well? How would that work?

The questions filled my mind, making me worry more and more that this was a bad idea. "Yeah, maybe."

"Look, I can tell you're mostly all feet and hands out the door, not even one foot in and one out. I get it. I sprung this on you. But I honestly have been thinking about this and think it's time you left and made a name for yourself outside of Florida Airlines." Something about his tone reminded me of Leslie in the call today, when he said he'd happily work with me again, but not John. Like he was reading my mind, Henry continued, "When John was promoted to CEO over you, you should have quit. I hate watching you continue working there when I know it's holding you back—and you never get to see Grace."

He was right about that. One thing I would love was to spend more time with Grace. Have her stay with me every second week or something. Living in a house instead of an apartment also sounded nice, even though I could do that now if I really wanted to. All of the things he was proposing were intriguing ... but Sophia. I just couldn't. And Tahlia? I couldn't throw her to the wolves.

"I still don't know, Hen." I felt bad. He had obviously put a lot of work into this idea, wanting it to be perfect before even telling me, and here I was shitting on it.

"No stress, Ry. Just think on it, will you?" He filled up a glass of water and headed back to his room.

"Yeah, okay. I'll think about it."

Chapter Thirteen

Tahlia

"Ms. Walters!" Orion shouted. All heads in the office turned and stared at me, pity in their eyes. I rushed to Orion's door and poked my head in.

"Yes, Mr. Ariti?" His smile was smug, like he thought his performance of asshole boss was working. I wasn't so sure.

"Come in, we need to talk." He spoke louder than he needed to, making sure others could hear what he was saying. I entered the room, my shoulders drooping, and turned to close the door. I caught the eye of someone at their desk, they looked worried, pitying maybe. Surely, they weren't already feeling bad for me? It couldn't be this easy.

"How can I help you, Mr. Ariti?" I smirked as I made my way over to sit in front of his desk. We hadn't been doing it long, but it was kind of fun to have this secret, to act like he was an asshole and then laugh about it behind closed doors.

Orion looked fresh today—maybe he'd gotten a haircut? His hair looked more styled than normal. It suited him.

Orion looked amused at my continued use of his surname. "How are you going with the merger?" His face conveyed no telltale sign of it if he was worried about it, not worried about it, excited. Nothing. Nada.

"I've actually been doing some digging," I started. "We aren't the only ones trying to merge with them."

Orion looked surprised, his eyes widening.

"I should have expected this." He seemed far away, his voice detached.

I sat up straighter in my chair. "So we need to get them to choose us." I really had no idea what that meant. I assumed Orion would be able to give some guidance—he knew so much. He should be CEO, not the saltless pretzel, John.

"There are a few things we could do to address this." Orion began, his eyes now focused and locked on mine. "We could change nothing and hope that they merge with us anyway. We could try to adjust the merger offer, all the percentages of who owns what, but I doubt the board would let them retain any more control than what I've been able to procure in our current offer. Or we could change our plan, come up with something else to intrigue them."

I considered the options, but our only real choice was the third one. But how would we manage to do that? I needed to fix this. I had to. If we could pull this off, they might even make Orion CEO. As the thought occurred to me, I found I was even more determined to make it happen.

"Do you have any suggestions on how we can change our plan?" Orion smiled at me, like he was ... proud?

"I do, but I want to see what you can come up with. If you're smart enough to know the first two options weren't really options, then you are smart enough to think of something. I believe in you." He grabbed his water bottle from his desk, a metal insulated one that said, "World's Best Dad", and took a big drink, the bottle clanking against his desk as he put it back down.

"What do you know about the leadership at Air Mexicana, about Leslie?" Orion looked surprised at my line of questioning, but intrigued, like he was impressed that I was asking questions to help with my research.

He considered for a moment, looking past me into the distance. Why was his concentration face kind of ... hot? "Leslie and I are old friends, he's genuinely a great guy. They have a similar leadership structure to us, but Leslie definitely takes more charge of things than our CEO does."

"That's because John shouldn't be CEO." The way Orion worked, all the extra shit he did and the respect people like Leslie had for him made it clear to me he was the man for the role, not John. "I have an idea on how to get you the position that you deserve."

He didn't hide his confusion, his face screwing up as he leaned back in his chair. "What are you talking about?" He crossed his arms over his chest, the rolled-up sleeves of his shirt holding on tight. Jesus, this guy needed to think about sizing up in his shirts—those forearms should have been illegal.

I cleared my throat. "If we can get this merger through successfully, there's no way you couldn't fight for the CEO position. We will have so much proof." Orion's head was shaking as I continued. "We will have proof that you made this merger happen despite John's mismanagement, but we will also have so much evidence that you've already been doing the job, on top of the COO job. This merger is already one big example. It should be him leading it, not you. But we can prove that you have been doing half of John's job, all the stuff he has been palming off to you; we have emails and meetings invites, not to mention comments from various people about his rudeness recorded in meeting minutes."

"Tahlia, I appreciate all the thinking you have put into this, but you don't need to worry about this, about me." He looked conflicted. I wished I could know what was going on in his mind.

"Orion, this is your shot." It looked like he was fighting himself in his head, but I wasn't sure about what. Surely this was what he wanted, or had I missed something?

"Let's get the merger done first, and then we can look at a takedown of John." He smirked. I could tell he wasn't completely on board, but I left it. I knew what it was like to confront people like John, and it wasn't easy.

"Okay, I'll come back to you shortly with some ideas." I nodded, trying to convince myself I would figure it out. I wasn't confident in my ability to figure out how to fix this problem, but I didn't have any other choice but to try.

"Now, Ms. Walters, out. I'm busy." Orion couldn't hold the laugh back as he tried to keep the act up. I joined in as I stood up, pushed my chair in and made my way to the door.

There were little wrinkles next to Orion's eyes when he laughed. I hadn't seen them before.

I winked at him as I grabbed the door handle, switching my expression to a sadder one before making my way back to my desk. I held on to the feeling of laughter and lightness even though I had to pretend to be miserable and tyrannized by my "horrible boss". It was hard keeping this act up, especially given that our relationship had changed a lot in the last little while. We had fun together while working, laughing, smiling, and joking around. Work had become more fun.

Was it worth even doing this act? Did I really want to try and make friends with others at work who didn't even give me a chance?

It didn't matter at that moment, though. All that mattered was this merger and getting Orion his CEO position—and kicking that ass-wipe to the curb.

By the time lunch came around, my brain was total mush. I had been researching what we could do to fix the merger and was coming up empty. I searched Orion's emails for other similar situations, but there was nothing. I was starting from scratch for this.

Making my way down to the café, I was going to grab something quick for lunch so I could get back to figuring this out. There were an array of paninis, wraps, and sandwiches on display. I wasn't sure what to have, and panic ordered a pesto chicken wrap and a coffee. I considered getting Orion one, but he didn't usually have more than one coffee a day, so decided against it. I asked to eat in; I needed to take a proper break from work and not just sit at my desk.

The café was small, with only five or so tables. They had a large display case of food, as well as some snacks on the bench next to the register, which I tended to buy when I got our morning coffees. I couldn't help myself, the donuts looked so good. There were plants all around the place, giving it a homey garden feel.

"Tahlia." I looked up to find someone approaching me. I recognized them as someone who worked on the same level as me, but I had no idea who they were or why they were coming up to me. My food arrived at the same time. I wanted to dig right in but held back, waiting to hear more from this person. "I'm Lily, I work in the finance team."

"Nice to meet you." She asked if she could join me. I wanted to ask what she wanted first, but gestured for her to sit. Lily's hair was tied up in a tight bun, glasses adorned her nose, and she was wearing a matching blue pantsuit with court heels.

"I'm sorry you have such a scary boss." I had to quickly school my features; our plan had already worked. I just nodded, my mind coming up empty. "I also wanted to apologize for not speaking to you. I've noticed you're all alone most of the time, and I feel this could partially be my fault. I should have invited you to join us."

My heart swelled in my chest, my throat getting tight. I didn't expect to have this reaction to someone admitting I was left out, purposefully. "It's fine," my voice came out hoarse. Shit, I didn't want to sound upset by this.

"I wanted to say hi on your first day, it's usually what I do ... but Rachel said not to, to let you settle in." Of course, Rachel was the reason I was not included, the reason I wasn't a part of the team. I should have put it together sooner, but didn't want to think it. "And then I guess I wanted to, but Rachel somehow managed to stop me, calling me over when I was trying to talk to you."

Lily's shoulders were drooping, her face scrunched up as she picked at her fingernails, obviously uncomfortable with the whole situation.

"I'm not going to say it hasn't sucked, especially with Or—Mr. Ariti being the way he is. But it's not your fault by the sounds of it."

I didn't know why I felt the need to make her feel better, but it was like I saw the weight lift from her shoulders, and she smiled. "I'll make sure we invite you to the next team event, and I'll introduce you to everyone."

"Will Rachel be there?" I looked around, wondering if she was near. It felt like something she would do, sniff out when people were talking about her and stop it.

"Probably ... she tends to take charge of things." Lily also looked around, her eyebrows drawn together.

"Do you all not like her?" I wasn't sure if she would answer my question. Would she trust me?

Lily shook her head. "Not really. When she started she was okay, but she's since become closer and closer to John and become colder towards us."

"Oh." Rachel *was* very close to John, which seemed odd. I spent a fair bit of time with Orion, but not nearly as much as Rachel did with John. I swore half the day they were in his office, conspiring or something.

"But it works in our favor," Lily looked around again and lowered her voice. "Since she started, John takes less of an interest in us." She emphasized the 'us' with a gesture between the two of us. What did she mean?

"Like he stopped asking for your help?" I knew I wasn't thinking the right thing, but for some reason I couldn't figure out what she was talking about. "Did he not have an assistant before she started here?"

Lily lowered her voice even more, which I wasn't sure was possible. I could barely hear her. "He stopped looking at us ... in a way that a boss shouldn't." I instantly lost my appetite as I felt my face pale.

"Did he ... did he do anything to any of you?" The thought made me glad I hadn't eaten yet because I was sure it would be on the way back up.

"No, no." I nodded, feeling the sudden nausea ease slightly. "But since he and Rachel got close, that all stopped so ..."

Holy shit! Rachel and John are sleeping together.

I wondered if Orion knew ... Surely?

"I'll let you get back to your lunch." Lily stood up and pushed her chair under the table. "I'm sorry again." She smiled softly and left the café.

I couldn't believe I didn't put it together that Rachel and John were sleeping together. It made so much sense. It was gross, but could help me with my plan. If I could get proof, there was no way with that and all the other evidence they could deny giving Orion the CEO position.

My plan was coming together. Now I just had to think what we could do to make sure this merger was ours.

Chapter Fourteen

Orion

WALKING INTO SOPHIA'S BAKERY brought a rush of delicious smells, cookies, cakes, slices, everything. I missed having the house constantly smell like baked goods.

I had to speak with Sophia and wanted to have the conversation while Grace was at school, so I'd left work early. Henry's business idea was stuck in my head, and I wasn't sure how I felt about it. I needed to talk it through with her. I couldn't think of anyone else to help me figure out what to do. Henry wasn't being pushy about it at all, he was letting me take my time and think about it. That wasn't like him. He usually annoyed me to make a decision. That's how I knew that he was being serious.

When Tahlia mentioned that she was determined to get me the CEO position, I became even more conflicted. Did I even want that anymore? It wasn't such a simple question. I had wanted to be CEO for as long as I could remember, but after everything I'd been through, then not getting it, was it still something I desired? Was it really where I still wanted my career to go?

The bakery was so packed, I didn't think Sophia had even noticed I'd joined the queue. The bakery looked small from the outside, but Sophia knew how to make use of space. She had a large glass cabinet filled to the brim with all of the baked goods. She had the regular stuff, as well as a section for the new things that her and the bakers made. They were always experimenting.

The bakery had a pastel theme that really made the space bright, open and welcoming. There were a couple of tables with chairs, and she had invested in a really good coffee machine, so people could grab one with a sweet on their way to work.

The back of the bakery was massive. I'd seen it many times before, but as a customer, you couldn't see much of the kitchen from the front, aside from the windowed section where bakers iced and decorated cakes so that customers could watch. I'd wondered how often that section would actually get used. But most of the time when I came here someone was in that spot decorating a cake, children stood watching, noses pressed to the glass, enamored. It helped Sophia sell spots in her cake decorating classes too.

She had two other staff members behind the counter with her serving customers. Sophia was a woman of many talents, smiling as she got it all done. She baked the goods and also served customers daily, not expecting her team to get through it all on their own. Not to mention while also doing all of the other stuff that came with running a business. And she was a single mom. She really was a super woman.

It weirdly felt like home being at her bakery. I was with her when she'd started it from just an idea. I remember her at home, pregnant, baking cookies and selling those through Instagram. When she was finally able to open a standalone store, even though we had separated by that point, I was still so proud of her.

At the grand opening, I was her first customer, and still visited as often as I could. A pang of regret hit me. If only I had been more present. I was there supporting her, but I wasn't there fully. I was always thinking about work, or rushing in or out to not miss a meeting or an opportunity. I should have been there with her, standing behind the counter taking customers' orders. I barely even knew how much she went through to actually open the store. She had started planning it when we were together, but my priorities were in the wrong place.

Sophia caught my eye and her eyebrows drew together in confusion before she replaced it with a smile. There were still a few customers before me, and thankfully the line behind me wasn't long, so Sophia may actually have a few minutes to have a break and talk to me.

"Just come around back, Ry," Sophia called, even though I was next in line, and she was putting cookies into a box for a customer.

"But how am I going to buy donuts if I'm waiting to talk to you out the back?" I laughed as her employee called me over. I wasn't sure if they knew who I was, as I hadn't been there in a while. I ordered a box of donuts for Henry and I to share, with one Grace liked too, as I was going to offer to pick her up from school and spend some time with her this afternoon. If I was going to leave work early, I would like to see Gracie.

Once I paid, I headed through the kitchen doors and around the corner into her office while Sophia finished up serving customers. When she came in, she hung her flour-covered apron on a hook on the wall. She looked tired but so happy. Her hair was in a messy knot on her head that was starting to fall apart, and she was wearing her signature Saltwater Cakes t-shirt with jeans.

"Did you get fired? Because there's no way you'd leave work early." Sophia laughed, taking a seat at her desk chair and taking a big drink of water out of her water bottle.

Her office was cozy, and I really liked it, especially compared to mine. People probably assumed that I loved having a big office, but it felt unnecessary. There were two sitting areas and for what purpose? I wasn't holding meetings or working bees in my office.

Sophia's office had a glass desk with two guest chairs similar to mine, and a bookshelf to the left of her desk. It was minimalistic. She had an eye for interior design; I'd assumed that's what she was going to go into, but then she went the baker route, which suits her even more.

"Not yet," I sat across from her, placing my donut box on her desk. "Can I pick Grace up this afternoon? I can bring her home before dinner."

"Of course Ry, she would love that." Sophia's smile was so genuine it could be mistaken for fake. But that's just how she was, the most genuine person I knew. "So you are here for a reason, especially since it's still a few hours from finish time for you. How can I help you?"

I wasn't sure how to start, anxious about her reaction to it all. "Henry has suggested something to me, but I need someone else's opinion."

"Be more cryptic, please." She laughed as she leaned back in her chair, waiting for me to continue.

I took a deep breath, trying to calm myself. "So Henry's been staying with me for a while and—"

"What why? What happened?" Sophia interrupted. Shit, I hadn't told her about his situation. They were friends ever since we were a couple but didn't talk much. I explained what happened to her. She went from sad to angry to furious. "I can't believe that happened, I need to text him." She got completely sidetracked, pulling her phone out and furiously typing a message to Henry.

"So, Henry suggested something." I chuckled, it could be hard getting her attention back when her mind was set to something else.

"Yes, yes, go on." She threw her phone onto her desk and gave me her full attention.

"Henry has a business idea; he thinks it's time I left Florida Airlines."

Sophia's face hid what she truly thought, staying silent and listening attentively as I explained his idea that had been replaying in my head.

"And what do you need from me? I think your mind is already made up." Sophia knew me more than I knew myself, I had no idea what my choice was, but apparently she knew.

"What if it doesn't work, and I end up having to go back or find a new job?"

Sophia's expression said, *stop beating around the bush and tell me what is actually the problem.*

I sighed. "I wasn't a good partner to you. I was distant, my mind was not there when we were together, always thinking about work. I was so focused on moving up the ladder, becoming CEO that our relationship was sacrificed, our chance to be a family. And there could still be potential for me to get the CEO position, so maybe I should stick that out and see how it goes. If I walked away from Florida Airlines now, not having achieved what I had been trying to for fifteen years, what did I sacrifice everything for?" I tried to catch my breath, avoiding Sophia's eyes.

"Ry," I looked up, a soft smile on her face, no sign of anger or disappointment. "Is this what you want to do?" She looked back and forth between my eyes, as if trying to catch any hint of what I really wanted.

"I'm honestly not sure. Working at Florida Airlines has become slightly nightmarish. But I've worked so hard to get there. This is what I wanted. I don't want to let anyone down." I felt heavy admitting this all, but lighter at the same time.

"You're not letting me down." She reached across the desk and pulled my hand into hers, the warmth from her fingers nice on my ice-cold hands. "Sure, it was hard when we were going through those things. But even if we didn't, we probably wouldn't have ended up together. We weren't meant to be a couple. We were meant to be Grace's parents, though, and I will never regret anything to do with that."

"She's my whole world."

"I would never want you to hold yourself back from an opportunity that would mean you could be happier, have more time with Grace. I would love for you to be able to have her with you for sleepovers more. If you did this, I think you would be able to. But only if it's what you actually want." One of her staff members called out for Sophia. "I'll have to head back out in a couple of minutes. But Ry, I forgive you. It's the past, and we've worked through it. I don't want you to not do this because you think it will hurt me. I promise it won't." Sophia walked around the desk and pulled me up into a hug. I felt a tear slip out of my eye, down my cheek and into her hair. I didn't expect this.

"Thank you," I whispered. Something changed, what was holding me back was gone.

She pulled back and kissed my cheek. "Any time. I have to go back out there, but feel free to hang out a couple more minutes before you head out." Sophia grabbed her apron and threw it over her head. "I also want to hear how it all goes." She rushed out, leaving me in her office.

I slumped back down into the chair I was sitting in and took a few deep breaths, feeling more overwhelmed than I expected. I never realized how much disappointing Sophia was holding me back. I hated how I was as a partner when we were together when I looked back. If I could reverse time and do it differently, I would, as long as it was guaranteed we would still get our little girl in the end.

I stayed a few more minutes before heading out, waving to Sophia as I left the once again busy bakery. This was what I wanted, something I could be proud of, something that worked for me, for my life. I wanted to see my daughter. I wanted to move to a house, have her stay with me every other week or whatever arrangement Sophia and I would come too. I wanted to be a better dad and do what worked for my family. Florida Airlines didn't.

How did Henry figure this out and I didn't? Fuck, I didn't know what I'd do without him or Sophia.

I got in my car, placing the donuts on the passenger seat. I was tempted to eat one now but figured I'd hold off and have one with Grace when we got home.

I made my way to her school, and parked outside. I was about to go in, but I knew I needed to talk to Henry now, before I somehow talked myself out of it.

I dialed his number, but it went to voicemail after ringing out. I hung up and figured I'd just try him later or talk to him when I was home.

I got out of the car and started to walk into the building when my phone buzzed.

It was Henry.

"Hey, Hen." I walked back to my car and leaned on the passenger door, not wanting to pick Grace up while my attention was elsewhere.

"Orion. For what do I owe this pleasure? A call during business hours, it must be important." I could hear the smugness in his voice. *Asshole.*

"You're right, it can wait till I'm home tonight." A parent and their kids walked past, laughing and talking, which Henry picked up.

"You're not at the office, are you, Ry?" He was curious, much like Sophia. Did I really never leave work early? I needed to fix this.

"No, I left early, I just left the bakery. I'm picking up Gracie." I shook my head, realizing that Sophia had probably texted him, and he already knew exactly where I was and why I was calling him out of the blue instead of waiting until we were both home tonight.

"Spit it out, Ry. I'm busy." No, he wasn't. I could hear the TV in the background watching football reruns.

"I'm in."

I think Henry dropped his phone, static coming through the line. "I knew you would be. Great, we can talk more about it later. Are you bringing Gracie home, I miss that little snot ball."

"My daughter isn't a snot ball, you prick." I laughed, glad to see he was back to his joking self, not being so serious. "I'll bring her home so you can see her."

"Yes! She's going to be so excited to see Uncle Hen Hen." I barked out a laugh; he'd never called himself that before.

"You are not Uncle Hen Hen. I have to go. I have sweets melting in the car."

"See you soon, daddy." I heard Henry laughing at himself as I hung up.

I was excited about the possibilities for my future. After talking with Sophia I knew this was the right move. The only worry that popped up was Tahlia. I couldn't leave her there with the vulture, John. I had to figure something out for her.

I brushed off all thoughts of this change, wanting to be fully present with Grace. I signed her out and took her back to my apartment for our afternoon with donuts and Uncle Hen Hen.

Chapter Fifteen

Tahlia

WALKING INTO ASHTON'S BIRTHDAY party was slightly less nerve wracking with Jeremy by my side. He insisted I come, saying I was now a part of their group and I didn't have a choice.

Since moving to Tampa, I hadn't really explored or done a lot except work. Starting a new job in a new city where I needed to make new friends was more exhausting than I thought it would be. So going to this party was definitely daunting to say the least.

The art class I had booked was how I had planned to get out more and meet more people, but it wasn't starting for a few more weeks. It was soon, though, and I was excited. It would be nice to do something for me, and do more drawing and painting.

The party was at some boujee restaurant, with lots of small tables set up around the place. Jeremy didn't have many details about the event when he told me I was coming. He'd only invited me at the last minute because they'd all apparently only found out an hour before it started, with Steve, Ashton's boyfriend, organizing it.

"Jeremy! Tahlia!" Ashton came up and greeted us as we came in. It looked like Ashton's family was here, as well as Jeremy, Liam, Suzie, and September, and some other people I didn't recognize. "Thank you for coming. Grab a drink, we'll have some food soon." He disappeared, off to talk to the others.

"He loves parties," Jeremy explained as he guided me over to his friends. "He loves to host, so we might only get a few minutes with him here and there—he likes to make sure he talks to everyone, even though it's only his family and close friends." I nodded as we walked up to September, Liam, and Suzie.

"I'm not a close friend," I whispered in his ear, which was responded to with an eye roll. I was pulled into a hug by Suzie, got a head nod from Liam, and a small wave from September.

"What are we drinking?" Jeremy waggled his eyebrows at us, looking like he was ready to party. I had work in the morning, so I definitely couldn't drink too much. I wasn't usually much of a drinker. But at a party where I knew basically no one, I was definitely going to have something.

Jeremy took everyone's orders, beer for him and September, Liam an Asahi, and me an Espresso Martini. I may not drink much, but I knew what I wanted when I did.

Liam went up to help Jeremy with the drinks. "How have you settled into living in Florida?" September asked.

"It's good. I mean, I haven't really done much but work, but it's nice. I like the weather." Was it weird that I hadn't done anything? Tried to make friends or meet people?

"Did I hear you talking about the weather?" Liam handed out drinks, his face screwed up at that thought. The espresso from my martini made my mouth water.

We all laughed as we tried our drinks. My martini was strong, but at least it would take the edge off quickly.

The group quickly fell into a conversation as I looked around. I'd never had anything like this. No parties, definitely not this number of people I could invite to anything. It was strange. I hadn't really been invited to anything like this either, not having a whole lot of friends growing up. I had been slightly worried when getting ready for this party. Jeremy hadn't given me any sense of a dress code, but my casual jeans and a top seemed to fit in with what most people were wearing.

"Hey guys." I was pulled from my thoughts when a guy walked up to the group, Ashton rushing up behind him. There were murmurs of greetings from the group, the conversation immediately fizzling out. He turned to me. "I don't think we've met. I'm Steve, Ashton's boyfriend."

Oh. He was not what I expected, not that I'd known what to expect. He was short with cropped, blond hair, and no facial hair. He was dressed so formally, not casual like everyone else. I guessed that Steve wasn't really a part of the friendship group. He wasn't in the book club, but maybe he'd just missed that one.

"I'm Tahlia, I live with Jeremy. Nice to meet you." He pulled me in for an unexpected side hug, our shoulders squishing together, making it more awkward than it needed to be.

"How are you guys going?" Ashton came up next to Steve, looking a bit worried.

"How come you didn't tell me your friends were here?" Steve asked, aiming a pointed look at Ashton.

"Sorry, babe, I didn't even think about it." Ashton blushed, looking incredibly uncomfortable. Steve didn't say anything and turned and walked away. What the hell? Wasn't this his boyfriend's party, why was he being cold? "Sorry, I'd better ..." Ashton pointed in the direction Steve went and followed.

I turned to Jeremy and lowered my voice. "Is that normal?"

He nodded, his eyes drooping. "Steve doesn't like us, so Ashton tries to keep him away. He didn't want us to not come—he insisted, even though it would probably be easier for him."

"That's awful." How could he be with someone who hated his closest friends? It didn't make sense to me.

"Let's do shots!" September called, a tray of tequila shots in their hands. I hadn't even noticed them sneak away. "Looks like we are going to need it." They mumbled as they picked up their shot, and everyone followed suit. I hesitantly grabbed one, only having just finished my first drink, and worried about being hungover tomorrow.

"Just worry about the now and have fun." Jeremy nudged my shoulder. "You deserve a break."

With the cheap alcohol still burning holes in my throat, we headed to a small table to sit together, not being approached by anyone else after Steve and Ashton had run away. Jeremy said it was unlikely that Ashton would come back tonight, trying to avoid any more conflict.

The vibe in the group felt off. I could tell September was trying to keep everyone talking, but Suzie and Liam were whispering to each other and Jeremy was there ... but not. He was zoning out of the group, his eyes following Ashton, who was talking to some other people with Steve's arm around his shoulder.

The food started coming out, the smells of the bowls of chips, halloumi sticks, chicken satay skewers, and jalapeño bites making my stomach grumble. I was ready to stuff my face, but no one else seemed to grab anything as I filled up my paper plate.

I looked around the loud room filled with chatting people as I ate my food, amazed at where I was. I was so grateful to be surrounded by these people who had somehow become my friends. I could feel myself choking up, even though I wasn't trying to say anything. I was definitely tipsier than I had been in a while. Two drinks and I was already almost drunk. Typical Tahlia.

I had been apprehensive about moving to Florida. Honestly, I'd been worried I would end up a total loner, constantly being drenched in sweat because I couldn't get used to the humidity, eating takeout every night in my bedroom in my sad-girl pajamas. But I somehow was so lucky to have Claire connect me with Jeremy and his amazing friends, who'd accepted me with no questions. Knowing that Steve was making Jeremy's ... no, *my friends* feel like they had to tone themselves down at a party that was for an integral member of the group, pissed me off.

"Guys, guys," I heard myself call out before I realized I did. "Can I tell you about my boss's asshole boss and his assistant, who, I think, is sucking him off in his office during the day?" Everyone's mouths dropped open, except Jeremy. The words made their way out of my mouth before I even had a chance to think about them. My plan was to try and distract them from the shitty situation that was this party, and that was the first thing I blurted out.

"Babe, you'd better after that opening." Jeremy handed me another martini, which I immediately took a sip of. Everyone laughed, but then gestured for me to continue.

"So my boss, Orion, is getting fucked over by the CEO, John, the dirtiest ass-wipe of all ass-wipes. His assistant, Rachel, is just as bad as he is, making people exclude me from events. But I have a plan." I finished my drink, finding everyone waiting with amused, interested, curious looks. "We're working on a massive project, and I'm going to use it to get Orion his job."

"Her boss, Orion, is dreamy." Jeremy jumped in. "I found him on socials and he is HOT. He also pretends to be this tyrant boss, so others will be nice to our Tahlia."

Orion's on social media? Maybe I should find his acc—no, you shouldn't Tahlia, that's inappropriate and crossing a line.

"That's so hot, he is so into you Tahlia." Suzie nodded her head excitedly.

I wanted to tell them how he actually was with me. He was nice, funny, so, so good at what he did, and honorable when it came to business. But he was so fucking sexy, it was getting harder and harder to ignore.

"No, no way Suzie."

Everyone nodded in agreement with Suzie. "Sounds like he might," September interjected.

I shook my head. "Guys, no. He's my boss, there's no way he's into me—and he has a kid, so he probably has a wife."

"Didn't you just say his boss was sleeping with his assistant?" Liam added as he finished his drink. Suzie elbowed him in the ribs.

"It doesn't matter how hot he is, he is off-limits!" I shoved more food into my mouth, noticing the others were starting to fill up their plates and eat too. The mood had shifted, people moving to the music, being louder and more like themselves. "But help me think of an idea. I need something to wow the client to make the project successful. This is a big deal to Orion, and it's going to take something big to make it happen. I can't think of anything." I slumped back in my chair, having no idea where to start.

Suzie started spit-balling. "Airline, air, fly, plane, travel, vacation."

"Vacation! That could work." I racked my brain thinking about a vacation, why would it be a vacation?

We all went back and forth, as we kept drinking and eating. Ashton never came back, which I could tell made Jeremy sad, but the others were all distracted with my problem and didn't seem to notice.

"What about a … cruise?" September stood, pretending to be on the bumpy sea, their drink sloshing over the rim of their glass.

Everyone sat in silence, thinking about their idea.

"There are so many things to do on a cruise." Suzie's eyes lit up. "When we went on one, we went to the spa, the theater, the spa, the room a lot …"

"Yuck, gross!" Jeremy shouted. "We don't want to hear about your nasty sex life."

"September, I think you're onto something."

Would Orion go for it? A vacation, a cruise to bring us together, show them we would work well together. Leslie had said they were a family-oriented business, and lots of cruises were aimed at families.

Was it crazy? Yeah, probably. But could it work? *Maybe.*

The next morning at work was rough. I wasn't super hungover. No vomiting, thank fuck—which was surprising—but had a monster headache. Claire had responded to me last night, but I only managed to look at the message on my lunch break.

Claire: How was that party last night?

Me: Good, hungover though…

Claire: let me guess, too many espresso martinis?

Me: nooooo… never…

I missed Claire. It was strange being so far away from her. But the longer I was here, I knew it was the right move for me. I just hoped she could come and visit. I could go back, but not for a while. I needed my space from Boston.

I also woke up to so many texts about the cruise idea. It sounded crazier sober, but I promised I would pitch it to Orion, and I had no other idea, so what else could I do?

My plan was to catch him after the meeting he was in. He had been back-to-back all day, the only time I had seen him was when I gave him his coffee. It was probably a good thing. I was so tired, I probably could have fallen asleep at my desk.

All morning I had looked into cruises to get a general idea of timing, costs, and the length. I prepared a presentation to show him. It wasn't my best work, but something to at least show him what I was thinking rather than me blurting it out and getting lost.

I waited until it was five past three before knocking on his door. I swore I could feel eyes on me, waiting to see what Orion's reaction was. A moment later, he opened the door, raising an eyebrow at me. No words spoken.

He audibly huffed, waiting for me to speak.

"Do you have a few minutes, Mr. Ariti? I'd like to discuss the merger project." I could see a smile he was trying to hide starting to escape. He walked into his office and left the door open. A silent invitation to enter.

There were faint whispers from behind me as I followed him, closing the door. A lot of people were staring, including Lily, who gave me a thumbs up.

I sat in the chair in front of him, as I always did.

"How are you, Tahlia?" His smile was out now. It was sexy. Shit. Everyone's thoughts from last night were getting in my head. Did he like me?

No, he's your boss, Tahlia.

He was hot, though, and it was so hard to deny. His hair was ruffled like he had been dragging his hands through it, his shirt sleeves rolled up to just below his elbows—Christ, save me from those forearms—his five o'clock shadow forming around his chin. I had an insane impulse to brush my palm against it.

I violently pushed all thoughts of that out of my mind. He was hot, sure, but it didn't matter. "I'm good, you've been busy today."

He sighed, leaning back in his chair. He looked exhausted. "Yeah. So how are you going with the merger?"

Excitement bubbled up. I was nervous, but couldn't wait to tell him my idea.

"How about a cruise?"

Orion raised that one eyebrow that made my stomach turn to jelly, which I knew meant he was intrigued. "So I think we can expect that our competition will run with the standard pitches, hosting them for weekends in their cities to wine and dine them, maybe some kind of corporate retreat with a golf course. But what if we did something different. Something a bit more personal, family-oriented?"

I paused, taking a sip of water, trying to calm my nerves and slow my speech. I spoke really fast when I was nervous and wanted him to actually understand what I was saying. I turned my laptop to face him, my presentation playing. It would probably be more impactful to do this in a meeting room, but I didn't want to risk John seeing.

"Air Mexicana is a company that's driven by strong core values. They care about their staff and their families. I think if we show we not only respect but share those values, they would be interested in us. A cruise is one of the most family-friendly holidays you can take." As I changed the slide, I chanced a peek at Orion. He looked excited, which gave me a boost of confidence to keep going. "We could take them on the cruise, spend time getting to know each other, work through any problems we have while also having fun together, going out for dinner, going to the theater. And they can bring their families."

"Tahlia." Orion stopped me. The silence that surrounded me as I waited for him to continue was deafening.

He hates it. Shit.

"Stop that, I can see what you're thinking all over your face. This is great. How did you come up with this idea?"

I felt instant relief, I couldn't believe he liked it. There was no way I could tell him my friends and I came up with this drunk at a party last night. "I actually have a bit more." He laughed and gestured for me to continue. I went through the very basic data I had on when we could go, costs, and how long the cruise would be. More research and work would need to be done on this, but it would help give him an idea.

"No need to convince me any further. This is amazing, I would never have thought of it." Orion grabbed my hand, his smile so big I was sure his cheeks were going to hurt later.

"Thank fuck for that," I mumbled, and we both fell into laughter.

"I have an idea, only if you're up for it." I nodded as I pulled my hand back into my lap, noticing how it was tingling. "To kill two birds with one stone, we should work overtime this weekend. Firstly, it will help us make progress on this cruise, I think we need to get it done ASAP to keep being competitive. We will need to pitch this to the board. But this will also help keep up our charade."

"Ah, big mean Orion is making me do overtime."

"That's Mr. Ariti to you." He winked. My stomach filled with butterflies that were apparently having a party. Who was this guy? Suddenly, he was excited, like I wouldn't be surprised if he jumped out of his chair. He'd held my hand, and now he'd winked at me. The wink was not helping me forget how hot he was.

"Let's do it, Mr. Ariti."

Chapter Sixteen

Orion

THANK GOD IT WAS Friday afternoon. I closed my laptop at exactly five o'clock and started to pack up to head home. Even though I was now going to work the weekend, it didn't feel the same. I had a feeling it wouldn't be so bad.

I wasn't sure why I was shocked when Tahlia pitched an idea that was so different, so wild, that it might actually work.

As she'd pitched her idea, and I'd realized how good it was, my nagging worry of leaving her behind resurfaced. I needed to have a solid plan for her, someone for her to work with that wouldn't treat her the way John would if he got his hands on her. Tahlia was already gone for the day by the time I left my office, closing the door behind me. I was glad, I hoped she had left a bit early—she deserved it. Her ingenuity and focus made it obvious to anyone with eyes that she had a big future here, if that's what she wanted. It was probably part of why the others had excluded her to begin with. And it was why I was feeling torn about leaving. The place needed brains like hers, but she needed guidance to reach her potential.

What could I do to ensure her career wouldn't be affected once I left?

For once, I'd actually brought my lunch but then had been too busy to eat it, so I made my way into the kitchen to take it home again.

I wasn't sure I'd be able to get Tahlia in the room when this was pitched to the board. If that was the case, I would make sure they knew it was all her idea. I wasn't going to take credit for something that wasn't my idea.

"Orion, heading off already?" Phil, the Chief Financial Officer, had come into the kitchen without me noticing while I was putting my lunch container in my bag.

"Working this weekend, so figured I can have an early one today," I replied. Phil was a really good guy, very business savvy, by the book. He'd been in his CFO position a long time and had helped me when I was on my way up.

"Enjoy, I'll see you next week." Phil headed out, smiling at people as he did.

That could work. I could get Tahlia reassigned to Phil. He could mentor her like he did for me. With his help, I could honestly see her becoming the first woman CEO for Florida Airlines—if she wanted it, that was.

Everyone avoided eye contact and gave me a wide berth as I left the kitchen and made my way to the elevators, unlike they had with Phil. I chuckled internally. Really, how had I got such a reputation as an asshole? Was it my face?

I was feeling more confident in leaving now that I had an idea of how to help Tahlia keep progressing without me. Now, I just wasn't sure when I should tell her about me leaving. Probably before I resigned, but not until it was ready to go. I didn't want to freak her out in the middle of this project, I wanted her concentrated and not worried about what would happen to her when I left. My plan for her would be solid before I told her what was going on.

If she told me she didn't want to stay, I would help her find another job. She had no contacts in Florida, and I was confident I could get her something else.

I pressed the basement level button in the elevator, looking forward to dinner tonight, and strangely, coming back tomorrow.

"Thanks for coming out again, Ry." Henry tipped his beer at me before taking a swig. When I suggested a night in, Henry had scoffed and eventually convinced me to go out with him. Takeout and reality shows had turned into dinner and drinks at a bar. "So, who do you think I have a chance with?"

We had just finished our burgers, which were nothing more than you'd expect from a bar. Picking at the last few fries on my plate, I looked around. Henry really had wanted me to help him, be his "wingman". He was finally getting back to normal after everything Charlotte put him through, and he felt it was time to get back out there.

The room was dimly lit, a few people sitting at the bar like we were. The rest of the high tables were filled by groups of friends chatting and drinking. A couple of pool tables to the right were taken, with a few groups hovering nearby, obviously hoping to take them once they had finished their game. Near the pool tables, there was a dartboard that a couple of guys were using. The speakers buzzed overhead with too loud music, causing my head to thump with the beginnings of a headache. I'd much prefer the comfort of the couch at home and reruns of *Desperate Housewives*—but Henry needed me, and so I'd suck it up.

"What about her?" I nodded at a woman who was just walking up to the bar, another friend in tow. She was dressed in a tank and shorts, had short red hair, and was already eyeing Henry off.

Hen had always caught women's eyes, whether he was out with Charlotte or with me. He was a bit of a lady magnet, but never seemed to believe it, no matter how many times I'd tried to point it out to him. He had only had eyes for Charlotte.

Henry looked over his shoulder to the redhead, a smirk on his face. He nodded at her and she smiled in response. "You're good at this."

"I really didn't do anything." I chuckled, finishing my beer and ordering another round.

"Why don't you two come sit with us?" I looked over as the redhead and her blonde friend gestured for us to join them at a free table away from the bar. Henry grabbed the beer I'd just ordered and headed over. I hadn't really come out to meet anyone, but I couldn't leave Hen hanging.

"I'm Henry," he introduced himself as we sat down.

"Cat." The redhead introduced herself as she sat next to Henry. "And this is Polly."

Polly smiled at me, a blush creeping up her neck.

It kind of felt like we were in high school, having to introduce ourselves at the start of a new school year. At least no one had asked for a fun fact—I would have had no fucking clue what to say. "Orion. Can we get you anything to drink?"

"We already ordered. They said they'd bring it over." Polly explained. I wasn't surprised, even though it wasn't the kind of bar where they brought you drinks. The bartender always tried to get into women's pants. It was disgusting. I wasn't sure why we came here; this was one of my least favorite places to go.

"Boys' night out?" Cat raised her eyebrows at us, an amused look on her face.

I tried to hide my laugh at the thought of calling Henry and I going to the bar a "boys' night out".

"Not exactly." I hadn't heard the tone in Henry's voice before. I think he was trying to flirt. "What brings you two out tonight?"

"It's been a shit week, a drink—or five—is required." Cat took a long pull of her beer as Polly just nodded along. Polly had a kind face, minimal makeup on, and wore a mid-length black dress. Her blonde hair reminded me of someone I was definitely not supposed to be thinking about outside work hours. I cleared my throat, trying to focus back on the conversation, *not* on how long until I saw her aga—

Henry led the conversation with Cat and Polly, very obviously more interested in Cat, if the way he leaned towards her was any indication. Asking them all about what they did for work, if they had pets, what their favorite movie was. It was a little bit obvious to me that he hadn't done this sort of thing in a little while, but he was having fun and so was I, so I wasn't complaining. The number of beers I'd had was also helping.

"We should play pool," Cat suggested during a pause in the conversation. I looked over and, surprisingly, there was a free table.

"Let's do it." I led the group over and racked the balls up. Henry grabbed the cues from the rack on the wall.

"How should we team up?" Cat eyed Henry, and I tried to hide my smirk.

"You two can team up, Polly and I are going to whoop your asses," I said with a laugh as I took a sip from my new beer, which probably needed to be my last.

"If you're so confident the two of you will win, we should get to break," Henry said.

I agreed, and Henry gestured for Cat to break, leaning on his cue to watch. I pulled the ball rack off as she lined the cue ball up and smacked the ball into the others. I couldn't deny I was impressed. The balls shot out in different directions, two falling into pockets.

"Shit," Polly muttered. "Maybe we won't win."

I smiled at her; her nerves from earlier seemed to have lessened.

"Nah, we've got this."

"I'm not sure." Polly looked around before lowering her voice. "I haven't played before. Cat knows, I think that's why she asked about teams."

Maybe we weren't going to win then. But I guessed it didn't really matter. The competitive side of me was trying to convince me otherwise.

"Your turn." Henry pulled us from our conversation. Polly passed me the cue, obviously avoiding going yet. I wasn't entirely sure why she'd agreed to play, considering she clearly wasn't confident in her abilities. Maybe she wanted to learn.

Henry and Cat were chatting and laughing to my left, but I could feel Polly's eyes on my back as I approached the table. Cat had sunk one striped and one solid ball. She chose solids, leaving us going for the striped balls. I lined up my shot, took a breath, and hit the ball.

"You got it!" Polly cheered. She high-fived me as I passed the cue to her. Usually if I sunk the ball I'd go again playing in a team, but since she hadn't played, I thought maybe she could have a go rather than waiting for Cat and Henry to wipe the table.

"Give it a go. We got another turn because I got it in." I explained how to shoot, how I hold the cue and line it up.

Polly lined the ball up and tried to hit it but slipped, causing the ball to only move an inch with a sad little plink. "Shit."

"You'll get it. It's hard to learn, so you did great for the first go," I reassured her.

"Could you show me again?" Polly stepped closer to me, a bit closer than I liked.

On our next turn, I walked up to the table, lined up my shot, explaining what I was doing to Polly. I turned back to see her attention fully on me, more than I had expected. "And then you gently hit it and ..." the clanking of the ball falling into the pocket had me straightening up, already looking for my next shot.

"Wow, impressive." She went to pull me in for a hug as I gestured for a high five. It was awkward. Her face turned a dark shade of red, while I laid the cue against the table.

"Sorry, you're great and everything, I just ... I'm not really looking for anything." Fuck, I hated this stuff.

Tucking her hair behind her ears, a shy smile on her face, she waved off my stilted apology. "No worries."

Henry taking the next shot pulled my attention back to the game. I could feel his gaze on mine, he must have witnessed the uncomfortable exchange between Polly and me.

"So, how do you like being a pilot?" Cat asked Henry as he finished his turn.

"I love it, best decision I ever made." I gestured for Polly to have another go as I had more of my beer.

We continued playing until Cat and Henry won, unsurprisingly. Polly did get a bit better as the game went on, but it was obvious Cat had played a fair bit.

The girls went to the bathroom as Henry and I finished off our drinks.

"How's it going?" I placed my bottle down on the bar.

"She's nice, and I'm having heaps of fun, but ... there's no spark there or anything. I don't think she feels anything really, either." Henry shrugged, not seeming too bothered. "What about you?"

"Me?"

"Yeah, you." He shook his head at me. "And the blonde?"

"I'm good. I didn't come here to try and get laid or meet someone." It felt weird even thinking about it. It wasn't something I had actively done for a while. My priorities in life were elsewhere.

After Cat and Polly came back from the bathroom, we let them know we were heading off. I was glad that we'd caught a lift over here, as there was no way Henry or I were in the shape to drive after the number of beers we had.

"So you didn't like her?" Henry waggled his eyebrows at me as we got into our Uber.

"She was nice, sure, but no, not in that way."

"Is that because there's someone else on your mind, maybe?" he prodded, a devious smile plastered on his face.

"Like who?" I couldn't tell him that she'd kept popping up in my mind all night—that Polly's blonde hair and short stature reminded me of her.

"Tahlia," he deadpanned. "Don't lie to me, Ry. I'm drunk, so probably won't remember it anyway."

"Fine." I huffed out a breath, wondering if I'd regret this in the morning. "Maybe I like her, just a little bit. But it doesn't matter."

"And why's that oh-so-serious, Orion?" Henry loved to mock me when he was drunk.

"She's engaged and my assistant, you jackass."

"So?"

"She's off-limits." No matter how often I had to fight that thought.

Chapter Seventeen

Tahlia

THE OFFICE WAS DEAD quiet when I made my way in on Saturday. As I walked up to the building, I had a thought that I wouldn't be able to get in, but I apparently had out of hours access on my building pass. I would have felt super awkward if I had to call Orion if I couldn't get in.

There were no security guards at the reception desk, no people rushing around on phone calls, and apparently no coffee. I stopped in front of the closed coffee shop. I hadn't considered that they would be closed on weekends. It made sense, but it sucked.

I sighed and made my way to the elevators. I could always go out and get coffee from another café nearby, but it was so hot outside, and I was already here. Maybe we could get delivery? I didn't even have to wait for the elevator; the doors opened as soon as I called it—somehow, that was even more eerie than the echoey lobby. Still, it was nice being there with no one else. Definitely kind of creepy, but nice. I didn't have to worry about keeping up the act of Orion being an asshole, or dress up. I was wearing a mid-length sundress, with puffy sleeves, that was covered in white, pink and blue flowers. It was way too casual for normal workdays, but seemed appropriate for a Saturday when no one else would be at work.

As I made my way over to my desk, I thought about yesterday afternoon. Lily had brought me over to meet some of her coworkers. They were all really nice, but definitely seemed cautious about what they could say around me. It was strange. I assumed they were still worried about me being another Rachel—or ending up on the receiving end of her spite.

They had asked me what my weekend plans were, which I was taken aback by. No one here, except Orion, had ever asked me about anything outside of work. When I told them that Orion was making me work the weekend, they all looked so sorry for me and gave me sympathy. Orion was definitely right about why they left me out, and his idea was working a treat. He knew exactly what we needed to do for them to let me join in.

It still felt wrong spending time with them. They were only inviting me over because they felt bad, not because they genuinely wanted to spend time with me. I wasn't sure this whole act was worth it. If we did become friends, could I even tell them that we were pretending? That we lied to them for weeks?

I shook the thoughts away as I unpacked my bag. I checked my phone; we said we'd meet ten minutes ago, and Orion still wasn't there, which wasn't like him. Had I gotten the time wrong? I couldn't even check as we had only spoken about it, there was no email, message, text—nothing.

The elevator dinged just as I was about to open my laptop and double-check my emails to see if he had sent anything about the time, and Orion strolled out. He had two coffees in one hand and a pastry box in the other, an easy smile on his face.

I almost did a double take, he looked so different. Hotter, somehow. His usually well-styled hair was wet like he'd just gotten out of the shower, blue jeans hung low on his hips, a short sleeve button up clung to his chest. But the one thing that really stopped me in my tracks was the glasses he wore. They were black rectangle glasses, rounded on the corners. Maybe Ray-Bans? I didn't even know he needed glasses. He probably usually wore contacts. But holy shit, he should wear his glasses more often. Or maybe not, actually, it was way too distracting.

"Morning, Tahlia." He walked past me into his office, somehow opening the door with no hands. I grabbed my laptop and made my way into his office. Who was Orion out of the workplace?

"Morning." I'd been too in shock about how different—how hot—he looked to respond. The smell wafting from the pastel-green box he carried thankfully caught my attention as I followed him into his office. "What do you have there?" I asked, gesturing to it.

He passed me one of the coffee cups he brought, which said my order on the side: caramel latte. How had he known my order? I was always the one to get us coffees.

"I have a few different pastries, cookies, and donuts from Saltwater Cakes." He opened the box and showed off what was inside, like he was doing a YouTube unboxing.

Holy shit, they looked delicious. There were Danishes, croissants, cookies, cupcakes, and donuts. Fuck, I was in heaven. First, sexy Orion arrived at the office, then second, he'd somehow known my coffee order and brought me one, and third he'd brought the best looking pastries I'd ever seen.

"I've never heard of that bakery before."

Orion shook his head as he placed the box down. "That's your loss, it's the best bakery in town," he explained as he went to the kitchen and got some plates. Orion passed me one as he came back into the office. "Overtime Saturdays mean we start with a pastry. So, pick one. We'll eat the rest later."

I wasn't going to argue with that. It was an incredibly hard choice; they all looked and smelled amazing. But I went with my gut and chose the fluffy glazed donut. I had obviously chosen right—Orion looked disappointed, as if that was the one he wanted most. But he didn't say anything.

We sat in his lounge area, as I now called it, eating our pastries and drinking coffee. "This is the best donut I've ever eaten. And this coffee is so good."

"Sophia is a boss in the kitchen." Orion nodded as he devoured his Danish.

"Is Sophia your wife?" I blurted the question that had nagged at me ever since I saw the photo of his daughter on his desk.

He seemed to think over his choice of words. "No, she's my friend. So, are you ready for today?"

"I have one more question, and then I'll be ready to get into it." A grin was forming on my face, even though I was trying to hide it.

"Alright."

"How blind are you?" I wanted to ask if he wore contacts, but that was a stupid question. If he was wearing glasses today, then surely he had to wear contacts.

Orion rolled his eyes at me, which was somehow hotter with the glasses. "Blinder than you probably think." He passed them over to me, which was the last thing I expected. I wiped my sticky, glaze-covered fingers on a napkin before grabbing them and placing them on my nose.

The glasses were too big for my head, so I had to hold them. "Shit, Orion, you are so blind." I couldn't see out of them at all—no wonder he wore contacts.

"You look ridiculous right now, you have to see it." He pulled out his phone and pointed it at me. "Smile." I smiled at his phone—well, at least in its general direction—before I gave him his glasses back.

Orion turned his phone to show me. I looked like a child who put on an adult pair of glasses, but was smiling like an idiot in the wrong direction. I couldn't hold back my laugh.

"You need to get laser surgery or something." I finished off my coffee, the cup rustling the paper bin bag as I managed to throw it into the trash can by his desk.

"Maybe." He chuckled as he finished off his food.

"We can get started now." I moved to the table near the door. I booted up my laptop as I thought about what we were actually going to do today.

Orion joined me so we could see each other's screens.

"So, where do we start today?" I felt a bit lost. We needed to figure out how to pitch the cruise to the board, but how would we do that?

"We will do a bit of a cost breakdown that we can present and then draft up the presentation, I think." Orion nodded to himself like he was checking off a list in his head.

"Let's do it." I started to open up my previous research, the presentation I pitched to him, wondering if we could reuse any of it.

"Tahlia?" I looked over and found Orion watching me.

"Yeah?" He looked so serious.

"How did you come up with this idea?" Oh. I blew out a breath through pursed lips. "It's not something that's so crazy that I'm surprised you came up with it, but I would have never thought of something like this. I'm curious."

Should I tell him?

I didn't want to sound like some dumb teenager who went around telling everyone about our plans. Would he be annoyed that I told people? I didn't tell them any details.

"I was at a party with some friends, and we came up with it together." I shrugged. If I didn't tell the truth, I wouldn't know what to say.

"Were you drunk?" He looked amused. It was my turn to roll my eyes at him.

"Obviously. I'm twenty-five and went to a party. It was Thursday night, though, so yesterday morning was rough." Orion barked a laugh, which made me laugh too.

"Twenty-five is where it all goes downhill, Tahlia. Just wait until you're in your thirties."

I fake-shuddered at the thought, earning another eye roll from Orion.

"Let's be honest, though. The good ideas only happen when we're drunk anyway. So I respect that." He bumped his shoulder into mine, which caught me off guard for a second before I did it back.

"Okay, let's get into it." Orion nodded and turned to his laptop.

We fell into a comfortable silence, the only noise filling the space the clacking of our keyboards.

Chapter Eighteen

Orion

TAHLIA'S STOMACH HAD BEEN rumbling for the last fifteen minutes. I hadn't said anything, but it was starting to get irritating.

"I'm thinking about ordering some lunch, are you hungry?" I locked my laptop and looked at Tahlia, who was furiously typing something out.

"Obviously, I'm hungry. Have you not heard my stomach?" She laughed.

"Thought it would be rude to mention it." I teased.

She snorted, pulling a face of mock offense before getting up and stretching. We had been sitting for hours, working side by side.

"What do you feel like?" I wasn't usually someone that could work with other people for long. I hated hearing other people typing, them making funny noises when they worked, or seeing them pull a thinking face out of the corner of my eye. It frustrated me.

It wasn't like that with Tahlia. Her typing wasn't annoying, I found comfort in hearing her sigh or when she would ask me questions, bounce ideas off me. Her thinking face was also kind of cute.

"Pizza would be amazing right now." Her eyes lit up as she rubbed her hands together. It wasn't exactly what I was thinking of having, but I had a feeling she would be pretty upset if I suggested something else.

I grabbed a menu from my desk. "This is the best place. Let me know what you want, and I'll call."

Tahlia took her time, choosing a margarita and I ordered a pepperoni. I ordered it to be delivered, which wouldn't take long, as they weren't far away and had only just opened for the day.

I slumped back down on the couch while Tahlia went to the bathroom. I couldn't believe how much progress we had made—the presentation was almost finished already.

I was starting to wonder what Tahlia normally did on her weekends. We hadn't really talked about our outside life, except when she'd asked about Grace. I knew nothing about her, what she liked to do, anything. It felt wrong that I didn't. We were becoming more like friends every day, and she knew a lot more about me than I did about her.

"You look deep in thought." Tahlia floated back into the office, her dress swaying around her. She looked beautiful in it. I'd never seen her look more like herself. The clothes she wore to the office looked nice, but this dress was made for her.

"Just wondering why you would get a pizza that has no toppings."

"Cheese is a topping." She narrowed her eyes, taking a seat next to me on the couch. "It also has basil and tomatoes."

I rolled my eyes, which she seemed to enjoy, a smile blossoming on her face. "Doesn't count. Where's the meat?"

"You also got the second most basic pizza, so you don't get to have an opinion." She tossed her hair over one shoulder and crossed her arms over her chest, not looking away from me.

"Touché." I chuckled. "So, what plans did you cancel to work this weekend?" Tahlia's expression faltered, her head turning slightly, like she was taken aback by my question.

"What do you mean?" She fiddled with the hem of her dress, picking at loose strands of fabric.

"I didn't think about it until now, but you probably had something fun planned with your friends to do this weekend." I rested my arm on the back of the couch.

Tahlia was quiet for a moment before she looked up, a conflicted smile adorned her face. "I didn't have any plans this weekend. Just catching up on sleep and trashy TV. What were you supposed to be doing?"

Nothing. "I was probably just going to clean, do groceries, some laundry. See Grace—nothing crazy." I liked my weekends for getting my house in order. I didn't have time for it during the week, usually I was too exhausted after work. I was lucky lately that Henry had been doing some of it, but he wouldn't be around forever. I hoped not, anyway, for his sake.

My phone rang, the pizza was downstairs. "I'll be back." I made my way to the elevator quickly, my stomach was now the loud one.

The boxes were hot, the pizza piping hot.

Tahlia was putting plates down on the table as I walked back in.

I had barely even made it in the door before she exclaimed, "That smells delicious," and snatched the boxes out of my hands, flinging them open on the table.

I couldn't hide my amusement as I watched her put a couple of pieces on her plate and tuck in, gasping from the too-hot dough. I followed suit and put some slices on my plate, even though I would normally just eat out of the box.

"Are you liking Florida?" I asked Tahlia as she shoved her pizza in her mouth, leaving an awkward few seconds while she chewed and swallowed.

"Yeah, it's nice, finally getting used to the weather." She took another bite of her pizza, looking at it adoringly. I'd never seen someone look at food like that. "I live with a really cool guy."

She lives with a guy? Does she mean her fiancé?

"How'd you meet?"

"My friend Claire knows him. Jeremy is so cool. He's made the transition heaps easier." There was no way Jeremy was her fiancé. It seemed weird she lived here and her fiancé maybe didn't. Was he back in

Boston? Or maybe he was here, and they just didn't live together. That was normal for some people, to not live together until they got married.

"At least it's not some random. That would be sketchy."

"It's been great. He introduced me to his friends at their book club, he's also the one I went to the party with the other day. It was his friend Ashton's birthday, but Ashton's boyfriend, Steve, had organized it. Steve didn't seem happy we were there—there's some tension between them all, I think." Tahlia looked up, realization dawning on her face. "You don't care about that." She laughed, a blush creeping up her neck and onto her face.

"So, what's Steve's problem?" My love of drama was my dirty little secret. I was a big fan of all the reality TV shows, and medical drama shows like *Grey's*. Nobody knew. It was hard with Henry living with me, having to hide and watch them in my room so he wouldn't find out. I knew he would tease me endlessly if he found me watching *Keeping up with the Kardashians*.

"I think he knows that Jeremy and Ashton liked, or maybe *like*, each other. I'm not really sure." She thought for a second before continuing. "Jeremy is into Ashton, like more than a crush. I'm pretty sure he's in love with him still, but Ashton got together with Steve before he could tell him. From the way Steve was acting, I'm sure he knows about Jeremy's feelings and maybe worries that Ashton feels the same, so he tries to keep them apart."

I was hanging on to every last word. This shit was my jam.

"Anyway, it was a fun party. We just didn't see much of Ashton."

"Do you miss Boston, your friends there?" Her expression changed. The smile that was previously there was shadowed by something else.

She sighed. "I do miss it. I lived there my whole life; it was a big change."

The sad look in her eyes hurt my heart. Did something happen that made it hard to think about? Did she leave for this job, or was she escaping something?

"Your new friends sound great, though." I tried to bring her back, not wanting her to get stuck thinking about whatever it was she had on her mind. It plagued her, I could tell. The look she had was haunted, more than just sadness. Something that was always there. That look inexplicably made me wish I could wipe any hurt away.

I realized I'd barely eaten any pizza and grabbed a few more slices from the box, digging straight in while Tahlia finished her plate and had a drink of one of the sodas she'd brought in from the kitchen. I ate my pieces, not wanting to get back to work soon. I was enjoying sitting there, getting to know Tahlia more. She hadn't said much, but I felt like I knew her better already.

"You've got something—" Tahlia leaned over, my eyes finding hers as she wiped some sauce off the corner of my mouth. She blushed as she pulled away, my cheek feeling cool at the sudden loss of her touch. My heart beat rapidly in my chest, my palms sweaty. I looked over at Tahlia who looked embarrassed. Her breathing quickened. She sat as far away from me as she could. The air felt electric, like her touch had awoken something.

I tried to calm my heart as I looked around the room. Both of our laptops had been closed and pushed to the side, random paper with them. Logging back in and continuing to work was the last thing I wanted to do.

I wanted to keep talking to Tahlia. I wanted to make her not feel so embarrassed about what just happened. I wanted her to touch my face again ...

"I think we've earned ourselves the rest of the weekend off." I barely registered that it was me speaking. I went automatically into problem-solving mode. Something was happening here that definitely couldn't. It needed to stop.

"But I told everyone we were working all weekend." She got off the couch and walked over to her laptop. "We have to finish the presentation."

Was I the only one who'd noticed the shift? The air was thicker, I felt drawn to her. But it couldn't happen, for so many reasons. One being that ring she wore on her left hand. She was taken.

"No one will know," I put a smile on my face, trying to hide how I truly felt. "We've done enough work today anyway. It can be our little secret."

She didn't look convinced but agreed anyway. Tahlia made her way over to the pizza boxes and started cleaning it up.

"I've got it." I touched her arm to stop her, but the same electricity sparked. We both pulled away, our breaths rapid and in sync. "You enjoy the rest of your weekend. I'll clean this up." Tahlia didn't even hesitate, nodding as she grabbed her stuff and ran out of the office like it was on fire.

It kind of felt like something was.

Chapter Nineteen

Tahlia

I BARELY SLEPT ON Saturday night, my mind whirring with thoughts of that day. My hand on Orion's cheek, the electricity that sparked between us, how he ended the day there even though we had so much more work to do.

I tried to shrug off the lingering feelings and thoughts as I dragged myself out of bed. I was tempted to stay in bed, but it was the first class of my art course today. I had completely forgotten about it when Orion mentioned working the weekend. It was lucky that we finished up yesterday. I was nervous but excited. This would be the first time I'd headed into the city for something other than work. It was time I saw a bit more of Florida. I'd been living there three months, too long to have not even explored the city.

I had a shower, blow-dried my hair and dressed in a floral knee-length dress. I didn't bother putting on any makeup, just some sunscreen, before putting on my ring.

The trip into the city was uneventful, but as soon as I got there I realized how early I was. I had a couple of hours until my class.

I wandered into a shopping center, had a look around and ended up buying a few new clothes. The pieces I'd brought to Florida were starting to feel less like me. Some, like the dress I wore today did, but so much of it just reminded me of my old life.

Looking through stores got boring very fast. My stomach grumbled, reminding me that I'd left the house so quickly that I didn't eat breakfast or even have a coffee.

I thought about the food Orion brought in yesterday, slightly cursing myself for thinking back to it. I think he said the cakes he got were from a bakery, Salt-something-Cakes. I searched it on my phone and Saltwater Cakes came up as the first result. It wasn't far!

Just the thought of those baked goods made my mouth water. I followed the directions my map gave me. The store stood out from everything else around it, making it easy to find.

The front of the store was painted a pastel-green, the writing for Saltwater Cakes standing out in a bright white. Inside the store was just as nice, the walls also pastel, but this time in a pink, with sketches of baked goods and coffee on the walls. People were sitting at tables throughout the space, the doorbell chiming each time the door opened.

I had never been to a place that felt so welcoming.

It was busy, a few staff working behind the counter, making small talk with the customers. I joined the short queue and thought about what I wanted.

Behind the counter there was a window where you could see into the kitchen. I got distracted by someone decorating cakes. The baker placed the fondant over a cake, smoothing it out and trimming off the excess.

"Can I help you?" I looked back over to the counter and found it was my turn. I walked up to the lady, a smile on her face, her blonde hair was tied in a messy knot on the top of her head, and her apron was covered in flour.

"Hi, um ..." I looked at the display case of sweets and had no idea what to get. I really should have been deciding this while in the line instead of watching the baker decorate a cake.

"Take your time, love," she smiled at me. I looked and was conflicted between getting a donut, muffin, croissant, or cookie.

I looked behind me and realized no one was waiting to be served, which made me feel better about taking so much time to pick what I wanted. I was always someone who knew what they wanted or decided in line so that I wouldn't hold anyone up.

"It all looks so good, I don't know what to have." I was tossing up between getting a box to take some home or just get one thing to eat. "My boss brought some in yesterday, and they were so good."

"Everything is delicious. Well, of course I would say that." She chuckled. "This is my bakery."

I looked up. The owner had the brightest and proudest smile on her face. "Wow, that's amazing. I didn't expect to be served by the owner." I laughed.

"I'm a bit different from a lot of business owners." She looked up and waved at someone. "I like to get my hands dirty. Now, if you still aren't sure and maybe want to take a selection, I can make you a box full of sweet surprises?"

"That would be great. Can I also order a coffee, please?" She nodded, and I rattled off my coffee order as someone came up next to me.

"Can I have an oat cap too, please, Soph?" I recognized that voice. I looked up and found Orion next to me, a small smile on his face. "Fancy seeing you here."

"What are you doing here?" Well, that was great. My plan of avoiding all thoughts of Orion and yesterday was ruined. He had those goddamn glasses on again and was dressed even more casually, in a pair of jeans and a hoodie. I felt my heart rate increase just from his proximity. Oh boy.

"I come here most weekends." He shrugged as Sophia walked back over with my box of sweets and two coffees. He handed her his card. I reached into my bag for my money when Orion stopped me, his hand on my elbow. I looked down at where our skin was touching, shivers racing up my arm, before looking up at him and pulling away. "I've got it." I didn't say anything else as he paid, the noise from the bakery, mixers whirring, the coffee machine steaming, the scrape of people's chairs on the concrete floor, drowning out the sound of my beating heart.

"Thanks, Soph," he passed me my coffee and handed me my box of goodies. "Tahlia, this is my friend Sophia. Soph, this is Tahlia who I work with." I smiled at Sophia, suddenly feeling a bit awkward, but not really sure why. Something seemed to dawn on Sophia's face.

"It's lovely to meet you. I've heard a lot about you." Orion talked about me to his friend? Why would he talk about me to her? What was their relationship? Were they actually friends or something more? So many questions ran through my head, I didn't even notice Orion had spoken to me.

"You too." I smiled at Sophia. "Thank you for this." I walked out of the bakery, not sure what to do, or where to go.

I heard the bell of the door behind me and Orion walked up next to me. "Are you alright?" I turned and looked at him, his features scrunched up, worry lines on his forehead.

"Yeah, why wouldn't I be?" I acted as normally as I could, not sure why I was feeling so strange all of a sudden.

"I asked what your plans were for the day, and you ran out of there like your tail was on fire."

Oh.

A nervous laugh bubbled out of me as I brushed my hair behind my ear, my coffee balancing on the box of sweets. "Sorry, I didn't hear you. I'm just so excited about these." I lifted the box up, the sweets jiggling around. Would Orion think my art course was strange? That it was childish? Surely not, he wasn't like that. Right? "I have an art class soon. I got here way too early."

"Oh nice. Before you go, do you want to sit and have your coffee with me?" I looked up at the sincere expression he had on his face. The corners of his eyes crinkled as he smiled at me, everything else about him so relaxed. I wasn't sure that spending more time with him was a good idea. I came to the city for art class, I really needed to not be thinking about him, but there I was considering having coffee with him. The way he looked at me apparently made me forget what I should do. I found myself nodding and following him to one of the free tables outside the bakery.

"What did you end up getting?" He pointed to the box in front of me.

"Honestly, I have no idea." I chuckled, already feeling more relaxed. I didn't know why I was panicking about having coffee with Orion. That wasn't against the rules. Coworkers hung out outside of work all the time. It was a little different because he was my boss, but I was sure it was fine. "I couldn't decide, so she picked for me."

I opened the box, very happy with the selection of sweets she'd chosen. There was a glazed donut, a chocolate éclair, a blueberry muffin, and what looked like a salted caramel cupcake based on the frosting.

Orion leaned over and peeked into the box, looking pleased with the selection. I went to grab one, when I remembered he'd actually bought these for me.

"Would you like one?" I turned the box to him, letting him have the first pick.

He grabbed the donut, leaving me stumped. That would have been my first choice. After careful deliberation, I chose the chocolate éclair and dug in.

"I can't believe you have a baker as a friend and are"—I gestured to his physique—"as fit as you are."

Orion laughed before he shoved the remainder of his donut in his mouth. "You learn to only eat one every time you go, which is not easy." An easy smile spread on his face as he leaned back in his creaky chair and took a long sip of his coffee. The air puffed out of it as the cup popped back into shape when he placed it back on the table.

Why was the sight of him eating a donut ... sexy? Jesus Christ, maybe I just needed to get laid or something.

But the thought of putting myself out there after so long made me feel nauseous.

"How did you and Sophia meet?" I tried to distract myself from the rabbit hole where I could feel myself falling down.

Orion looked surprised by my question. "We met in college; we had a class together." I wanted to know so much more than that. Were they the kind of friends I thought they could be? Or was it truly a platonic friendship? But there was no way I could find any of this out without outright asking. There was no way I was doing that.

"What did you study?"

"I ended up studying business, even though that wasn't the original plan." He checked his phone before placing it face down on the table. "Sorry, just checking if Grace's grandma messaged." I smiled. It was cute that he worried so much about her.

"What was the original plan? You didn't always want to be where you are?" Even though I didn't know much about Orion, and hadn't known him all that long, I couldn't imagine him as anything other than what he was. He was so good at his job, it was like it was made for him.

Orion took a breath before answering. Maybe it wasn't something he liked to talk about.

"You don't have to tell me if you don't want to." I cut him off before he could respond.

My heart picked up at the shy smile he offered. "It's fine. It's been a long time since anyone asked me this." I didn't say anything further and waited for him to respond, the sound of people walking past us, having conversations filling the silence. Orion took a long drink from his coffee, avoiding my eyes, seeming to delay responding. He seemed ... nervous. I didn't think I'd ever seen him nervous before. "The plan was to be a pilot."

I felt my jaw drop before I could stop it. That was the last thing I expected to hear. "That's so cool. Why didn't you do it? Why did you want to be a pilot?" I could feel more questions bubbling out of me but tamped them down, as Orion was smiling and shaking his head at me.

"I haven't had anyone react quite like that when I've told them." A blush crept up my neck and onto my cheeks. "My best friend is a pilot.

It was something we wanted to do together. But there were ... factors stopping us."

"What?" As soon as I said it, I cringed. He probably didn't tell me initially, as he didn't want to talk about it. I assumed that there were many things that could stop you being a pilot; it could be something personal that he wouldn't want to share with his assistant. "You don't have to answer that."

"It's fine Tahlia." He assured me. "I'm color-blind."

"You're color-blind and a terrible boss?"

He nodded, his mouth quirking up, not seeming phased at all.

"That must suck. Whoever created you really wanted to make life hard for you." I couldn't believe the words that had just come out of my mouth.

"Yeah, I definitely wasn't made with sugar, spice, and everything nice." A smirk formed on his face, seemingly unphased by my stupid comment.

"Unlike me." Where the fuck was this confidence coming from?

"Whoever made you definitely put all the right ingredients in." His voice dropped an octave as he said it, his eyes on mine.

I suddenly felt very hot, sweat forming on my brow. I poured myself a glass of water from the bottle that was on the table and gulped it down. A smirk crept its way onto Orion's face as he watched me start a game I couldn't finish. He leaned back, not looking away, his eyes shining with the same amusement that was on the rest of his face. He seemed barely affected by our conversation. "You're a hard worker, with great ideas that are improving business."

His comment seemed strange. Was he trying to bring the conversation back to something more appropriate?

I ignored that and asked, "How come you picked the line of work you're in, then? It seems pretty far off being a pilot."

"It is, but I was able to get a job as a baggage handler and worked my way up. Sometimes I still wonder what it would have been like if I was a pilot. Would I have even liked it? I see the hours Henry, my friend, works, and it definitely wouldn't work with a toddler."

"Was Henry upset?" Orion crossed his arms over his chest, considering my question.

"A little, but there wasn't really anything either of us could do. You need to be able to clearly see certain colors, particularly for landing, so it was not an option." I hadn't thought about color blindness being a barrier to being a pilot. I guessed I'd never really thought about pilots and what they need to do the job. The only time I had thought about pilots was when I was on a plane, and even then, it was mostly hoping they landed smoothly, or traversed the turbulence well.

"So, how about you?"

"What about me?" Orion was obviously not interested in sharing more about his life, or he wanted to know more about mine, which I highly doubted.

"When are you getting married?" Orion's eyes were locked onto mine.

"What?" Where did he get the idea that I was getting married?

He gestured at my hand, the one that adorned the engagement ring. Ah. Of course. "Oh, yeah. I'm not engaged."

Orion looked confused, very confused. Naturally, since we hadn't spoken about it before now. "Is it a promise ring or something then?"

"It's an engagement ring, I'm just not engaged." I spun the ring around my finger, surprised it'd taken Orion that long to notice it. For some reason, I'd felt the urge to tell him more. Maybe it was because I hadn't spoken about Tim in what felt like forever. I took a deep breath, begging myself internally to hold it together. "My fiancé died. I still wear the ring to feel closer to him." I looked directly behind Orion, not wanting to see whatever was on his face. If I didn't look at him, there was less chance I would fall apart. "I don't really have any other family, he was it. I'm just not ready to let him go yet." I felt a lump form in my throat.

"I'm so sorry, Tahlia." He pulled my hands into his, his touch warm and comforting. "I wouldn't have asked if I had known."

"You wouldn't have known if I didn't tell you." I smiled. "You shared your deepest, darkest secret with me—so I think it's only fair I shared too." The lump in my throat started to go away as Orion pulled his hands back.

"I have got to get going." Orion looked regretfully at his watch. "I am supposed to pick Gracie up in about ten minutes." He stood, grabbing our coffee cups and putting them in a trash can. "Thanks for having coffee with me. I'll see you Monday?"

I smiled, somehow feeling lighter after the time we'd spent together. "See you."

He stayed with me even though he knew he had to pick Grace up. I hoped he wasn't going to be late. I grabbed the rest of my pastries and shopping bags and decided to make my way to my class. Even though I'd hoped to not think about Orion, it was quickly ruined not long after I got into the city, but I still had a great time. I already could feel thoughts about that interaction and yesterday swarming my mind.

Stop it Tahlia, he is your boss.

I couldn't have these thoughts, I needed to stop them in their tracks. He was not available, and he was my boss. It was so wrong in so many ways.

If Tim could see me now, crushing on my boss, he would laugh and tease me about it.

Chapter Twenty

Orion

AFTER TAHLIA LEFT WORK on Saturday, I couldn't shake the feeling that something had changed between us, a spark was there that wasn't before. I did anything I could to distract myself, cleaned my house, went grocery shopping, and offered to take Grace for the night Saturday, so Sophia could have some time to herself.

But I felt … weird. Ever since she'd touched me. It was nothing, though. I had no idea why it stayed with me. It's something anyone would do. You don't let people go into meetings or whatever with spinach in their teeth, it's the same if you have pizza on your face. Right? Most people did that, didn't they? I could never let anyone continue on if I saw toilet paper stuck on their shoe or something.

I couldn't help but think back to the moment, how soft her hand was, the focused look on her face as she'd dabbed the corner of my mouth. I had tried to drag my gaze away from hers in and after that moment, but it was like we were in a trance. She had the cutest pink cheeks, a blush that had started creeping up from her neck. Immediately after she pulled away, her breathing had picked up, she'd seemed unsure if she should have done what she did.

After I dropped Grace off at her grandma's early on Sunday, I went for a run to clear my head, a fairly long run. It generally helped clear my mind, but as soon as I was home and showered, the feeling came back.

I needed a better distraction. So, I headed to Saltwater Cakes, which was usually a great distraction. But as soon as I walked in, the doorbell chiming above me, I recognized the woman talking to Sophia. Tahlia was wearing a dress covered in flowers that I struggled to drag my eyes from. Her soft blonde hair was the giveaway, though, I would recognize it anywhere. I took a breath, not surprised the universe was doing this to me. Of course, I'd run into her when I'm trying to distract myself. My mind started to race, sweat forming on my brow.

I wondered if I should just turn around and leave, but Sophia looked up and waved at me. There was no way I could leave, she would just call me out. There was no one else waiting, and I thought it best to just bite the bullet.

I walked up to the counter next to Tahlia and ordered a coffee. I didn't want to just say hi to her as I walked up—she might think it was weird that I recognized her without seeing her face or something.

I saw her look at me out of the corner of my eye, her eyes wide and that signature blush of hers creeping up onto her cheeks. She recovered quickly, wide eyes being replaced by a soft smile.

Before I even introduced Tahlia to Sophia, she had a cheeky look on her face that said she already knew who she was. I was sure she was going to text me about this later.

Asking her to have her coffee with me was the stupidest idea I had. How was I supposed to ignore the thoughts and feelings that were bubbling to the surface?

As soon as we sat at a table outside the bakery, I knew I'd made a mistake. Sophia was watching, giving me a thumbs up. Tahlia's chair was positioned so she couldn't see inside the bakery. At least, I hoped she couldn't.

When she asked me about what I studied at college, I didn't expect it to take a turn to me telling her I was color-blind. It wasn't something I told a lot of people, purely because they didn't need to know. It didn't really affect my day-to-day life, just what I wanted to do for work. I loved her reaction to me originally wanting to be a pilot. She looked equal parts amazed, shocked and confused. I understood it all. I had a lot of feelings about it too.

When she mentioned taking an art class, I wanted to ask more, but I'd only just asked her to sit with me and didn't want to freak her out or something. I loved that she was doing something she enjoyed outside of work. I needed something like that.

But the last thing I expected to hear about was her late fiancé. She wouldn't look at me as she told me he'd died. Her voice held strong, not a single quiver, not one tear dropping from her eye. If I was in a similar situation to her, I wouldn't have been able to hold it together like that.

It pained me to not be able to pull her into my arms, tell her I was there for her, and protect her from all the pain in this world.

But I couldn't do that.

I had to force myself to leave and not offer her a lift home or something. I loved spending time with her, getting to know her better. I could have happily sat there all day listening to her tell me about her life, and answering any question she asked me.

I was excited for work tomorrow, which was fucking weird. I wasn't usually excited to go to work. But I wasn't excited to see her—no, I couldn't be. I was excited to work with her and see where our project went.

Even though she wasn't engaged.

But I had to keep reminding myself that it didn't mean she was available; she was still very much off-limits, she was still my employee.

As long as we worked together, there was no way we could be together.

Henry was on the couch watching TV when I finally got home. He offered up his leftovers to me, which I happily devoured, sitting on the opposite end of the couch—my regular seat. Henry was watching some drama show on Netflix, *Bridgerton* maybe? It wasn't my cup of tea. My mind raced with the events of the weekend, earlier that day. Of Tahlia.

"What's going on, Ry?" Henry kept his eyes on the TV, having always been able to read me just by being in the same room.

"Just work."

"Anything specifically?" Henry sat up and paused his show, giving me his full attention.

I didn't really want to tell him what it was, so I went with, "Just the bullshit that is John and everything he makes me do. I just can't wait till I'm done there."

"It shouldn't be too long." Henry assured me. He raised his eyebrows at me, a smirk on his face. Cocky as always. "We have some interest already. Some big clients are keen."

I felt a bit bad that I hadn't really been around helping in the planning part of the business. I had been so busy with work and Grace, and my thoughts preoccupied by someone they shouldn't be. I wanted to be more involved, but how much thinner could I spread myself until I snapped?

"Have you told them it's me?" I didn't particularly want any news of this getting back to John before I resigned.

"Not in so many words." I narrowed my eyes at Henry. "Don't worry, they won't say anything. I have it sorted."

"Alright." I was not super worried, and if it did get back to John, was it really that big of an issue? I was going to be quitting anyway, it wasn't really like he could punish me or anything. Having to work for him every day was punishment enough for anything I could do to piss him off. "So what's left?"

"You just need to quit." It couldn't be that simple, but the expression on Henry's face said it was. I just needed to resign from Florida Airlines—where I'd been working for years.

The thought of resigning, now that it was so real, made my stomach turn. I hadn't known anything else as an adult, except for working at Florida Airlines in some capacity.

Was I really doing this?

"And then everything will just fall into place, I assume?" I joked, masking the worry I felt taking over my body.

"Yes," he responded seriously. "Once you quit, everything will happen pretty quick—the clients are keen to get started. So once you resign, tell me when you want to start meetings and I'll help book them. But don't think I'm going to be your assistant forever."

I chuckled at that. Henry wouldn't survive as an assistant; I could guarantee Tahlia would run circles around him in that department.

"How is that assistant of yours?" I could tell that Henry was going to somehow ask me about Tahlia. He could read me like a book too, I was sure he could tell it wasn't just work bullshit that was bothering me.

"She's fine, working with me on that project." I really didn't feel like getting into it. This conversation today was one of the few times my mind had been distracted enough to not be thinking about her.

"How does she feel about you leaving?" The reminder that I would be leaving her in the lion's den brought that worry from earlier right back. I had to tell her soon, before I resigned. I didn't want her to find out the wrong way.

"I haven't told her yet. I'm sorting out where she'll go when I leave."

"Ah, don't want that boss of yours to get his hands on her." I shuddered at the thought, even though I knew that Henry didn't mean in the physical sense.

"Yep." The thought that Tahlia might not care I was leaving crept in. I was sure she would. But it was the 'what if' that I knew was going to keep running through my mind. "Once we finish this project and I have someone for her to work with, I'll resign."

"What else is it?" I looked at Henry, no amusement on his face. He always did this. Went all serious when he wanted to find out what was going on.

"There's nothing else," I said nonchalantly.

He laughed, obviously not convinced. Henry wasn't stupid, I knew he wouldn't believe me. "Ry, I've known you for how long? I can tell something—or someone—has gotten under your skin."

I shook my head. "Nah, I'm good."

"Tell me, Orion Ariti."

I chuckled. "Who are you, my mom?"

"Maybe. I'm gonna whoop your ass if you don't tell me." He narrowed his eyes as he tried to keep a smile hidden.

"Then do it." I stood my ground, crossing my arms over my chest.

"Oh come on, please tell me!" He was so dramatic. "You know all about my life drama, tell me some of yours. Give me something to think about that isn't Charlotte."

"You're evil." He knew that I couldn't not tell him after he brought up Charlotte. Henry shrugged and waited for me to continue. "I'm just thinking things I shouldn't about someone I shouldn't."

"Hmmm, would this someone be your assistant, Miss Tahlia?"

I threw a pillow at him. "Stop being a dick." I couldn't help the laugh that snuck out.

"What happened?"

I told Henry about Saturday at the office and earlier that day when we had coffee. I'd never really told Henry about 'girl troubles'—even though this wasn't what this was. This was just something that I needed to stop. It couldn't keep going.

"I shouldn't have had coffee with her today, it really didn't help." I groaned.

"You're right, it didn't. But you obviously like the woman." Henry handed me back the pillow I had thrown at him.

"But it doesn't matter. It's so wrong, I'm her boss. It's also such a cliché." I wished I didn't feel the way I did, but I had no idea what to do about it. "It didn't help when she told me she isn't engaged, even though she wears a ring on her left hand."

Henry's interest piqued at that. "She's single?"

"I'm not sure, but I think so. He died."

"Oh, that's rough." The silence in the apartment was deafening.

"But it doesn't matter either way."

Henry's face was engulfed with a devious smile. "And why's that?"

"She's my employee, how many times do I have to tell you this?" I felt like I was going around in circles.

"Once you resign, you won't be an employee at Florida Airlines, meaning she would no longer be off-limits."

Chapter Twenty-One

Tahlia

STIFLING A YAWN, I knocked on Orion's office door at seven o'clock. Working this late wasn't exactly what I had in mind, but if Orion and I wanted to finalize the finances for our pitch, then it was the only time we could meet.

He was almost in back-to-back meetings every day with the amount of shit that John was palming off to him. He somehow still managed to get all of his other work done, but I was sure it wasn't during normal business hours.

The board meeting was coming up soon, and we needed it to be perfect. If they didn't approve it, and we had to work on it further, we were screwed. The cruise we had picked was soon, so if they denied it we would end up back at square one.

My stomach grumbled as Orion called for me to come in. I was starving. I hadn't eaten since lunch and didn't pack dinner, as we'd decided earlier that morning that we'd have to meet later. I hoped it wouldn't take too long.

He was typing away furiously as I sat on the lounge and logged back into my laptop. I opened up the documents we were last working on, Orion having still not taken his attention away from his screen. He was engrossed in whatever he was working on, and I decided to give him a few minutes before I interrupted. He was obviously trying to finish whatever it was.

I was amazed at his ability to just push through and get things done, considering how John treated him and this place. If I were him, I would probably have left or be looking at other jobs—which he could be doing, but I highly doubted it. With the way he talked about this place, it was hard to imagine him working elsewhere. I couldn't imagine working here without him now too.

Orion was hunched, looking at his screen, his features drawn together, his eyes drooping. His suit looked all over the place compared to normal. His tie had come loose, his sleeves rolled up, and his jacket was laying across the back of his chair. He usually had all of those things in perfect order, but even his hair was sticking out all over the place, like he had been constantly running his hands through it.

"Fuck." Orion blinked furiously before rummaging through his bag. "Sorry Tahlia, just give me a second. These contacts have been in for too long today and are driving me insane." He turned his back to me, I assumed, so I didn't watch him hold his eyelid open to get his contacts out, before turning back looking like he couldn't see anything.

He grabbed his glasses and a bottle of solution from his bag, putting the drops in his eyes and the glasses on his nose.

"How are you?" He smiled at me, a smile that was way too sexy for my boss to be giving me on a Monday night in his office. Did he know how attractive he was? Especially with those glasses. I really wished he had just suffered through wearing contacts until I'd left, it would have been so much easier to ignore him.

Who was I kidding? Glasses or no glasses, there was no way I could ignore him.

I smiled back as I tucked my hair behind my ears. "I'm alright." My stomach chose that exact moment to grumble, a sound similar to that of an earthquake. I pressed a hand over my abdomen, urging the sound to disappear, hoping that Orion didn't hear it.

The small chuckle I heard from him told me he'd definitely heard it.

"Have you not eaten?" I shook my head, annoyed at my stomach, as Orion laughed. "What do you feel like? I'll order us some dinner."

"All good. I'll get something on the way home."

Orion was unimpressed with my answer. "You can't work on an empty stomach." He shook his head at me.

I couldn't have him buying me more food. First the pizza, then my pastries and coffee, and he'd brought those pastries and coffees in on Saturday too. I knew that he earned a lot more money than me and I probably didn't need to worry about him buying food, but I was worried about the other stuff that came with it. The closeness when eating, the intimacy of it, how someone might have some food on their face and someone else might have the urge to wipe it off even though it's completely inappropriate.

I couldn't stop myself when it happened, my gaze drawn to his eyes as I'd cleaned the food off his face. I didn't want that to happen again.

Liar.

It shouldn't happen again, and the best way to stop it would be to remove the food from the situation. I would be fine being hungry for a little bit and would pick something up on my way home. It wouldn't be a problem.

"It's fine, honestly," I reassured him, looking down at my laptop, wondering where we should start.

"Do you prefer Chinese or Indian?" Orion was rummaging through his desk drawers before he pulled out takeout menus, looking at me expectantly.

I couldn't think of a way to turn it down; it was obvious he was going to order food whether I said what I wanted or not.

"I'm hungry too, Tahlia." He looked exhausted. Had he eaten today? I wasn't sure I'd even seen him really leave his office. There were one or two times he'd left for meetings, and others where he went to the bathroom, but he'd never gone to the kitchen or downstairs to get food. No delivery driver called up with food for him, either.

I should have noticed and brought him something. That was my job, wasn't it? Not to buy or bring him food, but to help him, particularly when he wasn't helping himself. No wonder he was so tired. I hoped he had at least eaten breakfast.

"I like them both." Orion handed me the menus he had fished out of his drawer.

"Pick what you want and let me know. I'll give you my card." He sat back at his desk, focusing back on his screen.

"You don't need to do this." I couldn't help the guilt that was gnawing at me at the thought of him buying me food again. And the anxiety building about ... the other stuff.

"You're hungry, I'm hungry. Don't worry about it Tahls."

Tahls? What the fuck? Since when did he call me Tahls? Only my friends called me Tahls. Orion had never called me Tahls.

I shook the thought off, deciding it must have been just a slip of the tongue. "Pork dumplings and spring rolls then." I didn't even bother looking at the menu. As soon as he'd mentioned Chinese, I knew that's what I wanted. I was curious if it was the same place Jeremy ordered food from.

"Great, just add some chili beef and rice."

The Chinese place picked up straight away and said it wouldn't be too long until it arrived.

Orion had moved to sit across from me as I hung up the phone. "All sorted?" He looked up from his laptop as he waited for me to respond.

"Won't be long."

His shoulders relaxed as he leaned back in his chair. "Thank fuck. I am starving." He ran his hands through his hair, making it even messier. Fuck me.

"We need to get the pitch done earlier than expected." I looked up from my screen to a very serious Orion behind his sexy-ass glasses looking me in the eye. There was no hint of a joke or anything.

"Earlier?" It already felt like we were rushing to get everything in order.

"Between you and me, Leslie gave me a heads-up that someone else made an offer. I don't want to lose our chance." He paused, taking a sip of water before continuing. "We need to pitch this to Phil, the CFO, get his feedback and backing before we even head into the board meeting. Usually, all these sorts of things need CEO approval before the board, too, but—"

"But given that John is the reason we're having to put together this second pitch in the first place, probably better not risk it," I said.

Orion nodded, my chest warming at his clear approval. "It's risky doing it this way too," he said, "but I think less so."

"Makes sense." I sighed at the stress of all this. I had never been so involved in a project—I had no idea if this was what it was usually like. Such tight deadlines, and the stakes were so high.

"Hey, don't worry about it. We are so close to having it all done." Orion assured me as he pulled out his laptop, and we worked away for the next twenty minutes until I got a call that our food had arrived.

Orion went and met the delivery person at the front door as he didn't feel comfortable with me going out there in the dark, late at night. It wasn't really something I had thought about until he mentioned it. I couldn't help but notice the warm feeling that tingled in my chest.

We both dug right in once he came back. I grabbed some bowls from the kitchen while he was downstairs. We shared our meals; I couldn't resist trying some of his chili beef, and I could see he was eyeing off my dumplings.

I could barely hold back the moans trying to escape at how much I was enjoying the food, which surprised me when I found out it wasn't where Jeremy ordered from. This was somehow a thousand times better.

"It's good, isn't it?" I nodded, not wanting to interrupt my eating. "I used to get this all the time when I was working late. I haven't been as much lately."

"That's good that you haven't been." I was curious as to what would have changed, as it wasn't his workload. Was it Grace? Sophia?

"I just realized it isn't worth everything. This place, I mean." He looked a little lost in thought, like there were so many clouds rushing by, and he wasn't sure which he wanted to watch. I didn't know what to say, so sat there quietly while I finished eating.

"Thanks for ordering this Tahlia, and for working late, and for everything else you have been doing. As resistant as I was to getting an assistant, I really don't know what I'd do without you." There was a fluttering in my chest at his words—his soft, kind words that I was sure were nothing more than a compliment from my boss on my performance, even though my brain wanted to take it a completely different way.

"Oh, thank you." The blush that always appeared when I was with Orion returned, while he held my gaze, that goddamn soft smile not leaving his face.

"I think we should call it for the night." There were a few telltale cracks as Orion stood up and stretched over his head.

"Why?" I was surprised at his suggestion, I thought we had so much more work to do.

"Well, for one, I'm tired, and two, after eight my productivity decreases significantly." He laughed, pushing his glasses back up his nose, them having fallen slightly after his cat-like stretch.

The yawn that took over my face made me agree with Orion. I was so tired and needed to get into bed as soon as I could.

I packed up my laptop and notebooks, taking them to my bag that was at my desk. I walked back over to the sitting area and began cleaning up the empty soy sauce-filled containers, my mind going back to earlier when he'd called me Tahls. He hadn't said it again, so maybe it truly was just an accident. He didn't even seem to notice. I really wanted to know why he thought to call me that.

I was so distracted in my own head that I dropped one of the containers that still had soy sauce in it all over the carpet.

"Shit." I grabbed some tissues and began blotting at the ground. Of course, he had beige carpet that would definitely now be stained. "It's not going to come out."

"It's fine, it's just carpet, we can just move the rug to hide it." His voice was more calming than I expected, considering I had just ruined the carpet. I kept blotting the carpet, trying to at least get some of it out, and failing. Orion's hand landed on my shoulder. "It's fine, just leave it. It's just carpet, it's not important."

The situation felt so surreal, like I had been in it before. Tim. His kind words, gentle touch, helping hand. It was like how Orion was with me. The attraction I felt for him too, even though it was so wrong, reminded me of how I felt with Tim. Tim, the man I hadn't thought about much recently. The man that I seemed to not think about while I was here, lusting over Orion.

"Are you okay?" I felt under my eyes, and found my cheeks wet. A few tears had slipped out while I knelt on the floor, my hand frozen holding a tissue on the carpet, realizing how much I hadn't thought about Tim lately.

"Yeah I'm fine. You're right, it's not a big deal." I pulled myself off the ground, threw out the rubbish and grabbed my stuff. "I'll see you tomorrow."

"Did you drive? Do you need a lift home?"

"All good, I'll call an Uber." Orion eyebrows scrunched together at that, probably not super keen about the idea of me getting in the car with a stranger at night.

"Are you sure? I'm happy to drive you, it's late."

"Nope, all good." I rushed out of his office, grabbed my things, and left the building as quickly as I could.

The drive home took an eternity. I felt numb. Everything that happened before then didn't matter, how Orion made me feel, us working late together, me wiping food off his face, the electricity I felt between us.

None of that mattered.

Ignoring a text I got from Claire checking in, I crawled into bed as soon as I got home, not bothering to shower or change. My mind went back to my earlier thoughts. I had pretty much forgotten about Tim in the last few weeks. Why hadn't I thought about him? Was I too occupied with this other man that I couldn't even have?

Was I changing that much being in Florida, that I forgot him? My best friend who'd left the world way too soon.

Were the feelings that arose when I was around Orion more than some stupid crush, or lust? Maybe it was something more. Feelings, real feelings. Whatever they were, they had been enough to make me forget Tim, even temporarily.

Orion was so kind, gentle, and funny. I could tell he was this amazing, devoted dad, even though I hadn't seen it in action. He was so dedicated to his job, even though he kept getting the short end of a shitty stick.

Thoughts raced through my head all night, of Tim and the life we had together before he was gone. The tears didn't stop, though. They continued until I at some point fell into a fitful sleep that was riddled with dreams of Orion and Tim.

Chapter Twenty-Two

Orion

GETTING UP FOR WORK was a struggle. I missed Grace, it felt like I hadn't seen her much lately. Knowing how to escape this place, but not acting on it made every day more painful. I had to stick it out though, for just a little while longer. I could see the finish line, feel it, just as long as the meeting with Phil went smoothly, I was confident that we would get board approval.

I got ready and went into the office early, grabbing a coffee on my way up, knowing I was in too early for Tahlia to be there already with our usual morning coffee.

My thoughts drifted back to Tahlia running out crying last night. I wasn't sure if it was something I did that made her upset, but I had no idea what to do. My heart hurt seeing the tears on her face, hearing the short, sharp breaths she was taking that I didn't even think she noticed. I wanted to comfort her, pull her into a hug and tell her it would be okay, even though I had no idea what *it* was. But it was inappropriate, especially in the office.

It was getting harder to ignore the pull I felt towards her—the more time we spent together, the worse it got. I wasn't even sure I was hiding it well anymore. I was sure she knew I was feeling something more for her than a boss should.

The office was quiet when I got out of the elevator, only a few people milling around, avoiding my eye contact as I made my way to my office. As I had assumed, Tahlia wasn't in yet, which was a good thing considering it wasn't even eight o'clock. I wanted some time to review everything before I got stuck in meetings all day, one of them being with Phil.

It would be fine. Phil was my mentor, a good friend, I had no worries at all that he wouldn't agree with our plan. I had another motivation for the meeting.

I hadn't specifically asked Tahlia yet, but I was hoping she would be comfortable to run the meeting. She knew all of it better than I did, and I wanted Phil to see her in action. I wanted him to have a chance to see what I see, see the potential she has—her drive, her passion.

Plus, having a confirmed backing going into the meeting wouldn't hurt either.

I left my office door open as I got to work, which was unusual for me. I wanted to know when Tahlia got in. I needed to see if she was okay.

I was deep in reviewing a document when I saw familiar blonde hair pass my door, heading towards the kitchen.

I called her into my office when she got back to her desk. She would usually pop her head in and say hi if I had gotten to the office before her. But not today.

"Yeah?" Tahlia stood at the door, her eyes wandering around the room looking at everything but me, her tone weirdly chirpy.

"How are you?" She probably still wasn't feeling her normal self after last night.

She looked me in the eyes, a forced smile on her face. "I'm great. Anything you need?"

"I have my meeting with Phil today. I want you to lead it."

"Okay, perfect, sounds great." She walked back to her desk, her slumped shoulders not matching her overly happy tone or massive smile on her face. She seemed to have no interest in talking about what had happened, but she was definitely not herself.

I wanted to go out there and try and get her to open up to me. But I couldn't, not here. I was her boss and if she wanted to talk to me about it, she would have already. I couldn't force her to talk to me, as much as I would like to help her.

Tahlia waited outside my office before the meeting with Phil. I hadn't given him many details about why we were meeting, wanting to give Tahlia the opportunity to take the lead.

Phil was … Phil, pulling me in for a hug with his usual affability, a rare sight in this workplace. That got an emotion out of Tahlia: confusion. It was better than the robotic cheerfulness I had been getting from her.

Phil was like an older version of me—tall, dark hair, a freshly pressed suit—but he had so much more wisdom than I could ever hope to have. We had known each other a long time and were now more friends than coworkers, with him being a mentor for me, and he would be for the rest of my life. He had given me so much advice and help over the years, I had never known how to repay him.

"Nice to meet you, Phil," Tahlia shook his hand, her movements cautious. Maybe she was worried about being pulled into a hug—or working here had just taught her not to trust the front people first present.

"Tahlia, it's a pleasure." He gestured for us to sit at his desk, as he made his way back to his chair.

His office was less cluttered than mine, with just a desk in the middle with one framed photo of his cat, a small cabinet to the right, and a small sitting area near the door. His office was smaller than mine, not for any reason other than he didn't want a big office or a lot of "unnecessary shit" in his space, as he said.

"What can I help you both with today?" I looked at Tahlia and gestured for her to begin.

Her demeanor from earlier was still in place, a smile plastered on her face, her tone light. But her posture was rigid, her movements shaky.

"Orion will be making a proposal to the board, and we would like your backing." Phil's eyebrow raised, his interest piqued. He nodded for her to continue.

Tahlia went through all the details, specifically the financials, with Phil being CFO. Phil was nodding along to it all, he was impressed.

I wouldn't say it was hard to impress Phil, but it wasn't an easy feat. One, I could confidently say John had never achieved.

"That's basically it in a nutshell. Anything else you wanted to add, Orion?" Tahlia looked over at me, her smile less enthusiastic now that she had done her part.

"No, you covered it all." I couldn't help the swell of pride at what she'd achieved. It might not have been strictly professional, but I was proud of her for getting through everything, even when she wasn't one hundred percent herself that day. "So, Phil, what do you think?"

Tahlia had offered to pick up some lunch from down the street. Phil and I insisted she didn't need to, but I could tell she just wanted to have some time alone and get some space. So, I gave her my card and she left the room as quickly as was polite.

We had just finished going over the finances, tweaking them and making sure they were airtight. Phil seemed pretty happy with it all, which was great. I was feeling less worried about the board meeting.

"Orion," Phil's tone was one I had heard before. His serious mentor voice, one where I was sure he was going to tell me something that I needed to hear. "What are you still doing here?"

I blinked in shock, surprised to hear that coming from Phil. "What do you mean?"

Phil sighed, leaning back in his chair and crossing his arms over his chest. "You've done all you can here. You're better than the shit that's here. You're young, it's time to move on."

"I'm surprised to hear you say this." Should I tell him my plans, that I was going to leave? I wasn't sure. I knew I could trust him, but what if somehow it fell through?

"I always told you, only stay somewhere if it's serving its purpose."

He wasn't wrong, but ... "I never made CEO." He knew that being CEO was always my plan, my goal, but I was starting to lose sight of why I really wanted it. Was it the title, the money, the work that came with it? I wasn't sure. I wasn't sure about a lot of things about my work these days.

Phil shook his head at me. "You're more a CEO than the hamster we have running on that wheel."

I chuckled at the image. "I'm just not sure." I wasn't ready to say my plan out loud, even though if there was someone I was going to talk about it with, it would be Phil.

"You're holding yourself back. You do too much for John, when you should be doing something for yourself."

"I've been thinking about changing it up but I just ..."

"You're worried about Tahlia, aren't you?" How the fuck did he get that? He wasn't wrong, but shit, he could really read my mind. Phil had always been like this, able to know what I was thinking, feeling, and get the answers he wanted out of me. "So you've been looking for other roles?"

"I've thought about it, sure."

"And Tahlia?" It felt like his eyes were boring holes through me at the intense stare I was getting,

"Of course I'm worried about her. She has so much potential, and I'm concerned that no one will mentor her." Even with my plan forming for Tahlia working with Phil, the thoughts of "what if" plagued me. John could find some way to block her working with Phil, he could find a way to fire her. She might want to leave, or maybe she wouldn't even care. For some reason, the last thought was the one that stuck with me most days. What if she didn't even care that I left?

Phil took a sip of water, something he always did when he was thinking. "If she wants a career here, I'm not going anywhere until I retire."

"Oh, so tomorrow's your last day?"

"Fuck you." We laughed, the room feeling slightly lighter. "I'll help her, mentor her like I did you, if that's what she wants. I'll make sure that John doesn't pull any of the shit you're worried about."

"Thank you." Hearing the words come out of Phil's mouth eased the gnawing sense of guilt I felt at leaving her behind. Not entirely, but to an extent. At least she wouldn't be left in the trenches with no support.

"You need to stop worrying about her and worry about yourself. Think about what's next for you, in your work, and at home. You've given everything to this company, it's time to focus on you, what you want, and what you need."

I didn't even know what to say in response, so I just nodded and gave him a tight smile. Knowing that Phil thought what Henry did, what Sophia did, that it was time for me to leave Florida Airlines, gave me a sense of peace. It made me feel like I was doing the right thing with Henry, starting the business, starting a new chapter of my life. I had always looked up to Phil, and knowing he would always have my back, and now Tahlia's, it felt like a weight had been lifted off my shoulders.

Chapter Twenty-Three

Tahlia

I COULDN'T CATCH MY breath—the fresh air wasn't providing any reprieve. My body felt like it was in fight or flight. I wasn't feeling like myself, and it was bothering me more than it should.

The meeting was great, Phil seemed keen about the idea from the start, but I couldn't shake feeling upset. I had forgotten about Tim, worrying too much about Orion, someone who I couldn't even have.

I wasn't even hungry. I'd barely eaten all day, but I needed to get out of that meeting room, so I used getting everyone lunch as an excuse. As soon as I'd finished presenting, I felt like I had to get out of there, I needed some space from Orion. How I felt about him wouldn't go away.

I made my way back to the office as slowly as I could, every step feeling heavier and heavier.

I knocked on Phil's office door, taking a deep breath before plastering a smile on my face and walking in with the takeout bag in my hand.

"That smells delicious." Phil took the bag back from my hand, thanking me for getting lunch.

"Can I talk to you for a second?" Orion looked at me with concern, putting his kebab back down on Phil's desk and following me out of the room.

We stood together outside of Phil's office, Orion's face drawn together, all of his attention on me. "Are you okay?" He reached for my hand, but pulled back at the last second. My heart started to race, that electricity between us filling the air.

"I'm not feeling well, is it alright if I go home for the day?"

Orion smiled softly at me—he was so beautiful it made my chest ache. "Of course. You don't have to ask—if you're not well, just tell me and head home."

I was relieved at his response, asking to go home from work was something I hated to do. The guilt ate me up, even though I knew that I would be better off heading home.

I walked away, not having it in me at that moment to say anything else, or hear any other words from Orion. His concern for me was sweet, but only made the pain worse.

Getting home was my only priority, I didn't even care that everyone was staring at me as I packed up my stuff and left.

When I walked through the door, I finally felt like I could breathe, like some of the heaviness I felt was left at the door.

When I got home, Jeremy was curled up on the couch in the lounge room, snuggled under a blanket with an array of snacks on the table, and a tub of ice cream in front of him with a spoon in it.

"Jer?" I had never seen him like this, something was definitely up.

Jeremy looked over his shoulder at me. His eyes widened before a soft smile landed on his lips. "Hey, Tahls, what are you doing home?"

"I was about to ask you the same thing." I dropped my stuff on the ground, kicked my shoes off and joined him on the couch. I grabbed another blanket from the basket next to the couch and draped it over myself.

"Don't worry about me and my regularly scheduled mope time. What's up with you?" He handed me a packet of candy and paused his TV show.

I shrugged. "Nothing really."

"Babe, don't lie to me. I can tell something is wrong."

I wasn't sure what to say in response, so I tore open the bag of candy, a bit too aggressively, sending the sweets flying through the room.

Jeremy and I both started laughing, the kind where it's hard to breathe, until suddenly tears were streaming down my face.

"Tahls." Jeremy pulled me to his chest as I cried. Everything came swarming in, my life with Tim, moving to Florida, Orion. "Do you want to talk about it?"

I pulled back from his hold and laid back onto the couch, looking up at the ceiling. I hadn't spoken about this, about Tim, in a long time.

"It's all gotten a bit too much lately. I'm not even sure where I should start." My words were so quiet I barely heard them myself.

Jeremy didn't say anything, I wasn't sure what he was doing, I couldn't bring myself to look at him. If I did, I would get overwhelmed with emotions again and not be able to speak.

I needed to talk about it, to get it out, but it was just terrifying. It felt like I was picking a scab off a wound that just wouldn't heal.

"Claire likely told you that my fiancé died." My breathing hitched when the words finally came out, a bit louder than my last. "It feels like just yesterday." Jeremy took my hand in his. The warmth from his palm, knowing that he was there for me, gave me the strength to continue.

"I'd known him almost my entire life, we were best friends, but more than that we were family. My parents and siblings never liked him, I never understood it, but I didn't care. He was my world, even before I knew I was in love with him." The TV turned off at that moment, the noise distracting me from my thoughts. "Finally, in high school Tim told me how he felt, and we became even more inseparable than we already were. We were gross, that couple in high school who were always together, all mushy, so in love. It felt amazing. Everyone told us that we wouldn't last. We were just in high school; we hadn't experienced life yet. Especially my parents.

"We got engaged." The feeling of when Tim proposed to me flooded in as I looked at the ring on my finger. "He proposed to me in this gazebo at this park we always went to. I hadn't been expecting it at all. But I was happy, happier than I had ever been in my life." It was almost silent in the apartment except for my words and Jeremy's breath. "When we told my parents, they reacted ... poorly, to say the least. They told us everything we'd heard before, 'it's not going to last', 'you don't know what love is', 'this is a stupid idea'."

I took a breath. I was in a safe space, but it was still so hard to talk about. "We'd been engaged for a while, I'd gone no contact with my family, and we had started to plan the wedding. Life was amazing. But on his way to work one morning, he slipped on the frost and hit his head." I swallowed down the lump in my throat, trying to stop the tears that wanted to spill. "It sounds so stupid and simple. Something hundreds of people would do every year and just stand back up again. But he cracked his skull in just the wrong place and—" my voice cracked, and I dragged my wrist under my nose to catch the drip. I couldn't bring myself to say anything more about it, or even think about that day any longer.

"Oh Tahlia, my love." Jeremy squeezed my hand as I continued to lay there, staring up at the ceiling, breathing through the tears that had escaped and the feelings that were rushing through.

"Lately, I think I've been forgetting about it all, about Tim, the amazing life we had together, even though it was short, with other ... things occupying my mind." I sat up, wiped my face and looked at Jeremy. He was crying too, sadness and shock on his face. "These stupid feelings for Orion, which I don't even know if they are real, how much I'm enjoying being in Florida. I feel guilty about it all." It was hard to admit that. I knew that I shouldn't feel guilty for living my life, for moving on, but it didn't make it any easier. "Am I forgetting about Tim? I haven't thought about him a lot in the last few weeks, does that make me a bad person?"

Jeremy looked me in the eyes, taking both of my hands in his, "No, my love. Moving on doesn't make you a bad person. He would be happy you continued living."

I nodded, the feelings suddenly stuck in my throat, making it hard to speak.

"Thank you for trusting me enough to share this with me," he said, giving my hands another squeeze.

I pulled Jeremy into a hug. It had been hard holding it all in for so long, but now I had a friend, a real friend I could share my life with, which made me happy through all the sadness. I truly did love it in Florida, the life I was making, the memories, the people I'd met. I couldn't imagine still being in Boston, even though it felt like I had left some of my heart there.

I woke up the next morning exhausted from yesterday. There were tears dried on my face, I had a massive headache, and just generally felt a bit shit.

I emailed Orion and told him I wasn't coming in. I didn't feel great about it, but I knew that today was an okay day to take off. The presentation to the board wasn't until Friday, and it was all ready to go as we'd basically had a run through with Phil. If there was anything that needed tweaking, I was sure Orion could cover it.

If I went in, I just knew I would sit there, half falling asleep, not getting anything done. I needed some more time to myself to just reset.

I had a shower, standing under the hot water for too long. My body was aching, but the warmth felt like it was helping.

After making pancakes for breakfast, I knew it was time to properly unpack. I'd never gotten around to it. My Boston clothes didn't really work in Florida, so I'd mostly been buying new things as I needed them.

I just wanted to go watch a movie or something, but I knew that if I finished this, it would feel completely real. I lived in Florida. This was where I was supposed to be. Having a room full of unpacked stuff made it seem like I was ready to run if I needed to.

I quickly went through the remaining clothes in my suitcase and found most of them I didn't even want anymore. I made a bag for donations and put away the few remaining pieces.

I only had two boxes to go through. I opened one, finding some pictures, toys from my childhood, and other random shit I obviously didn't need, having lived without it for this long.

There were a few frames in the box that I couldn't recall packing and wasn't sure what the photos were. I knew there was one of Tim and me, which I smiled at as I grabbed it from the box. I hung that one on the wall. It was a photo of us at the park, which a stranger took for us. Just the two of us on a normal day, smiling, laughing, enjoying life. I smiled at the memory of that day.

I got the other frames from the box, surprised that I'd kept them. One was a photo with my siblings, and the other of me with my parents as a baby. I didn't even remember packing these. Seeing my parents smiling while holding me brought up a weird feeling I really didn't want to deal with. It was a mixture of anger, over the fact I don't remember them being like that with me, but there was also sadness, knowing I would never have that. I threw them into a drawer, the frames clinking together as they landed among other random shit.

My phone buzzed on my bedside table, drawing me from my thoughts about my family.

Assuming it was Claire, I picked it up without looking. "Hey."

"Tahlia? Is that you?" My mind went blank, no words leaving my mouth at the sound of the person on the other end of the line. "Are you there?"

"Morgan." My voice was caught in my throat, my words barely a whisper.

"How are you?" This had to be a joke. No way my brother just called to ask me how I'm doing after all this time.

"Are you seriously asking me that?" I choked out.

"Why can't I?"

"Why can't you?" I scoffed. I really wasn't sure I was in the headspace for this call. I could feel anger bubbling up in me. "How long has it been since you have spoken to me? Hell, even thought of me before today."

"Okay, that's fair." Morgan didn't say anything else for a while. I was about to hang up when he said, "I'm not speaking to them anymore."

"What?" My voice was barely a whisper.

"I don't have anything to do with Mom and Dad anymore. They're terrible people." He took a breath, his voice shaky on the other end. "I wanted to apologize for not being there for you. For everything, especially after Tim died."

I pursed my lips, not really knowing what to say to that. It felt like too little, too late. "Why are you calling, Morgan?"

"I called you to tell you something." He sounded nervous. "Firstly, I wanted to make things up with you, I miss you, I miss my little sister. I want to fix what's broken between us, not just because of what I'm about to tell you, but because I want to. I've wanted to for a long time, but never had the courage. Connie pushed me to." The way he spoke reminded me of when we were kids, and he would nervously ramble off everything on his mind.

"Connie?" Hearing that he wanted to make up with me was the last thing I expected to hear.

"She's my wife." The nerves I heard previously were gone, a confident, proud Morgan replaced them.

I smiled at the thought that he was making a life for himself. "Congratulations."

"She's pregnant. I'm going to be a dad."

"Oh wow. That's so exciting, Morgan. I'm so happy for you."

Morgan told me all about Connie, the life he'd made, and asked about mine. I wasn't really sure what to say but told him about my job and Jeremy. I didn't mention Orion, not knowing myself what was going on there.

We were on the phone for over an hour before he said he had to go.

"I heard you moved away."

I nodded, before remembering we were on the phone. "Yeah."

"I'm proud of you for doing that, I know Tim would be too. He would be cheering you on from above." Fresh tears spilled down my cheek. After how much I cried yesterday, I was surprised I had more in me.

"Thank you."

"I really did think he was a good guy, you two were great together."

"Morgan—"

"You deserve to be that happy with someone, Tahls. He'd want that for you."

If someone had told me when I woke up today I would be on the phone with my brother, talking about our lives, I wouldn't have believed them. But I think it was exactly what I needed. Hearing my brother's words of approval, even if Morgan hadn't known Tim as well as I did, that he'd want me to move on … it was like I could feel the healing power of the words on my heart.

I felt lighter for the rest of the day, and was finally able to relax.

Chapter Twenty-Four

Orion

THE BOARD MEETING WENT off without a hitch.

Tahlia was back at work and presented to the board confidently. She seemed happier; I was glad to see her mostly back to her normal self.

Her presentation was brilliant, and the board hung off every word. Everyone, except John, voted yes. I couldn't say I was surprised; that was why I'd brought the idea to the board without passing it by him first, after all.

After the meeting, a few members came up to me and asked where I'd found her. I relished the way their jaws dropped when I told them my assistant had come up with the idea, pulled together the pitch herself, then presented it to a board without even looking nervous.

There were a few jokes about me needing to watch my back because she was coming for my job. Even though they were joking, knowing other people saw how good she was, how much potential she had, gave me a sense of relief. She was on the entire company's radar now. If they found out I left and John somehow got past HR and fired her, there would be questions.

John was shady, I knew that—so did many people—but this worry about Tahlia somehow flipped a switch in my mind, unlocking the door on so many buried thoughts. This whole time, I was constantly taking on extra work I shouldn't have, responding to him calling me when he knew I was off, and covering his ass to the board and when dealing with our key stakeholders.

He'd been pulling all this shit since he became CEO, and I had just rolled over and let him.

Anger was building up in my chest, my mind unable to focus on much else but John being an absolute asshole. I'd have to get over it and keep going. The last thing I wanted to do was work with John and Rachel to organize this trip, but I had to, for Tahlia's sake at least. Once this merger was sorted, I would be free. In the meantime, I couldn't let him walk all over me anymore.

At least the hard part, getting approval, was done—in theory. But my gut told me that what came next would be near impossible. Even though Tahlia and I would do all the leg work, everything from here on out had to go through John and Rachel. He was CEO, not me.

This newfound anger was going to make it real fucking hard to get through this.

He shouldn't be CEO, he doesn't act like one. I've been doing all the work for months, and now what? I had to basically hand it over to him to piss on and destroy everything Tahlia and I worked for?

I couldn't let that happen.

The cruise we had proposed was only a month away, which meant there was no time to waste; so we met with them that afternoon. Tahlia and I were nervous about the outcome, given John had been so thoroughly out-voted at the board meeting. We were first to the room, unsurprisingly. John and Rachel were generally late.

We didn't speak to each other. Tahlia looked like she was going over things in her head, probably similar to me. With the cruise not far off, everything needed to be actioned now, but we just had no idea how this meeting with John was going to turn out.

"I want to discuss the budget," was the first thing John said when he sat down—forty-five minutes late.

"Even though the board just approved it?" My eyebrow raised in question, I was unable to keep my tone from becoming sarcastic.

He was not looking as put together as he should. His hair was ruffled but looked like maybe he had tried to smooth it down. I also noticed his tie was off-center and looked like it had been tied in a rush. Rachel looked like her perfectly styled self as she took her seat next to him, but she was suspiciously flushed. It was obvious what they had been doing. I wasn't surprised, just disgusted. They made Tahlia and I wait almost an hour so they could fuck?

"The money going towards staff attending this trip. Who is coming, why are they coming, and why should we be paying for them?" Rachel's smirk she quickly hid behind her hand caught my eye.

"As Tahlia explained in the presentation," I said evenly, "the main reason we have included a large amount of the staff is we want to show them that we care about our employees. In turn, we will care for theirs. This is a key concern for them in the merger process as a family-founded and run business. If it's just you, me, Rachel, and Phil, then what does that say about us?"

"And how can we afford to pay for everyone?"

Before I could respond, Tahlia said sweetly, "Would you like me to run through the presentation again? I realize it was a bit complex, it might have gone over your head."

I choked on a laugh, covering it with a cough.

John choked on the sip of water he had taken, the tips of his ears turning a fiery red. I had to hold back my laugh at the thought of steam coming out of his ears and nose, as I was sure that would happen now if it could. "I don't think it's the right move."

"Why?" Tahlia prompted.

"Well, Ms Walters," John huffed, exchanging a look with Rachel. "We can't waste all of our money on bringing the whole company. We also can't have everyone come, regardless—who will run the place?"

Did he seriously think we hadn't thought of any of this?

"Firstly, it's not a waste," I said. "Phil has calculated how this fits in the budget himself—it will be a part of our employee culture and team building budget."

"Secondly, not everyone is going." I went into the specifics of who would have the opportunity to attend, a few from different departments, that had to include a variety of levels, ages, and diversities.

"It's a terrible idea."

"It was approved by the board."

"But not by me, the CEO."

There it was, the other shoe that I knew was going to drop. How had I ignored the conceit of this asshole for so long? I held back from snapping at him, taking a breath before continuing. "What do you suggest we do, then?"

"Staff will have to pay for themselves. We cannot fork out hundreds of thousands of dollars paying for a trip just to impress some people because the board wants their company. It's just not viable. I won't have you spend all our money on some employees no one knows."

I could see Tahlia squirming in her seat next to me—at least it wasn't just me on the edge of losing my cool.

"Well, what's your plan then, John?" If he wanted to change everything, I wasn't going to be the one to make the decisions. Sitting here, looking at him, it was like I was finally seeing him clearly after walking around with a bag over my head since I was turned down for CEO.

It was his minty breath that really caught my attention. There was a hint of something behind it. Something that shouldn't be there in the workplace. It was then I noticed some other things about him. The way his eyes were distant, the sweat-stains under his armpits, the pimples on his chin. What was he doing to himself? Something had changed, he was no longer the smart businessman we had both set out to be, competing neck and neck for years. He had become nothing but a bored exec with nothing better to do than create petty drama and sleep with his assistant—a cliché.

I watched John exchange another sly look with Rachel as he leaned back in his chair. Whatever he was going to say, we weren't going to like it.

"The company will pay for executives, as long as we continue to work while on the ship," he said importantly, then waved a lazy hand at his assistant. "Rachel will obviously be paid for, since she is basically an executive. However, everyone else will be required to pay for themselves."

The room was silent after he dropped that bomb—except for the rattle of John's mints. He jangled the tin as he popped two into his smirking mouth with a cringe-inducing crunch.

He had to be fucking kidding. He might as well have painted a giant banner to hang in his office that said, "I'm sleeping with my assistant". When I looked over at Tahlia, her face was carefully schooled. She'd put all of her attention on her laptop, acting unbothered as she typed up minutes. But I knew her better than that now. I wasn't sure when it happened, but somehow over the last couple of months I'd come to know every expression on her face. And that blank expression, the careful lift of her eyebrows ...

She was devastated. She'd put her heart and soul into this project, it was all her idea, for Christ's sake. Now they wanted her to have to pay to go.

Well, fuck that.

"If the company is paying for assistants," I said, looking deliberately at Rachel as I said it, "then it's only natural that Tahlia's place should also be covered. She is completely across not just this aspect of the process, but the entire merger, and has an existing relationship with the Air Mexicana execs—no one can do what she does. I need her."

Tahlia looked at me, her eyes wide.

I probably ruined the argument by tacking on the last part, but it was true. While she was off, I was able to do my job, but I had gotten so used to her help that I struggled. I really missed having her there.

"You were fine when you didn't have an assistant before—you'll be fine for a week if Tahlia feels she's above paying her way."

Tahlia shrunk into herself before my eyes. It took all my willpower not to throw myself across the table at John like some kind of caveman. But that's what he wanted. Clearly, at some point, what's between us stopped being just a professional rivalry to him and became something ... else. I'd be lying if I pretended to understand what was behind this churlishness.

He was taking aim at Tahlia just because I'd stood up for her, because he saw her as an extension of me. I could try to defuse the situation, but it was clear it didn't matter what I suggested—no matter how reasonable—he was going to reject it just because it came from me.

"Now," John continued when neither Tahlia nor I said anything further, "I will have Rachel take over organizing everything from here. As you know, this is her specialty."

"Tahlia should help," I said, careful to keep my eyes on John, though I sensed Tahlia turn toward me again, felt her eyes on my face like her touch that day in my office. "This was her idea. She should be able to see the project through."

Tahlia hadn't looked away from me, but I didn't dare look at her, my feelings about her bubbling to the surface. I didn't want any of that to be seen by Rachel and John, even though nothing was happening. They didn't need any more ammunition.

"Of course," Rachel said sweetly. "I wouldn't mind some help from Tahlia. I have a lot on my plate, and it would be good experience for her." I didn't buy the act Rachel had put on, and I could tell Tahlia didn't either. We both knew Rachel didn't like her. In fact, I was sure she felt threatened by Tahlia, so I wondered what her play was.

"This doesn't mean she gets a free ride, Orion." It was clear that John was over this meeting, bored because I wasn't fighting him anymore. "My decision is final."

That was my cue. I couldn't sit there any longer, listening to him speak about Tahlia that way. I gestured for Tahlia to grab her things and follow me. "Thank you for your time, John. Rachel."

Tahlia followed me out of the meeting room to my office. We said nothing, walking side by side, our arms occasionally brushing. Sending shivers down my spine.

I could feel anger emanating from Tahlia. She looked straight ahead, avoiding everyone's gazes as we approached my office. I shut the door a bit hard behind us, the noise of it slamming reverberating through the room. Other employees were staring from their desks, but I didn't care.

"That was fucked," Tahlia said as she slumped onto my couch. Her words were fiery, but she looked defeated, her shoulders hunched forward, her gaze turned downwards.

"It was complete bullshit." I agreed.

Tahlia sighed, kicking her shoes off and tucking her feet under herself. "If you didn't end that meeting when you did, I was sure I was going to lose it at them."

"I'd love to see that," I chuckled. I knew that Tahlia wouldn't back down once riled up, but it was for the best that we both kept our cool. I made my way over to her, sitting on the opposite end of the couch to her, making sure to leave a respectable distance between us.

She crossed her arms over her chest, some of that spunk returning. It was pretty hot, if I was honest.

"You're allowed to be angry." I looked away from her, willing my thoughts to remain professional. "You should want to scream, yell, cry. Well, probably don't scream in the office."

She huffed, eyes flashing. "At least people would still think you're an asshole if I did."

I couldn't hold back the laugh that escaped my lips. Only Tahlia would be able to joke when she was definitely more upset than she was letting on. "You did great—though I should technically reprimand you for insulting the CEO."

She looked concerned for a moment before she realized what I meant and laughed. Her head tipped back, hand lifting to cover her mouth—it was so cute that she was self-conscious—the pinch in her brow melting. I basked in it.

"What can I say? He made it too easy," she quipped, and I wanted to bow down at her feet.

"Don't worry about what he said. I'll get it sorted, there's no way you are paying for a trip that was your idea to begin with."

She waved me off, tucking her feet back into her shoes before standing up and smoothing her dress out. "It is what it is, don't worry about it."

I regretted bringing it up. Any trace of her regular self that had returned was gone again.

I needed to fix this. She should get the recognition. But, more than anything, I knew I couldn't have her hurting like that.

I reached for her hand and she let me take it, warm and soft in mine. I focused on my thumb as I smoothed it over her knuckles. "I promise I'll work something out," I said, then looked up and found her staring at our hands.

"Sure thing." She nodded, her voice thick, and pulled her hand from mine before she left the room, not looking back.

Chapter Twenty-Five

Tahlia

I CONTINUED WALKING AFTER leaving Orion's office until I was in the bathroom. My right hand tingled where Orion had held it, my left hand heavy where the ring encircled my finger. Once I was alone, a tear slipped free, followed by a downpour.

The roller coaster of the last few days was just too much. All of this was too much.

After I cleaned myself up, I went back to work. Even though all I really wanted was to go home.

It had been interesting being in a board meeting. A lot of them were young, like Orion and John. Phil was one of the oldest in the room. I really expected them to all be old, white men. But there was also some diversity within the group. I guessed I also thought Orion would be older before I met him, that he would be this old man who didn't care for anyone but himself. Maybe Orion being who he is, and Phil being at the company as long as he had, should have given me more of an indication of what the other executives would be like—they hadn't disappointed.

After being in the meeting, I had even more questions about how John became CEO. It was obvious that the majority of people in the room didn't respect him, especially when he'd voted no. In comparison, they had all tripped over each other to talk to Orion, to shake his hand.

There had to be something more I could do to help him push John out. Orion should be the CEO. I was sure he still wanted it, and it was obvious a lot of people in that room wanted him in that role, treating him like he was CEO already.

No wonder John was so pissed.

Orion was so good at his job, but also just a generally nice person. The way he comforted me, telling me that he would do everything he could to get me on the trip ... it melted my heart, even though I felt like it was a pointless fight. John had made his position clear.

But I couldn't help but hope when he grabbed my hand and looked deeply into my eyes. He was so sincere and true. The feel of his smooth hand in mine, only a few calluses—probably from weight-lifting, I thought absently. The way he held my hand longer, not wanting to let me go. Even now, just remembering it, my heart skipped a beat.

I tried not to let the sad feelings creep back in, holding on to what Morgan had said. It was beyond obvious to me now that whatever I was feeling for Orion was very real. I still wasn't even sure I was ready to move on. But even if I was, I couldn't be with him. He was my boss.

Was it even worth staying at my job?

The thought had knocked persistently at the back of my mind for the last week. It was getting harder every day to work so closely with him. Maybe not going on the trip would be a good thing. A week away from him to clear my head and understand what I should do would be good for me. But Orion aside, the other thing that bothered me about this job was the way everyone acted, Rachel and John especially, but the others as well. It felt like I was back in high school with the rumor mill, everyone gossiping, cliques everywhere, everyone too scared to stand up to the bullies. I wasn't really sure I wanted to keep working somewhere that this was considered normal.

The fact that Orion had to pretend to be this awful boss for people to just talk to me, to include me in team events, was actually ridiculous. I had never worked somewhere like this, where everything was childish, where everyone followed the one mean girl, not wanting to get on her bad side. It was so fucking stupid.

It was getting late in the day and I hadn't eaten, so I headed to the café downstairs to get some food. The line was really long, so I popped into a bathroom on that level while I waited for it to die down.

I had almost finished up when I heard Rachel and someone else walk into the bathroom, so stayed in my stall to avoid them.

"Somehow, the board approved her ridiculous plan that's going to send the company bankrupt—honestly, I don't know how she ever came up with something like that. But JJ and I have a plan to push them out, so she'll be gone soon," Rachel said, obviously very proud of herself.

"What do you mean you plan to push them out?" A voice I recognized, but couldn't place, responded. She sounded hesitant, like she didn't want to be involved in this but knew if she said anything negative she would join Orion and me on the wrong side of the tracks. "Orion and Tahlia?"

"Yes, obviously Orion and Tahlia." I could imagine Rachel fixing her lipstick or something in the mirror, rolling her eyes at the other person. Of course, she was talking about us. Did she have nothing interesting in her life to focus on? She just had to be hellbent on trying to ruin everyone else's lives. What were they even doing using the bathroom downstairs? It felt like a whole new low, even for this place, if they just came down here purely to gossip.

Also, JJ? Gross.

"What plan?" The other woman pressed.

"Easy—make their lives a living hell until they quit." A hand dryer started, making it so I couldn't really hear what she said next.

"Wow," her companion responded when the dryer stopped, her tone flat.

Someone else walked in and said hi to Rachel, who then left, or at least it sounded like it. I finally left my stall and washed my hands, wondering how often she did this sort of shit. Sleeping with the CEO must have made her think she's invincible, to feel so comfortable talking about Orion like that where anyone could have just walked in.

There was no sign of Rachel when I joined the café line, but there was someone familiar. The woman that came up to me a while ago and apologized for not including me more—I couldn't remember her name—but I was positive it was her I heard with Rachel.

I was not surprised to hear Rachel talking about me in the bathroom with coworkers. It did make me sad to think that I could have had such a different experience at Florida Airlines if it wasn't for her. But knowing that this was the reality of things, that I was a common topic of bathroom gossip ... this environment wasn't one that I wanted to continue working in.

It was time to find somewhere else to go.

After collecting my food, I sat in the café to eat, not feeling ready to head back up and potentially see Rachel. I didn't have a great poker face and was sure it would be all over my face. But maybe that wasn't a bad thing. Maybe she needed to know I knew, but didn't care.

You do care, though.

I had never worked somewhere where I'd been so blatantly disliked—that I knew of, at least. I could pretend I didn't care, knock her down a couple of notches. But I wasn't sure I wanted to give them all even more to gossip about. I just needed to go.

I racked my brain with where I could try and go. Did I want to move to a similar job, or something different? Could I do something with my art? I was learning a lot at that course. No, I didn't think that would work. I wasn't that good. Would it be the same somewhere else, would the grass actually be greener?

I could talk to Orion about it. Would he be upset if I said I was going to try and find another job? Maybe, surely not. Especially after what happened today. But I wasn't sure I was ready to talk to him about this. How I felt about him was just too ... overwhelming.

I needed to think on it, decide what I wanted for my life, where I wanted to go, and then go in that direction. If I kept to myself and did my work until then, it would be fine. I'd somehow managed to mostly avoid Rachel and John up to this point, despite their so-called "plan", I could for a bit longer.

My phone buzzed as I was finishing up my food.

Orion Ariti: I'm sorry about what happened earlier Tahlia. I don't know where you've disappeared to, but if you want the rest of the day off I support you. Just let me know if you need anything from me. I will fix this, I promise.

My stomach fluttered in a way it hadn't in a long time, just from seeing that he'd texted me—I hadn't even read it yet. He'd never texted me before, we mostly spoke over email, only a few times over office messages, but never texting ... on our personal phones.

Even though I wasn't sure what to make of it, the smile it brought to my face was hard to tamp down. It somehow made what I'd overheard, what happened today, and all the roiling thoughts fade away.

Knowing that I at least had one person in this company who cared for me and would make sure I'd be okay brought me a sense of peace. I didn't respond, not knowing what to say, but knowing that he wouldn't be expecting anything.

This guy deserved more than he had.

A plan was starting to form in my head. It was time Orion got his CEO position, and I knew how to help it along. I'd hold off leaving this place, build up evidence of John and Rachel's relationship, and if Orion wanted the CEO job, I was sure that he would be able to get it—especially after he secured the Air Mexicana merger. Because I knew he would.

Then I could leave, knowing I at least did something good while I was here.

I was sick of being a pushover. Orion and I both deserved more. Fuck Rachel and John, it was time to get what I wanted, what Orion wanted, and stop letting them screw everyone else over.

It was finally getting close to the end of the day and I couldn't wait to go home. The anger had settled throughout the rest of the day, not much, but slightly. Even though Orion had said I didn't have to stay, it felt like letting them win if I went home. That's exactly what they wanted, me to feel upset, to be isolated from everyone. I might be going to quit, but it would be when I was ready to. Not when they pushed me out.

But they were succeeding at wearing me down. Orion had to pretend to be this asshole, people avoided me still, and I was being excluded from the trip. Not entirely, but I couldn't afford to go. There was no way. I had spent all my savings moving here from Boston. I didn't have any extra money to spare—and I knew that had been their plan.

Nothing I did could distract me from it all. I looked at the clock for what felt like the millionth time. It was getting close enough for it to be almost time to go home. Fuck it. I wasn't staying any longer. I just needed to go home, watch some trashy TV and eat junk.

"Leaving so soon?" I didn't even have to look up to know who it was. Ignoring her, I continued to pack up my things, pens clinking together as I dropped them in my bag, my laptop sliding into the sleeve.

She was hovering.

Rachel was standing directly in front of my desk when I looked up, staring down at me, her arms crossed, and one hip popped. Her eyebrow was raised, mouth held in a smirk. Nothing about her said she was here for anything but a fight.

She probably thought I would just shut up and take whatever it was she was there to throw at me. Little did she know, I saw her for what she was. A mean girl. All she wanted was to make sure everyone she didn't like had an awful time. If I had to guess, she probably peaked in high school and never grew up.

The way she acted really showed how immature she really was. I knew children who could regulate their emotions better.

Well, Rachel was in for a rude shock. She hadn't met all of me, and I couldn't keep my filter in place anymore. If she'd just get out of the way, I could come back tomorrow with my smile fixed back in place. But no, she'd started this.

"Can't take a hint?" I said.

"Excuse me?" She flicked her hair over her shoulder, just like the mean girls in all those high school movies, and I had to stifle a laugh. She and John deserved each other.

"I said, can't you take a hint?" I rolled my eyes, zipping up my bag and flicking my eyes quickly to check Orion was still in his office—I didn't want him involved in this.

Rachel scoffed. "You better watch your tone, Tahlia," she said, looking around at everyone watching. She was embarrassed, the tips of her ears bright red. If she were a cartoon, I'd imagine she had steam coming out her ears and nose. This really would be hilarious if I wasn't so mad.

"And why's that?" I stood, walking around the front of my desk so that we were eye to eye. She wasn't going to look down on me any longer. "Are you going to try and make me quit or get fired or something? Oh wait, you're already doing that."

Rachel said nothing, her mouth opening and closing like a fish as she apparently racked her brain for something to say.

"She doesn't even deny it," I said to no one in particular, looking around at everyone pretending to not listen from behind their little cubicle desks. The braver ones exchanged hushed whispers. When Rachel still said nothing, I gestured for her to confirm.

"How dare you," she finally managed, her back ramrod straight.

I did laugh then. "How dare I what? Tell the truth?" I copied her, crossing my arms as I raised my eyebrow at her, enjoying the way my body weight tilted on my heels as I popped my hip.

"You're making it all up—you're just jealous of me." She waved a dismissive hand, throwing a false smile for her audience.

"Why would I be jealous of you?" I really wished at that moment I could see what was going on in her mind, what she was thinking. Did she really hate me, or was she just so insecure she had to take it out on everyone else? "I'm not jealous of people who spread rumors or talk about others and their plans to ruin their life in a public bathroom where anyone could hear."

Before she could say some stupid retort to try and restore herself, I continued. "Just worry about your own life for once."

I could feel eyes on me, more than before. Rachel looked like a deer caught in headlights, her eyes watery. The floor creaked behind me. Shit.

"Tahlia!" Orion's voice boomed through the space. "What's going on?"

"Nothing." I didn't look back at him.

"Oh." Rachel's eyes cleared, and a snarky expression overtook her face, her gaze focused on me as she smirked.

A thought had been niggling at the back of my mind all day, and seeing the way she was looking at me made it click into place. Rachel knew Orion wasn't an asshole. He tried so hard to get me on the trip, defending me in front of John. There was no way either of them would still believe our ruse after today.

As if she could read my mind, Rachel said, "Aw, big strong Orion coming to save you? How sweet—he mustn't be such a bad boss after all." Her voice dripped with sarcasm, loud enough that any spectators would hear perfectly.

This was why I hadn't wanted him to intervene. I didn't need to look like some damsel that needed saving—but now that was exactly what had happened.

Rachel said nothing further, walking away with her head held high.

"Tahlia, a word?" Everyone else scrambled back to their desks as I followed Orion back into his office. The door closed behind me, the room silent except for the roaring in my ears.

I sat in one of the chairs in front of his desk. Orion walked back to his chair. He looked at me with a sad look, his eyes drawn together. Was he disappointed? I squirmed in my seat, feeling uneasy. "I don't need a lecture right now," I said.

"I wasn't going to lecture you," he reassured me as he leaned back in his chair, rolling the sleeves of his shirt up, exposing those forearms. Fuck. My mind went blank, and I forgot why I was there, thinking about his arms, how strong he must be, how the rest of him would lo—

"Are you listening?"

A blush creeped up my cheeks as I shook my head.

Orion sighed. "Is everything okay? I only caught the end of that—I'm sure she deserved it—but this isn't you." I went to interrupt, but he continued. "You know you can talk to me about anything? I know that all the cruise stuff is frustrating, and I'm working to fix it, but this high school shit normally doesn't get to you so bad. There has to be something else bothering you."

He seemed genuinely worried, stress lines evident on his forehead. I looked in his eyes, he was looking between mine, but I wasn't some puzzle for him to figure out. I couldn't do this anymore.

"High school shit? Is it high school shit to have weeks' worth of work ripped away from me and then have it rubbed in my face by that ... by that ..." I squeezed my hands into fists and took a deep breath. "You don't know me, Orion. Don't try and make assumptions about how I'm feeling or how I react to things."

I left before he could say anything else, grabbing my stuff and heading home.

I could feel his eyes and everyone else's on me as I stormed out.

But I really couldn't shake his words as the elevator stopped on the first floor and I walked out into the balmy Florida air.

I know she deserved it, but this isn't you.

Maybe he was right, maybe he wasn't. But maybe I'd changed and this was me now.

I couldn't stop thinking about it the entire trip home.

Chapter Twenty-Six

Orion

WE'D GOTTEN BOARD APPROVAL just in time. I was actually excited about it, even though I still had to work while onboard and John was making things impossible. It would be the first vacation I had been on in a long time. When I finally got to start my new chapter, that was going to change. I wanted to see the world, bring Gracie along—and Sophia, if she wanted to come—and just enjoy life for once.

I pretended that I didn't also picture Tahlia by my side on these holidays. Seeing her marvel at art galleries, smiling with a gelato cone in her hand ...

Stop it, Orion.

I closed my laptop with a snap and rested my head in my hands. It was eating me away that Tahlia's spot on the cruise wouldn't be paid for. I would give up my spot for her, if I didn't think John would destroy everything if I wasn't there. I would happily pay for her myself, but that wasn't the point. She deserved to be there more than anyone else.

While Tahlia was gone, I had tried again to change John's mind—offering to do more work, to give him credit for the merger outcome—but nothing worked. So, I'd gone over his head to other board members to see if there was some way they could help me, but their hands were tied. They could vote on initiatives, but it was the CEO's prerogative to see them implemented. As long as John and Rachel didn't want her there, she wouldn't be at this rate.

That was also eating away at me. How had I put up with his bullshit for so long, all for the sake of loyalty to a company who had passed me over for CEO in favor of him? I really should have let them deal with the consequences, instead of covering for him for all this time. But if I had walked away back then, I wouldn't have met Tahlia.

"Just worry about your own life, for once." Tahlia's voice caused me to look up. She and Rachel were standing in front of Tahlia's desk, her back to me, the look on Rachel's face like she was about to eat Tahlia alive.

I got up and popped my head out. "Tahlia, what's going on?"

"Nothing." Tahlia didn't even look at me, obviously annoyed that I butted in.

"Aw, big strong Orion coming to save you? How sweet—he mustn't be such a bad boss after all." I didn't like the way Rachel spoke to Tahlia, even with me there. I didn't respond, staring at her with my most deathly expression. She walked off, acting unbothered, without saying anything else. Everyone in the office was staring at us.

"Tahlia, a word?" She sighed and followed me into my office, refusing to meet my eye. I closed the door behind her, not sure where to start as we sat across from each other.

"I don't need a lecture right now," Tahlia said defensively, crossing her arms over her chest.

"I wasn't going to lecture you." How was it that she was obviously pissed off, partly at me, and it was somehow so hot? Fuck me. I had to roll my sleeves up before I made a panting idiot of myself. "I'm sure she deserved that. But I can tell something is really bothering you ... are you listening?" Tahlia looked up and shook her head, clearing her throat as a blush crept up her neck. "Is everything okay? I only caught the end of that—I'm sure she deserved it—but this isn't you." I could tell she wanted to interrupt, but I pushed on anyway. "You know you can talk to me about anything? I know that all the cruise stuff is frustrating, and I'm working to fix it, but this high school shit doesn't usually get to you so bad. There has to be something else bothering you."

She finally looked me in the eye, not a hint of the happy, funny Tahlia I knew and lov— missed. "High school shit? Is it high school shit to have weeks' worth of work ripped away from me and then have it rubbed in my face by that ... by that ..."

She paused, and I tried to interject to say that wasn't what I meant, but she plowed on with a punch to the guts. "You don't know me, Orion. Don't try and make assumptions about how I'm feeling or how I react to things."

With that, she walked out of the office, grabbing her things on the way out.

She was obviously upset with me, on top of everything else, but at what? It had to be something I'd done. I'd really thought we were becoming closer, even almost friends when we were working through the cruise, before we pitched it. I wished we could go back to before then, when she smiled regularly, laughed and seemed to enjoy talking to me.

It may be partially me, but I knew she was upset with John and Rachel—particularly after that chat she just had with her.

I stormed out of my office, anger propelling me forward before I could think better of it. My footsteps were heavy, everyone looking at me with wide eyes as I barged into John's office, not having a care in the world for what he was doing.

He wasn't there.

I looked around, my anger still simmering. Would he be back soon?

Unsurprisingly, his laptop was there, unlocked for all to see.

I checked his calendar to see where he was, which said he was at some meeting which didn't end for another thirty minutes.

I sighed, looking around at his bare-bones office. No one could see me; it wasn't a fishbowl like everyone else's.

I had planned to interrupt John, tell him how big of a prick he was, and demand he have the company pay for her. She should have had the number one spot in my opinion.

As my anger started to subside, I wondered what length I would have gone to, to force his hand. I had a few pieces of dirt on him, one being the fact that he was sleeping with his assistant. But did I really want to stoop that low? If I tried to blackmail him, would that just make me as bad as him? Worse? I didn't want to be anything like him. Besides, I didn't really have any solid proof of his and Rachel's affair.

I was grateful he wasn't there—it was for the best. I straightened up from looking at his laptop screen and started to re-button my jacket when another idea occurred to me.

I wanted to pay for Tahlia to come—I had been thinking about it since John dropped the bomb of not everyone being paid for. I had money. More than I needed. But I had a feeling that Tahlia would never accept that.

I sat down, opened John's inbox and clicked 'compose a new email'. If John realized I was sending emails from his computer, I would be in a lot of shit. But I didn't care. I was almost done, almost out of here.

That thought brought some sadness to my mind, thinking about how far I had come at Florida Airlines. But I had outgrown this place, and it was time to make a change for the better. I wanted more from life. Nothing would change here.

I had already been in John's office longer than I should have, so I pulled myself together and quickly typed out an email to the travel team. Making sure to cc myself, I instructed them to book Tahlia's ticket on my personal expense account and to simply notify me, not John, when it was done. Then I deleted it from his sent folder once it had left the outbox.

As I was about to set his screen back to where he left it, an email popped into his inbox from Rachel.

I wasn't really someone who snooped. I was tempted at first, but when I saw the subject, I knew I wasn't interested and that I needed to get out of his office ASAP.

Subject: JJ office now. ✎

It was weird helping Henry move out of my place. I hadn't admitted to him, but I would miss having him there. I had gotten used to him being around all the time. It got lonely in the apartment; having someone else around warmed the place up.

It made me really wonder if I should find somewhere out of the city to live, a more family style home, with a nice office and just a cozy feel. Rather than staying in this bachelor style apartment. I definitely didn't feel like a bachelor. I'd loved the place when I bought it, and still did, but it was starting to feel like my life had moved down this more mature track, but I wasn't keeping up. It felt like time for a change.

The couch Henry had ordered had just been delivered, along with his refrigerator, bed and some cabinets. He had decided to start fresh, letting Charlotte keep all the furniture. He said it was too much of a reminder, how they went and bought it all together. There were memories in every piece, so he wanted a fresh start.

Henry grabbed some water and sandwiches from the cooler bag in the kitchen and sat on the still wrapped couch, gesturing for me to join him. The sound of the plastic scrunching wasn't my favorite, but it beat sitting on the floor.

"Thanks again for helping." Henry took a swig of his water before unwrapping his lunch. I followed suit.

"Don't sweat it." Honestly, it was good. It was keeping my mind occupied. All I had been thinking about was Tahlia, and it needed to stop. So having some heavy lifting to do, driving between places, and even just spending time with Henry quietened the thoughts.

"Have you asked her out yet?" he said, so nonchalantly I almost believed it was just a stab in the dark for something to talk about. Almost. So, I decided to play dumb.

"Who?"

"Tahlia." He wasn't even phased, the asshole.

I sighed, putting my sandwich back in its wrapper. "I've been trying to avoid thinking about her, so thanks for reminding me."

"You're so welcome, Ry." Henry was one smug bitch.

I laughed, not able to help it. "No, I haven't asked her out." I gave him a look that said "you know this". He knew that I couldn't ask her out when I was her boss, when she worked with me. That would make me no better than John. I had become a cliché of falling for my assistant, but I didn't need to act on it. I couldn't, it wasn't the right thing to do.

"Have you planned how you will?"

I rolled my eyes. Henry was such a slut for gossip, always squeezing whatever he could out of me. "No, I haven't. Can we talk about something else?"

"Fine, but you should think about it. How you confess your love. You can't do it in some boring-ass way, which is totally your style."

"Fuck off." I threw my water bottle at him, and it smacked him in the arm. "I'm not in love with her."

Henry's raised eyebrows and taut lips said he saw right through me. But he didn't say whatever he was thinking, instead dramatically pretending to nurse his arm.

Time for a change of subject.

"How's the setup going? Any more clients on board?" I was starting to get excited about this new venture, with the end at Florida Airlines now in sight.

"Plenty of clients want your expertise. I can tell you, they are sick of talking to me." He chuckled. "But seriously, it's ready. Are there any specific projects you want to work on? It might help with weeding through some clients. We may have too many for just starting up. I haven't committed to anyone yet, but everyone is keen for a meeting with you to discuss their options."

"I'm pretty good at mergers now." I laughed, thinking that the only reason the one I was working on was going well, not that it was finalized, was because of Tahlia. How was I going to do this without her? "But no, not really, just stuff within my wheelhouse, which you already know."

I helped Henry move for the rest of the afternoon before heading over to see Grace. She was so excited to see me—I missed her so much—reminding me of what I was going to have when I quit Florida Airlines for good. More time with my Gracie. More time in general. I could choose what I worked on, and who I worked with.

And Tahlia. As much as I was trying to deny it to get through these last few weeks, I had feelings for her, strong ones. I'd almost said something a few times.

I was ready to talk to her.

I was counting down until I was done with this job and could finally tell Tahlia how I felt. But my fear was that maybe she didn't feel the same. I was almost sure she did until our last conversation, but now I wasn't so sure. Maybe I was imagining it all.

I tried to shake the thoughts off again. There was nothing I could do about it. I could just hope she felt the same.

Chapter Twenty-Seven

Tahlia

MY PHONE STARTED TO buzz as I left the art studio and headed to Saltwater Cakes at lunch for some sweets and another coffee. I recently found out that during weekdays, the studio was available for students to use, and I was definitely going to take advantage of that on the off chance I wasn't working.

Saltwater Cakes had quickly become my favorite shop. Whenever I had the chance, I was there. I swore that most of my paycheck, besides what I paid for rent, ended up in this business.

I was getting emails, work emails. I regretted adding my work emails onto my phone. I'd never used it for work, but these last couple of weeks I had honestly stopped caring about this job. The only good thing was Orion—but even that was awkward now. I needed to stay away from him and get these feelings to fuck off.

I initially ignored the email, but something was telling me I'd want to see this one.

It was to me, with Orion cc'd, from the travel team. Weird.

Subject: Confirmation of your company cruise attendance

Hi Tahlia,

Please see below your confirmed ticket and itinerary for the company trip; your ticket has been covered, with all benefits included.

I almost dropped my phone.

What. The. Fuck.

There was no way this was real, but I kept reading.

There is no need to respond to this email. If you have questions,
reach out to Orion.
Regards,
Tiara Smith
Travel Consultant, Florida Airlines

It had to be real—that was the company signature. And Orion was included. What did he do to get this to happen? There was no way that my "substantial contributions" were the reason, even though they should have been. John didn't back down on this decision himself, someone made him. I knew who, but how?

I couldn't even ask him today. He had the day blocked in his calendar for something, he wasn't working. Truthfully, I didn't go in because of that. I had sent an email that morning saying I wasn't coming in. I knew he wouldn't see it until tomorrow, but the thought of being there when he wasn't made me nauseous, especially after what happened with Rachel last week. I could have called or texted him to tell him, but that felt too … intimate.

When I walked into the café, it was quiet. Probably because it was the middle of the day. Sophia was alone behind the counter and smiled at me as I made my way over to her.

"Tahlia, welcome back." She winked at me, her signature messy bun bobbing on her head.

"I've never seen it this quiet before." Sophia started making my coffee while I looked at the cabinet for what I wanted. I came here so often now that she remembered my order. Most of the time I couldn't pick what to get, and she would just surprise me.

"It's nice in these times." Sophia started to steam the milk as she continued. "I love the busy times, but in these quiet stretches I can admire what I've built here, what I have to pass down. This is one of my greatest achievements."

I smiled at her, her face covered in pride. "I second that." I was amazed every time I came here how busy it usually was, and ninety percent of the time Sophia was either serving customers or decorating a cake in the viewing window. I had never known a business owner to be so involved in the day-to-day running. There was only one time I didn't see her at all, but I was sure she was just working away somewhere in the back I couldn't see.

"Are you looking forward to the company cruise?" Sophia handed me my cup before starting to select some pastries and cookies for me, not even bothering to ask. Obviously, she was beginning to recognize the signs of an indecisive day as well.

"Yeah, I haven't been on a vacation in a long time." I couldn't remember the last time, if I was honest. It was probably some holiday with my family when I was a kid that I was begrudgingly brought on. "A cruise, too. I'd never imagined I would be getting on a ship and willingly spending time out in the middle of the ocean."

I was glad that I'd checked that email, my excitement had quadrupled since reading it. I felt like I could actually enjoy it now. I could go, have a great time, see Orion swoop in to become CEO, and then take my leave. The smile that had appeared on my face as I read that email probably wouldn't leave until I disembarked the ship back in Florida.

"I'm excited too." I blinked at Sophia, her response throwing me off. "I'm excited to spend time with Grace, but also to drop her off to have fun in the kids club while I treat myself to some much-needed downtime in the spa." My thoughts seemed to go haywire that second, so much new information getting muddled up and just not making sense.

Did she say Grace?

"I didn't know you were coming." It was hard to keep the shock from my voice. I was worried it would come off like I didn't want her there, which would be ridiculous—I barely knew her.

"Yeah, Ry insisted Grace and I come. He wants to have some family time." Sophia handed me over the box of sweets. My hand was frozen on the box, but I didn't take it from her. She looked confused.

Sophia, Grace, and Orion. Sophia was Grace's mother. Sophia and Orion were together. But he'd said they were friends. Was he lying? Surely not. But maybe he was. Maybe he didn't feel comfortable sharing that part of his life with me.

But why did I care that much? I knew he was probably in a relationship, and he's my boss.

"You're Grace's mom?" It made sense, but didn't at the same time. I should have put two and two together. It was staring me in the face this whole time and I just didn't pick it up.

How could I have, though? Sophia had never mentioned Grace before, and Orion had never mentioned Grace's mother.

"Yeah, I thought you knew."

I shook my head, unable to shake the confusion. It made sense, but didn't. "I didn't realize you two were together, either." I tried to sound as casual as I could, but it definitely came out strained. I hoped she didn't notice.

The sound of the door opening sang throughout the space, dragging me back to the present. Sophia called out behind her, untied her apron, and made her way around to my side of the counter.

"Let's go for a walk." She brought my box of sweets and opened the door for me expectantly. We ended up sitting on a park bench, the world bustling around us, the sound of car horns, people on their phones, children crying loudly, but it quickly fell into the background as Sophia turned to me.

"Ry and I aren't together." My stomach fluttered at the words. "We had Gracie, yes, but we aren't together anymore."

"Oh." But they were going together. They were having family time.

"We were together a long time. We met in college, sparks were flying. You couldn't separate us." She smiled at the memory. "Orion went straight into working at Florida Airlines after college, while I was still figuring out what I wanted to do. Saltwater was just a pipe dream at that point. But I knew I wanted to travel, Orion not so much."

"Let me guess." I shook my head, knowing exactly why he wouldn't have wanted to travel. "He was in love with his job?"

"Bingo." Sophia laughed. "He loved it, everything about it. Being a baggage handler, working his way up, it was everything he wanted once he knew he wouldn't be a pilot. We had planned that once he was set up, his career on track, we would travel Europe. It was my dream. I wanted to eat my way through Europe—still do."

"What happened?"

"Gracie happened." The adoration on her face was hard to miss. It was obvious how much she loved her daughter. "Funnily enough, we had planned and booked our trip to Europe, but then we found out I was pregnant. We couldn't afford to go with a baby on the way, and it was just too risky."

"I know this isn't what you are trying to tell me, but one day you will get to go, I'm sure of it." I squeezed her hand.

"I hope so." She smiled at me. "Ry was working really long days. I wouldn't even see him sometimes, and I had the worst pregnancy. Even thinking about being pregnant makes me feel sick. I was put on bed rest at one point."

"I'm sorry you had to go through that." I couldn't imagine that, it sounded like it was really hard on both Orion and Sophia.

"It was tough. Ry tried to be there for me, but I don't think the reality of what I was going through was really all that present for him—he was just so career focused. That was just as the competition between him and John was beginning to really take a toll, as well.

"Anyway, Orion and I split not long after Grace was born. We weren't working, we weren't happy. It was hard, but the best decision for our family. It took some time, but we eventually became good friends again."

This was not what I expected. I'd envisioned Orion as a devoted dad, a doting partner, someone who was there, helping, like he was now. And, "John and Orion?"

"You haven't heard about that? They started at the company at around the same time and were always pitted against each other for promotions, constantly compared to each other, although Orion usually came out on top. Until the last CEO retired. Orion had been assured he was a shoo-in behind closed doors, but when the announcement was made publicly, it was John. Some kind of underhanded deal, everyone is sure. Except Orion, at the time—he felt so betrayed, like he somehow hadn't measured up. That was a year or so ago now."

What the fuck? I desperately wanted to know how that had happened. But the worst part was, Florida Airlines was pitching family values, that it was a place of integrity, respect, flexibility, but with John as the CEO it could never be anything like that.

It was cool to get an insight into it all, especially considering how confused I was earlier, but Sophia and I weren't friends, this was not information I needed to know about my boss. It felt like I was intruding on his life. "Not to sound rude or anything," I said, "but why are you telling me this?"

Sophia looked at me, a mischievous look in her eyes. "I just felt like you needed to know."

I didn't really understand her response, but didn't question it. We got up and started walking back to her bakery.

"Is Grace excited about the trip?"

"Oh, we haven't told her yet." She looked guilty admitting that to me. There was no way I was going to judge the way she parented. I had zero idea what that would be like. "She will just get so excited, which is great, but you know, she'll fixate on it, not want to do anything else but go on the trip, even though we can't go yet."

Yeah, that didn't sound super fun. "I get it." I laughed.

The bakery had gotten substantially busier since we had left. We stopped on the curb and Sophia handed me my box of sweets.

"I have to get back to work," she said. "But I hope you're a bit less confused now," she added with a wink as she started toward the bakery door.

What did she mean by that?

"If you see me on the cruise, feel free to say hi," I called after her.

Oh my god, who was I? Since when did I say, "come say hi"? I outwardly cringed, which made Sophia laugh as she opened the door.

"For sure, I'll say hi." She waved before heading back into Saltwater Cakes.

The trip home felt long; I was still processing everything that Sophia told me.

Orion wasn't with Grace's mom, so he was single? Maybe?

It doesn't matter, Tahlia.

I would only know if I asked, and I couldn't ask my boss if he was single. But it was unlikely he was with anyone else. He had never mentioned anything, not that he was a big life sharer, but he'd never gotten any calls that I knew about, or had anything in his calendar or emails. Surely, if he had a girlfriend, she would email him and I would know. Right?

Maybe he was with a guy?

You're spiraling.

There was definitely something between us, whether he was with someone or not. But it didn't matter, not while I was working at the Airline.

But you're going to quit.

I almost yelled on the train like a madwoman. All because of my stupid thoughts that were trying to make me go into a panic.

I couldn't quit because I wanted to get with my boss, that was gross. I could quit for a better opportunity, and I would. But I had my plan to get Orion his CEO job, so it would all have to wait. But I could barely be around him without losing my mind—even though I didn't actually know whether Orion liked me back. Or if he even liked girls, for that matter.

Oh my god.

Taking a deep breath, I blew it out slowly, consciously counting to four before holding it for four ... box breathing, did they call it? It didn't matter, it worked.

I knew what I needed to do. I had to pretend I didn't have a conversation with Sophia. I didn't know all this new, interesting, juicy information about his life that made me think he could be an option—even though he definitely wasn't an option. I just needed to stop thinking about it!

As I walked up to my apartment, I knew it was time for a wine. It was five o'clock somewhere.

Chapter Twenty-Eight

Orion

WATCHING GRACE WITH HER eyes wide as we made our way onto the ship made me wish I could have done something like this when I was a kid. The way her smile lit up her face as we walked through the promenade, how she started drooling at the line-up of pizzas, made me so happy I was able to bring her. She had wanted to jump into the pool instantly, and I basically had to drag her away. It was like Grace was emulating how I was feeling—giddy, happy, overwhelmed with excitement. We had already completed our safety briefing, found our room, and had something to eat. It was time for Sophia and Grace to have fun, but I was waiting for something ... someone else.

It was close to the time Tahlia was supposed to embark, and my nerves were getting the better of me. With her ticket being bought so close to the trip, I was on edge something might have gone wrong. I could only hope there were no issues because I hadn't spoken to Tahlia properly in days.

Things had been weird with us since Tahlia ran out that day—she'd been distant, withdrawn. To be fair to her, the whole office had been filled with tension since the board meeting, so much so that even I had noticed—despite being largely checked out myself. Those going on the cruise were excited and grouped together, Rachel often in the center of them. But there was this pervasive uneasiness hidden underneath. Tahlia had come back to work—I honestly wouldn't have been surprised if she'd quit—and had been avoiding everyone like the plague, including me. As much as she could, anyway, as my assistant.

It would be a lie to say her avoiding me didn't hurt, but it was probably for the best. I was struggling to keep my feelings under wraps—I wanted to be real with her, tell her how I felt.

Soon, Orion. Soon.

I loitered in the atrium until it was time to meet Tahlia, right near the center of the ship, where all the duty-free shops were. The number of stores was amazing. They ranged from jewelers to a merchandise store, and a 24/7 pizza place. I already knew I would probably go there every day of the trip. I generally tried to eat healthy, but I couldn't resist 24/7 pizza.

I wandered around the area, worried I looked a bit strange just waiting there, not buying anything, when I could be out on the pool deck or doing anything else, really. Looking down at my watch, I realized Tahlia should have boarded an hour ago—at least that was what the time indicated on her ticket.

My heart rate picked up, sweat forming on my brow. Was she even going to come? I really wished I had spoken to her. Maybe I should have messaged her this morning, just a "see you on the ship" or something to check in.

You're overthinking.

Surely, she was coming. There was no way anyone would give up a fully paid cruise. Right?

My nerves got worse the longer I waited. I should have just spoken to her, been up front about my feelings. Maybe then everything would have been fine between us—or maybe that would have made it worse. Maybe we had become too close, too soon, and I blew it. Me being her boss obviously wasn't ideal, but I could have told her that soon, that wouldn't be a problem. I just—

There she was.

My mind had been buzzing non-stop, but when I saw her, it was like everything went silent. She looked beautiful. Her smile was the brightest

I had ever seen, her face free from any makeup, her wavy hair flowing behind her, matching her long floral dress.

My nerves quickly melted in relief, before they kicked up into excitement. She'd showed up. But I needed to tamp it down. I didn't want to freak her out or anything. It was just so good to see her, to finally have the chance to spend time with her as Orion and Tahlia. Not the exec and his assistant. I wanted to be nothing like John.

She was on her phone as she made her way onto the gangway, keeping close to the railing and out of people's way as she typed furiously, a determined look on her face. I didn't approach her. I wanted her to have a moment to herself, to enjoy the space and finish whatever she was doing on her phone.

When she looked up, her eyes immediately locked onto mine. My heart beating so loudly I was sure others could hear, even over the noise of the crowd. I waved at her as she started walking over, the smile she had before still there—now directed at me. I was dumbstruck before I remembered to smile back ... and wave. Waving was the right thing to do here, right?

"Orion!" She pulled me into a hug as soon as she made it over. Had we ever hugged before? I was frozen for a second before my body caught up and hugged her back. If I had my way, I'd have pulled her in tighter, kissed her in front of everyone. But I couldn't. Not yet.

We pulled back from the hug, her eyes lingering on mine before dropping to my mouth. Oh.

"How was the trip here?" Fuck me, what was I doing? Making small talk? Surely, we were past this part of our relationship.

Tahlia gave me a quizzical look before gesturing us to walk over to a quieter section, as we were really in the way of people trying to get on the ship.

The people around us though didn't really seem to care. The excitement was buzzing from everyone, even though it was only a three-night cruise, a taster.

"It was easy. How long have you been onboard?" Her voice was light, bright. I wanted to know what had changed since the last time we had talked, but didn't want to ruin it. Maybe I was imagining it all, and nothing was wrong? Fuck, I wasn't sure.

"Oh, not that long." I shrugged.

"I know things have been weird between us ..." Tahlia met my eyes, her full attention on me. A shiver ran down my spine at the intensity of her gaze. "But this feels like a fresh start."

I had no idea how to respond, so I went with, "Yeah, okay. Sounds good." I wanted—needed to know more, but I didn't want to push.

Things were hopefully going to change between us soon enough. But in a better way.

"I better do my safety briefing thing." I followed her as she made her way to her muster station.

"We actually have a company meet and greet really soon, so we might have to head there straight from this." Tahlia nodded, looking at her phone and then around the ship, determined. I had already gotten lost twice, so I had no idea where we were going. But I wasn't going to admit that.

We walked in silence to her muster station, and I hung back while she spoke to the staff and completed it. My mind went back to her wanting to have a fresh start. Maybe her taking the same day off as me was what she needed—some space, or something. I had been initially surprised when she took it off, but now I was glad she had. Almost relieved. Even though she had said all was fine and to start over, how bubbly she was threw me off. It was like the shadows that had come over her the past couple of weeks were finally dissipating. I tried not to think too much into it, I was just glad that it was passing.

"Let's go." Tahlia pulled me from my thoughts as she bounced back over to me

"You seem like you are feeling better." I commented as we walked to the room where the activities were happening.

"Yeah," she smiled at me, her hand brushing past mine as we walked in tandem. "Much better."

We walked the rest of the way in silence, closer to each other than we needed, our hands constantly brushing each other's.

I needed to quit and tell her how I felt. Now.

I could barely imagine Rachel's presentation to the Air Mexicana going much worse than it was. Having to sit there, eating my dinner, pretending that she was presenting the merger correctly was frustrating.

As much as I didn't want to care about it, I did. This would be my final project, and I wanted it to go well for Tahlia. She had worked so hard on it and Tweedledee was here destroying it.

It was obvious she hadn't practiced, that she clearly no idea what was coming up next or what was even on the slides. What was John thinking? He was making her—us—look stupid. I now knew the full extent of John's fixation on destroying me—but this was directly getting in the way of company goals. The company he was the CEO of, for fuck's sake.

The Air Mexicana executives didn't seem impressed at all.

Tahlia should have been up there. Her charm would have won them over, but how smart she was and how much effort she put into the presentation would have sealed the deal.

I wished she was sitting with me, but Rachel organized the tables. We were in a private room for this dinner meeting, with a main table for the higher execs and their families. Leslie and his family on my left, closest to Rachel while she was presenting. Sophia and Grace were on my right, followed by Phil and Andre, who was Leslie's right-hand man next to them. Directly across from me was John, and Rachel's empty chair. Tahlia was sitting with some other staff from both Florida Airlines and Air Mexicana behind John and Rachel. She was facing me, though, and I could tell she was equally unimpressed.

I was initially surprised that Sophia and Grace were sitting with me, but it made sense when Air Mexicana was all about family—Rachel got that right, at least. Maybe they were trying to be sneaky about how they ruined the deal, not making it obvious it was them.

Even though Tahlia looked disappointed—she wasn't even trying to hide it—I couldn't get over how beautiful she was. She had changed into a long sleeve button-down shirt, which she had tucked into a black pencil skirt. I think I preferred her earlier, more casual outfit. But it didn't matter what she wore. She was still Tahlia.

At that moment, Tahlia looked over at me and subtly rolled her eyes. I grabbed my drink to take a sip to hide the smile forming on my lips. I didn't want to hide it, I didn't want to be sneaking around like John, but we weren't. Nothing had happened. I wasn't John and she wasn't Rachel. We were nothing like them.

"Any questions?" I looked away from Tahlia and around the table of execs, as Rachel sat back in her seat—finished her bumbling at last. Leslie looked professional as always, no hint of his actual opinion on his face, even though I had a pretty good idea of what it would be. Andre, however, was the opposite. Leslie's loyal pitbull, ready to protect the interests of Air Mexicana from fools—like Florida Airlines.

"John," Andre began. "Tell me more about how this merger will actually look. What you—well, your assistant"—he inclined his head to Rachel—"has presented seemed to be a whole lot of hypotheticals. In concrete terms, how will this merger benefit us?" He waved his hand broadly between the Air Mexicana team and ours.

"Leslie, you se—" John slurred slightly before he was interrupted by Andre as I cringed at the obvious error.

"It's Andre, I asked the question."

John's slurring words worried me. He was beyond drunk. I hadn't thought about it until then, but he had been drinking non-stop all night, consistently calling waiters over for generous top-ups.

"Andre, then." John rolled his eyes, swaying slightly in his seat as his mind worked slowly—it was like I could see the cogs in there getting stuck. "It should be obvious—money. We will, you know, expand your business with ours. Make us all rich." He was flushed, had sweat marks on his shirt, and was now slouching over the table, unable to string a proper sentence together. It was embarrassing.

I could see the relationship between our companies fraying before my eyes. Leslie looked sidelong at me as Andre shook his head and leaned back, crossing his arms.

"What does that mean?" Leslie asked. I could tell Andre and Leslie were silently communicating, probably saying "no fucking way are we merging and having to work with this idiot". I didn't blame them.

John, the asshole that he was, had still always been a professional. He'd always liked to drink too much, but I had never seen him get to a state like this at a work event. He knew where to draw the line. But it seemed that he'd forgotten about it once he reached the top—or just didn't care anymore.

"Well, you know," John downed the rest of his drink, not even seeming to realize how bad he was fucking this up. He wasn't just fucking up the deal, it was now the reputation of Florida Airlines.

"So, we are currently expanding beyond being a domestic airline and tha—" Rachel tried to add, before John spoke over her.

"We will work together to make money."

I sighed before deciding I couldn't let this get any worse. "Andre, Leslie, we are looking to expand business with you, before we start offering international flights independently. This will allow us to create a 'home base' at your location, but also provide you the same option with our access to airports across the US. We want to work together to—"

"Orion, did I ask you to answer?" John stood as he gestured for another drink.

I turned at the touch of a hand on my shoulder. "I'm going to take Grace to the room. I don't want her around this," Sophia whispered in my ear. I nodded and leaned down, giving Grace a kiss on her forehead.

"Goodnight, sweetheart."

"Goodnight Daddy." Her tired smile melted my heart and almost let me forget that I was still stuck in the middle of a shitshow.

I was about to respond to John and shut it down when Phil caught my eye. He gave a small shake of his head, his eyes seeming to tell me not to engage. I could also see Tahlia watching me, a curious but concerned look on her face. I wasn't sure she could hear the actual conversation happening at the table, but I was sure the visuals were enough of an indication that things weren't going well.

I decided to listen to my mentor and stay silent, sit back, and watch John dig himself in deeper. I gestured for him to continue as I settled back in my seat.

The room had gone uncomfortably silent, the only noise was people putting their glasses down, or taking long gulps of whatever alcohol they could get their hands on. I had decided not to drink tonight but was starting to regret that.

"I was just about to say what you were, Orion, if you'd let me get a word in."

John's drink was delivered by a waiter who looked like they wanted to be anywhere but there. I didn't blame them. He probably shouldn't have even been served any more alcohol, but I didn't want to even imagine what he would have been like if they refused.

"If you want to be able to actually answer our questions and still have a chance at this merger, you need to cool it on the drinks, John." Leslie crossed his arms over his chest, his family sitting silently next to him. His kids were older than Grace, in high school, but I still wished his wife would take them out of there. This was shit kids shouldn't have to be exposed to.

"Lucky I'm not interested in joining your family affair." John downed his entire drink, turning to Rachel. "This is the only affair I'm interested in." He bent down and forced a kiss onto Rachel, his tongue flying out. It was obvious she didn't want it—it was disgusting. He kept kissing her as he drunkenly threw an arm out for balance, knocking plates and glasses off the table in the process.

I didn't even know what to do at that point. I just knew I was done with whatever circus this had become.

Chapter Twenty-Nine

Tahlia

Everyone at my table was stunned into silence while we watched the clearly drunk CEO of Florida Airlines slather his tongue all over his assistant's face. If I was a better person, I might have felt sorry for her. But Rachel had made this particular bed.

I desperately wanted to know what was being said at the main table, but I was just too far away. Were they telling him to stop? At first, it was so frustrating to not be sitting with Orion. But now, I was also glad I wasn't as the contents of the table went flying under John's weight.

Orion looked detached, like he didn't care. A few minutes ago he seemed worried, but something had happened around when Sophia left with Grace because his expression had changed, the shutters slamming closed over his face. What had John said?

Fuck, this was so frustrating.

Rachel finally pulled herself free from John, her lipstick smeared around her mouth and her hair aggressively mussed. She looked around at all of us before her chin wobbled and she ran from the room. One of the women at my table got up and followed her—I didn't pay attention to who.

John didn't seem to be that bothered that Rachel had run out of the room, clearly upset. He was still making a mess, knocking shit over, calling for another drink. The people sitting closest to John had moved their chairs as far from him as they could. The shock of what just happened was beginning to wear off and the room was filling with quiet murmurs. Though, as I looked at the Florida Airlines team at my table, they didn't seem all that shocked. Most of them looked tired, some stoic, all of them avoiding the eyes of the Air Mexicana staff at our table.

Where Orion's face was studiously blank, Leslie was clearly pissed off, his eyes rolling as he shook his head and pushed his food away. He looked nothing like he had when Orion and I met with him, all kindness from his face gone. Whatever John had said before he made a scene must have been beyond unprofessional. And well, I mean … looking at the state of the Florida Airlines CEO, it wasn't a stretch to imagine any number of things.

"If this is how you represent your company to people you want to do business with, we want nothing to do with it." Leslie gestured for the man next to him to rise, and the rest of their staff followed suit. They looked insulted as they left, leaving only Florida Airlines staff. I hadn't realized that there were significantly less of us attending the trip than them.

I wasn't sure how to react, how to feel, as I watched them all walk out. Everything was catching up to me. I had worked so hard on everything, and John and Rachel went and ruined it in a matter of minutes. But I didn't know if it was worth worrying over, I was leaving—but Orion … I looked back over at the main table to check on Orion and found him watching me, the look on his face unreadable. Even surrounded by this stupidity, I couldn't get over how sexy he was. He had a five o'clock shadow, the top few buttons of his shirt were undone, and his hair was ruffled from running his hands through it.

You could hear a pin drop in the room now, except for John mumbling and chuckling to himself over his glass. Had he even noticed Air Mexicana leave? He tipped slightly to the side, his chair screeching loudly as he fought for balance, and the room flinched. But not Orion. He kept his eyes on me, seeming to barely notice anything else.

John hiccupped and released a high-pitched giggle.

I raised an eyebrow at Orion, the side of my mouth twitching.

Orion placed his elbows on the table, lacing his fingers and resting his chin on his thumbs to hide a smirk. Then he swiped his face and stood abruptly, not bothering to button his jacket.

"Fuck this," he said, throwing his napkin on his plate and walking out.

I promptly followed him, not caring that all eyes in the room followed us out.

Orion was making his way down to the fourth floor where all the shops were when I caught up to him. There were people everywhere, browsing the stores that were so bright and in your face, it was hard to not walk into them. Stalls were set up in the middle of the promenade, with people trying to sell their massage oils, beach wear, and other accessories. I ignored it all, keeping up with Orion, who seemed to have slowed down slightly for me, though he hadn't turned around. We didn't say anything to each other, walking down the stairs in silence, a few people passing us as we went.

To my surprise, Orion went outside, where there were a few chairs, some shuffleboard games, and not many people. The darkness made it hard to see anything beyond the ship, but I could feel it. The waves crashing against the ship, the way the wind whipped my hair into my face, getting it caught in my lipstick. There was no way I could forget I was out on the open sea, even though it was incredibly dark with only the ship's lights and the streaks of moonlight reflecting off the water.

Orion strode out onto the deck and leaned on the railing, overlooking the dark sea. I admired him for a moment, his hair ruffling in the wind, his jacket stretched over his indifferent posture and flying unbuttoned behind him.

How was a guy like him, who looked like that, as kind as he was, as successful in life, possibly single?

His ribs and back expanded as he took a deep breath, exhaling with what would have been audible force up close, before he straightened up a bit and turned slightly. He smiled over his shoulder at me, gesturing to me to join him. There was no point in him asking me to join with how loud the wind was whistling. It was all I could hear. But I didn't care.

I kicked my heels off and picked them up with loose fingers, making my way over to him. With the already rough seas and the wind getting worse, I was sure that I wouldn't be able to walk on the deck in my heels.

"That was crazy," I said as I leaned against the railing. Our arms were barely touching, but it was all I could think about. My body came alive, goosebumps taking over. I tried to cover the shivers that followed, but Orion missed nothing.

"Are you okay?" he asked.

I nodded. "The wind is cold," I lied. The wind was cold, but that definitely wasn't the reason my body was reacting the way it was.

Orion shrugged his jacket off, and laid it over my shoulders. It smelled like him.

"Thanks," I mumbled shyly.

"What?" Orion said over the wind.

I laughed as I leaned closer to his ear, standing on tip toes. "Thank you for your jacket."

At that exact moment, a wave smashed into the ship and I lost my footing, falling into Orion.

"Lucky you took your heels off." He chuckled, placing a steadying hand on my waist. I couldn't tear my eyes away from his lips, even though I knew I needed to. Orion was definitely watching me, staring at his lips like a creeper. I forced myself to look up into his eyes instead, my heart skipping a beat when I found him staring right back at me.

I stepped back slightly and cleared my throat. "What happened back there?"

Orion shrugged, looking away into the darkness again. "John happened. Safe to say, the merger won't be going ahead."

"But that's not okay. We worked really hard to get it to where it was. It's only the first night of the cruise, and what? We've already lost the deal? Surely, the board will be pissed." I couldn't hold back, the anger bubbling out of me.

"It doesn't matter, Tahlia." He still didn't look at me, seeming deep in thought. I wished I could get inside his head and know what he was thinking. Was there something he wasn't telling me?

It didn't seem like Orion to not care about the outcome, about how this would ruin Florida Airline's reputation. There was no way Air Mexicana would work with them again, and when word got out about today ... I may not have been in the industry very long, but I was sure no one would want to work with them ever again. Unless they had someone at the helm who could turn it around. It might not be the way he imagined it happening, but ...

I turned to look at him, as he still looked out at the sea. "Well, at least after John's performance today, the board will surely make you CEO."

Orion looked at me with an intensity in his eyes, the creases in the corners deepening with his thoughts.

"Tahlia." He pulled me closer, the wind so loud now it felt like we had to shout to be heard. At least that meant no one else would be able to hear our conversation. "I don't want that job."

"What?" My brain didn't even want to process the words coming out of Orion's mouth. "What do you mean you don't want it? That makes no sense." I looked between his eyes, trying to figure out what he meant. "This was your chance, I made sure of it. I worked my ass off to make sure it was perfect. Not just because I wanted it to go well, I did, but I was sure that if we secured this deal, we could show everyone it was you, not the idiot CEO that currently appears to run everything. It might not have worked the way I thought it would, but they can't pass you over for CEO now." I could barely catch up my breath, the words rushing out before I really had a chance to think about them.

Orion sighed and tucked my wild hair behind my ear, a gesture that was sweeter than he probably realized. "I don't think you realize how good you are at what you do, and that you deserve so much more," I said.

He tilted his head at me, about to interrupt when I continued. "I know what happened with John getting made CEO, Sophia told me about it. I have no idea how you have worked under that piece of shit for this long and not lost it. It's rightfully your job, not his. You've earned it, he never did. So even if getting it this way isn't how you imagined …" I trailed off as Orion shook his head. He watched me, still saying nothing. I wasn't sure where to look—I hadn't meant to say all those things to him.

"I used to want to be CEO, a long time ago," he said eventually, then paused again. Then a thought seemed to occur to him, and he ran a hand through his hair, a soft smile on his face. "When I got passed over for John, I honestly didn't know what to do, how to bring myself back from it. I just kept going through the motions on autopilot. But then you started. You helped me realize … showed me that there's more to life than this shit. That it was okay for me to want more, good even. That when you get dealt a shit hand, you can pick yourself up and start over again."

"So … what are you saying?" I was never someone who was great at reading between the lines, but it felt like he was hinting at something more. My breath quickened, my heart beating faster than it should.

"I'm done, Tahlia." He visibly swallowed, seeming unsure, before he took my hands tightly in his. "Florida Airlines isn't for me anymore. I'm done. This trip, this deal, was my last project before I leave to start my own business."

I could barely hear, barely listen to what he was saying, my eyes glued on our hands intertwined above the swaying deck. The smell of him from his jacket enveloped me, his calming voice telling me things I was not expecting to hear.

"But don't worry," Orion tilted my chin up to look him in the eyes. "Phil is going to mentor you from here on out, to get you to wherever you want to be. He's a good guy."

My head was spinning. Orion was leaving. He had obviously been planning it for a while, starting his own business, making a plan for me. I needed to tell him I was leaving too.

"I could honestly see you as CEO, if you wanted it. Imagine, Florida Airline's first woman CEO, Tahlia Walters." Orion's smile was so big, so proud, he truly did want the best for me.

"I don't want that." He looked surprised at my blunt delivery, but didn't say anything, waiting for me to continue. I pulled my hands from his, suddenly remembering where we were, who we were. "I quit."

"You're not quitting because I'm leaving, are you?" The worry lines on Orion's forehead appeared.

"No, I scheduled my resignation to be sent earlier today—as I was boarding the ship, actually. I'm done too. I wanted to make sure you got your CEO job, and I thought this merger succeeding was how it was going to happen. But I can't stay. It's toxic, and now especially that you're leaving ... what would I even stay for?"

"I don't know what to say." He looked conflicted.

"Why didn't you tell me your plan? You left me in the dark this whole time!" I punched him in the arm before I could think better of it. "We could have avoided all of this."

"It wasn't even my idea." Orion laughed, pretending to flinch under my attack. "It was Henry, my best friend, who came up with the idea of going into business together. He saw how miserable I'd become, how this place was making it hard to see Grace, have friends, a relationship ..."

"That doesn't tell me why you didn't at least warn me." I still would have worked hard, I still would have tried, but maybe I would have cared less.

Maybe I would have quit sooner.

"Because I'm selfish." He rubbed his jaw. "I thought that if you knew I was leaving, you wouldn't care to work with me, spend time with me. I also wanted to help you with your career because you have so much potential, I think you have no idea the places you could go. I've worked with plenty of people in my time, and there's just something about you."

I was lost for a response, so many feelings bubbling up. Could I say that it wouldn't have deterred me from wanting to work with him?

Could I say that I wished for more time with him every day? Could I say I wanted more than he could offer as my boss?

"Tahlia?"

Something clicked in my brain, something that could change everything between us. I felt the nerves in my chest as I took a steadying breath. "So ... you're not my boss anymore, then?"

Orion's eyes locked on mine. "No, I guess not."

There was a sadness at the thought of not working with him every day, bringing him a coffee every morning, working late nights, but the way he was looking at me gave me hope there might be something else. Something better.

Orion took a step closer to me, my breath hitched as my heart thumped in my chest in anticipation. What was happening? Was what I thought was happening ... happening?

Orion's dark eyes searched mine, a lump forming in my throat. "You feel it too, right?"

I nodded, and his hands found their way up my arms, over my shoulders, and into my hair, a scorched path left in their wake. My entire body shivered from his touch; I couldn't speak, could barely think.

I knew that he understood. I felt everything, even though I had tried to push it all away, to not let myself go there with someone again.

Tim had been my everything for so long—I'd thought I'd met my person for life, only for him to be ripped away in an instant. But now, I had a chance to maybe start over. Tim would want this for me, I knew that, but it also felt like I was letting a big part of my life go. I'd felt like I had been forgetting him, moving on too early. Now, I wondered if maybe that was Tim. Maybe he was somehow telling me it was okay to move on, to be happy.

Orion had been on my mind since I'd met him, but this, this would change everything. It would cement what I felt about him, and what he felt about me. If he kissed me, I knew that I was a goner, that I was his.

My hair blew into my face again, the wind not letting down.

Orion tucked it behind my ear again. "We really need to get you a hair tie."

I laughed. That was the last thing I expected to hear from him. His warm breath mingled with mine as our noses touched, our eyes locked on one another as he pulled me closer. I could hear nothing but Orion's breath and my heart pounding in my ears. It felt like it was going to explode out of my chest.

"Is this okay?" he asked, and I nodded, bumping our noses and making him chuckle.

It was okay, the way his fingers lingered on my ear. The way his five o'clock shadow barely grazed my skin. The way my body buzzed with electricity at the thought of his hands on me more. It was all okay. It was more than okay.

My eyes dropped to his lips, barely a breath away. It was like time had stopped. Neither of us moved, neither of us made a sound, I could see nothing but Orion.

"Can I kiss you?" he whispered.

"Yes." I barely got my answer out before Orion closed the final distance between us, his lips so warm and soft against mine, which were cold from the ocean breeze. I could feel him smiling against my mouth as my lips parted for him, welcoming him.

I wrapped my arms around his neck, deepening our kiss, my body arching into him. His hand roamed down my body, resting on my hip.

Fuck, I didn't know what to expect, but he was a great kisser. I had no idea what I was doing, it had been a while since I'd done anything of the sort, but he led me effortlessly. I melted into him, let myself explore his body, my fingers tangling into his hair.

Orion moaned against my mouth, pulling me closer to him just as the ship hit another big wave and we both lost our footing, my bare feet slipping in the spray.

I yelped in surprise, gripping the open neck of Orion's shirt on instinct as I tipped backwards.

Orion's eyes widened and for a moment, I thought I was going to pull him down with me but, before I really knew what had happened, he'd caught the railing in one hand and me in the other—just before I fell on my ass.

We looked at each other in quiet shock for a moment, Orion kneeling above me, his damp hair hanging down. Then a slow, boyish smile spread over his face.

I burst out laughing as he helped me off the floor.

"Maybe that was a sign we need to head inside." He winked at me, pulling me in for one more kiss before leading me inside.

Chapter Thirty

Orion

As I followed Tahlia to her room, I couldn't help but think nothing compared to her as she was right now: wearing my suit jacket, hair tucked behind her ears, lips swollen from our kiss. It was surreal. Only days ago she was barely speaking to me, I honestly hadn't been sure she would show up for this trip, let alone kiss me where anyone could see.

Tahlia looked up at me shyly as she stopped to unlock her door. Her nerves made her miss the card slot at first, and she huffed a breath before eventually getting the door open and holding it for me. My arm brushed against her as I walked into the room. Her suitcase was opened on a couch, her floral dresses spilling out. As soon as the door clicked shut, it was like her nerves disappeared. My suit jacket fell to the floor with a whisper as Tahlia pulled my mouth to hers, almost desperately. I dragged her body flush with mine, groaning as she ground against me. My heart thundered in my chest as she slid her hand up and around the back of my neck, her fingers gripping my hair. Our lips stayed connected as I lifted her up and she wrapped her legs around my waist. I stumbled over to her bed and pushed the towel swan out of the way, falling back to sit with Tahlia on my lap. She pulled back from our kiss, almost like she was coming up for air. I admired her flushed face, the look in her eyes, the way her hands roamed my body.

She started to undo my shirt, as I sucked her neck. Tahlia's breathing became shallow as she melted further into my touch, and the sound of her erratic breaths had me straining against my pants in a way I hadn't in a long time.

My shirt was thrown unceremoniously on the floor, and Tahlia's hand roamed my chest as she brought her lips back to mine. Her other hand trailed down my body, feeling my cock through my pants. A strangled noise made its way out of my throat.

"Fuck," I hissed through my teeth, wanting her to not stop touching me, to be in this moment with her for as long as I could. But if we didn't do something soon, this was going to be over before it started.

I couldn't let that happen. I pushed her to stand, picking her up and laying her down on the bed. Seeing her spread out beneath me snapped any remaining restraint I had and threw it out the window. I ripped her shirt open, buttons flying everywhere. Underneath, her breasts were spilling enticingly out of a purple lace bra.

"Rude." Tahlia rolled her eyes at me as a grin spread across my face.

I couldn't help but kiss her—I loved her sense of humor. We were on the same wavelength—we always had been. "I'll buy you a new shirt," I said as I threw it off the bed. Her nipples tightened under my touch as I traced the lace pattern on her bra, and she shivered. "If I knew you had this on, I wouldn't have had such restraint."

Tahlia giggled, wiggling her eyebrows at me. "That was you with restraint?"

Fuck, her sassy attitude was hot.

"You going to take the rest off, or just stare at me?"

"Oh, baby," I breathed. "I'm going to do more than just take your skirt off."

Her breath hitched at that, a hunger in her eyes as her breasts rose and fell with each breath. There was no way I would last long with Tahlia looking this hot—and she wasn't even close to being naked.

She started to shimmy her skirt off, but I stopped her, taking both her hands and holding them above her head. She narrowed her eyes at me, but the small upturn of her lips that bloomed into a smile despite her best efforts, reassured me that she was just being Tahlia. Playing the game.

I couldn't suppress a grin in return. "I'll be taking that off for you, baby. So impatient." I leaned down and kissed her, making my way down to her breasts. I pushed the fabric away, exposing a perky nipple, before I sucked it into my mouth. Tahlia bucked beneath me, moaning. I let her hands free and they immediately found my hair, tugging at it gently as she tried to bring me back up to her mouth.

I reached under her and unclasped her bra, discarding it somewhere before feeling my way down her stomach to the waistband of her skirt, skimming my hands just under the hem, enjoying the way her stomach pulled taut under my touch.

"You're killing me, Orion." Hearing her use my name, her voice husky from my touch, made it almost impossible to hold myself back.

"If you have something matching that bra under here, you might just kill me." I kissed her stomach as I unzipped her skirt and pulled it down.

She didn't have matching underwear on. She had on white cotton panties, which were somehow sexier than a matching set.

I slipped my fingers under the band of the panties, finding her clit slippery from her arousal. "Mmm," I almost growled, knowing it was for me, because of me.

"Finally." Tahlia sighed, dropping her legs a little wider, a content look on her face. I kissed her as I rubbed her clit. She moaned and writhed as I flicked her nipple with my other hand. "Ry …"

I couldn't help the moan that escaped, the way my body bucked against her, begging for release. She had never called me that before, but I was pretty sure I never wanted her to call me anything else again.

I was certain Tahlia was close when she abruptly swiped my hand away, sat up, and pushed me off the bed, palms flat against my shoulders. My mind instantly reeled. Had I pushed her too far? Maybe she didn't really want this? Fuck. "Are you okay?" I drew back. Tahlia frowned as she looked at me and the distance I'd put between us, silence filling the space, until she noticed the clear concern on my face.

"Of course," she said. There was a sense of amusement to her expression, the corners of her eyes giving her away.

"Do you want this?"

Tahlia giggled, her head falling back, exposing her soft neck. "Uh yeah," she gestured to her naked body, her nipples tight, her thighs squeezed together. "I just wanted to get you naked." She reached out and slipped her fingers into my belt loops, pulling me to stand in front of her.

"Are you sure?"

"Yes, Orion." Tahlia smiled seductively up at me, her hair messy and all over the place as she undid the barely-holding-it-together zip of my pants. I couldn't take my attention away from her as she did, her arms pushing her breasts together, her eyes widening as she dragged my pants down my legs, leaving me just in my black boxers. Her face was level with my cock as she looked up into my eyes once more, my stomach tightening at the sight as she pulled my boxers down, leaving me completely naked.

She licked her lips, staring at my cock.

"Fuck, you can't do that." I was sure I was done for the second she touched me.

"Do what?" she asked innocently as she brushed her thumb over the wetness at the tip.

I almost fell forward at the touch, pleasure rippling through my body, and she'd barely done anything. She pumped my cock a few times before running her tongue along the length.

Fuck. Me.

"Tahlia." I barely breathed out. "What are you doing?" I didn't want her to do something she didn't want, or thought she ha—

"Fuck me." She sucked my cock into her mouth, her eyes locked on mine while she continued to pump the base of my cock, swirling her tongue over the tip. My knees wobbled, and I slid a hand into her hair on instinct, gripping for balance.

She moaned around my cock, and I watched her as her hand slid down to her clit, getting herself off as she got me off. I wasn't going to last.

I pulled her up and frantically kissed her as I laid her back down on the bed, spreading her knees with mine as I climbed onto the bed. I needed to be in her—now.

"Shit."

"What's wrong?" Tahlia sat up, a concerned look on her face.

"I don't have a condom." I hadn't bought condoms in a couple of years; why bother since I wasn't having sex. I sure as shit wasn't expecting to be having sex with Tahlia on this trip.

"That's okay." She kissed my nose as she got up and opened her suitcase, fishing around for a minute before she pulled out a pack. She held it up triumphantly, doing a small celebratory dance, which made me both laugh and get harder with her breasts bouncing around.

"You're prepared." Tahlia having a packet of condoms was the last thing I expected. "Were you expecting this to happen?"

She shook her head at me. "I wasn't expecting it to, no." She didn't explain further, but from the blush creeping across her cheeks, I guessed maybe she'd hoped something would happen.

Fuck, she was so sexy when she blushed.

Tahlia pulled a condom from the packet, placing the box within easy reach on the nightstand. Without breaking eye contact with me, she climbed onto the bed again, tearing the foil packet with her teeth before rolling it down my cock.

I laid her gently back down under me, hovering over her slippery entrance, barely able to hold back. I was on my elbows, keeping my weight off her, our rapid breaths mingling.

Tahlia looked confused at my hesitation. "I'm just savoring the moment," I reassured her, kissing her as I finally pushed into her. We moaned together, Tahlia's back arching off the bed. "Tell me if you want to stop."

"Don't you dare."

I started to slowly pump in and out of her, kissing her neck. She tugged my hair, bringing my mouth back to hers.

I flipped us over, Tahlia riding me without missing a beat while I rubbed her clit. Her head fell back as I moved her up and down on my cock.

"Ry, I'm going t—" Tahlia cried out, her body shaking from the pleasure, her pussy gripping me and sending me speeding toward my own release.

"Fuck," I grunted, pumping into her until I was completely spent. She collapsed onto my chest and I pulled her close as we both caught our breath, a comfortable silence filling the space.

I wasn't sure I could feel happier, more content, than I did at that moment.

We stayed like that for a while. I played with Tahlia's hair, not wanting to leave the moment. I thought back over everything that had led us to this point. John calling me into work on my day off, Tahlia spilling her coffee on me on her first day, Tahlia pushing me for more work, to give her a chance.

I couldn't help the smile that grew on my face thinking about who she had become in our time working together. But also at how I'd grown. I wasn't sure I'd be doing the things I was: starting a new business, making more time for my family, if it wasn't for her. Working with her showed me that there's more to life than sitting behind a desk, wearing a suit and tie, answering to the devil day in and day out.

My excitement had been growing every day for this new chapter, to do things the way I'd wanted, have more time for my family, more time for a relationship even. Knowing that there was now nothing standing between Tahlia and I made me feel giddy.

Tahlia turned her head to look at me, a satisfied smile on her face. She kissed me, so gently, before she rolled off me.

"I definitely didn't expect that." She chuckled as she got under the blanket.

"Can I stay?" I wasn't ready to go. I wanted to be with her all night, snuggle her, wake up to her morning breath and make lo—um, be with her again.

"I'd be upset if you didn't." She got up out of the bed, rummaging through the discarded clothes.

"Where are you going?"

Her eyes had turned mischievous. "Having a shower. Want to join me?"

My cock was already getting hard again at the thought of Tahlia in the shower. I chuckled as I got out of the bed and followed her into the shower. "You are going to be the death of me," I teased.

But I'd have it no other way.

Grace was making a very lopsided sandcastle but enjoying it nonetheless. I was so glad that Sophia and Grace were able to come on this trip with me, especially since it was very last minute. This was the sort of thing I was looking forward to doing more of now that I was done with Florida Airlines.

"Grace, my princess," I called, "come here, we need to reapply your sunscreen." Grace slowly made her way over, knowing that she needed to have more on, but not wanting to pause building her sandcastle. To be five years old again, without a care in the world.

I slathered her in probably more than she needed before she ran back to her sandcastle making. Sophia appeared, a tray in hand with a drink for each of us and some juice for Grace.

We had an island day that day. Sophia and I had gotten out here early so we could spend some time with Grace. The ship was docked not far from where we were. Groups were all around us, couples, families, kids, older people. I didn't recognize anyone from Florida Airlines, but I also didn't care anymore. I just needed to hurry up and officially resign.

"So, how was your night?" Sophia asked nonchalantly as she settled back into her beach chair. She didn't look in my direction as she asked, trying to hide the smile that was creeping onto her face.

"It was good." I had to hold back the grin that wanted to take over my face at the thought of the night before with Tahlia. It was so good, more than good. It was definitely not what I had planned, but I couldn't hide my feelings anymore. We were no longer working together, so it was okay, and she obviously felt the same.

"What did you get up to?" Sophia wasn't stupid. She knew what had happened, I was sure, especially since we were sharing a room and I didn't come back. I did message her on the cruise app to make sure it was okay with Grace and all that, I just didn't tell her why—or who I was with. But she had a brain and eyes and could put two and two together.

I wondered how long I could not say anything before Sophia came right out and asked.

"Nothing really."

"You piss me off." She narrowed her eyes at me. "Tell me!"

"I'm not one to kiss and tell, Soph."

She squealed, her excitement taking over. "I knew you two would be together eventually." She sat back, crossed her arms and looked out at the ocean for a moment before pulling out her phone.

"Me and who?" I could barely hold back the laugh as she shook her head at me.

She ignored me. "I need to call Henry."

"Leave my best friend out of this." I rolled my eyes at her.

"You seem happy, truly." Hearing this from Sophia, one person that I trusted wholeheartedly, warmed me even more. I was happy. I was never sure I would meet someone again that I wanted to be with like Sophia. Now, I'd found someone I wanted more than I did when I was with her.

I knocked my arm against hers, "I am." I took a big swig of my beer as Grace came running back.

"Mommy! Daddy!" Sand flew everywhere, into our open drinks. I guessed I didn't really want a beer anyway.

"What is it, sweetheart?" Sophia reached for Grace's juice bottle, opened it and gave it to her. She gulped some down before giving it back to Sophia.

"Will you swim with me?" She looked between us, adorable in her polka dot long sleeve one piece.

"You finally asked!" I feigned relief as I stood up and picked Grace up with me. She giggled as I turned back to Sophia. "Want to come?"

"You two have fun." She waved for us off. I put Grace on my shoulders as I walked down to the water, but as soon as we were at the water's edge, I put her back on the ground and held her hand as we went in. The water was freezing, but Grace didn't seem to care while we splashed in the shallows.

As I spun Gracie around, I wondered if things between Tahlia and I had moved too quickly. It had been barely a day since she was my employee. I wasn't one to make rash decisions, especially now that I was a dad—not that anything to do with Tahlia and last night was rash. I'd been thinking about it longer than I should have. But I honestly hadn't intended for anything to happen between us yet, not that I was upset it did. I was getting ahead of myself, the thoughts sitting at the back of my mind. We hadn't spoken about what we were, what we could be. I would love a relationship with her, but I would honestly be happy just spending more time with her if that was all she wanted.

But I really hoped she wanted more.

I looked back towards where Sophia was on the shore and saw Tahlia talking to her. She had no idea I had seen her. She was wearing one of those floral dresses, her bathing suit peeking out around her neck.

"Who's talking to Mommy?" Grace asked, curious.

"That's my new friend, Tahlia." She got excited, but seemed to forget about it as another wave came, and we jumped over it hand in hand. I looked back again and caught Tahlia smiling at me.

I waved, my heart leaping when she waved back.

Chapter Thirty-One

Tahlia

WHEN I'D SEEN SOPHIA on the beach in the morning, she invited me to the spa with her that evening. I wasn't sure about at first, but she convinced me. I had a feeling she wanted to know about what had happened the night before.

I left before Orion got out of the water, feeling awkward for some reason. Maybe awkward was the wrong word. Different.

His daughter was playing in the water. It was cute, it warmed my heart. I hadn't had the chance to meet Grace yet, but I hoped I would. It would depend on whatever it was we were. The last twenty-four hours felt like a whirlwind. I could barely believe what happened. When I woke up that morning, I thought I had dreamed everything—the dinner disaster, the kiss, and everything after. But then his arms tightened around me as he spooned me, both of us still naked, the hair on his warm chest tickling my back ... It was perfect.

I was contemplating whether I should go to the spa with Sophia when Claire called me.

"How is it?!" I pulled my phone away from my ear. She didn't bother with the niceties, but why would she? We'd known each other that long, we didn't need to bother.

"It's been great." My voice was weird, I was weird. I wanted to tell her about everything that had happened, but I didn't have enough time.

"Spill."

I almost laughed at her reaction. "I will, but I can't now. I'm supposed to be going to the spa with Sophia, Orion's daughter's mom."

"Okay, go have fun."

"But I don't know if I should go." My mind was telling me I should, it would be nice. But on the other hand, maybe she just invited me to be nice and I should cancel. Say I was sick or something.

"Tahls, stop." Claire's change in tone took me by surprise. "You're going. Go have some girl time, enjoy the spa, and then straight after call me and dish this gossip that I really hope is what I think it is."

Maybe Claire was right. I just needed to stop worrying and go enjoy myself. "Okay, I'll go."

"If I don't hear from you, I'll be getting on a helicopter onto that ship to come find out the gossip." I could imagine the look on her face. Fully serious with the slightest smirk. I missed her.

"I'll call you."

"You better," she huffed before hanging up.

I quickly grabbed my things and met Sophia outside the spa, no Grace or Orion in sight. It was probably a good thing. I needed to have some time away from him after being so swept up in it all. I just wanted to be in his arms, under the sheets, but it was so new, we needed to not be with each other constantly. I assumed, anyway. It had been a long time since I'd been in a new relationship. If that's what this was. I hoped it was.

Sophia pulled me into a hug, her messy bun bobbing around. She looked calm. Her face makeup free, she was in some comfy clothes, and had a big smile on her face. "Ready for some ultimate relaxation?"

We were ushered into a room for our treatments—I had no idea what they were. I was just happy to be there. The lighting in the room was dark, mood lighting almost, a lavender diffuser left the room smelling amazing, and it was the perfect temperature.

Sophia and I were lying on beds next to each other. I kind of hoped it wasn't a couples' massage—surely that would be weird? I didn't realize I'd basically shown my thoughts on my face until Sophia gave me a reassuring smile.

"Don't worry, I've booked facials and manicures."

Thank God.

I'd never really been to a spa before. Everything about it, especially the facial, was so relaxing. The silence made my thoughts take over, it felt weird to talk in this room. My mind wandered back to last night with Orion, how good it was, how natural and easy everything felt. I was so nervous going back to my room, not because I didn't want to do anything with him, but because I really wanted to. I hadn't been with anyone in a while. It felt big.

Everything had all moved fairly quickly, which didn't worry me too much, but I wondered what Orion thought. Had he told Sophia? Oh no, would things get weird between us now? She was his ex, the mother of his child. We were only new friends. Surely, she would be fine with it? She was the loveliest and understanding person I knew. But the speed of it all, I was curious what she thought.

Eventually, we were taken to another room for our manicures, which thankfully distracted me from my racing mind. "How are you and Grace liking the cruise?" I asked Sophia.

"Grace has been loving it. I have too, but it's exhausting chasing after her." She laughed as she showed the nail tech what color she wanted. "How about you? Seems like you've been having some fun." Sophia's suggestive tone and wink answered my earlier question. She definitely knew.

I could feel my face going bright red. I had no issues if Orion had said something, but I wondered what he'd told her.

"You don't have to tell me about it." I was so thankful for Sophia. I wasn't even sure if I could say we were friends, but she was a great one. Not pushy, there to talk about anything, I would love to get to know her better. "But I'd love to know."

"Isn't it kind of weird? He's your ex."

She shrugged. "Nah, just means I know how good he is in the bedroom." We both burst out laughing. It was the absolute last thing I expected her to say.

"I didn't expect it at all." I admitted. Last night was wild. I didn't expect I would tell him I was quitting; I didn't anticipate he would tell me he was too, and I definitely didn't think that would turn into sex. "But I'm surprised he's quitting."

It was like a light bulb clicked for her. "Ahh, that makes more sense." She must have seen my confused expression before continuing. "Orion is a good guy, too good. There's no way he would have done anything with you, no matter how much he wanted to, while he was still your boss. He didn't tell me anything! I thought we were friends." She pouted and I chuckled. "I'm sure he'd tell Henry all about it."

"That's his best friend, right?" I remembered Orion mentioning Henry was who he was starting this business with.

"Yeah, you'll love him." It was weird to think of Orion having other friends outside of Sophia and Florida Airlines. But we'd never really spent time together outside of the office, so what could I expect?

"Do you think I'm making a mistake leaving the airline?" I blurted before I could think about it. I hadn't really spoken to anyone about my decision—Claire had been too interested in my love life. Maybe it wasn't a smart move to leave. Orion said he thought I had the potential to be a CEO, and he said Phil would mentor me. Was it an opportunity I was throwing away?

"You have to do what's right for you. From all the shit I heard from Orion, it sounded like a pretty awful place to work." I stewed on that while Sophia washed her hands as directed by her nail tech. She had picked a pastel color, one that would match Saltwater Cakes beautifully.

"I don't know what I'm going to do next, though." I admitted when she came back. "I have no other job lined up—how am I going to pay rent? Oh shit, I shouldn't have resigned." I started to panic.

What was I thinking? God, I was fucking stupid.

"Tahlia." Sophia placed her hand on my shoulder. I looked at her, a kind smile on her face, which eased my panic. Slightly. "It will be okay."

"How?"

"Ry can help. He would love to, I'm sure." How she made everything sound easy and not stressful, I just didn't get. I wondered what it would be like working under her. Was she as calm of a boss as she was a friend, or was she stricter, tougher?

"I'm not sure." I was sure he would help, but we'd just started whatever this was yesterday. It felt weird asking.

"Just because you are together now doesn't mean he won't help you."

I sighed, feeling strange. "I know, but he's done so much for me already. He pretended to be an asshole boss to get people to be nice to me at work, he gave me opportunities, helped mentor me. I can't ask him for more."

"He's just a good guy, like how he paid for your trip. He won't mind." My stomach dropped. What was she talking about?

"Sorry, what?" Sophia looked at me, confused. "What do you mean, he paid for my trip?"

Her eyes widened. "You didn't know?" I shook my head, not sure what to think. "John wouldn't budge, and Orion knew you deserved to be here, so he paid. He makes more than enough money."

"I ... um ... What?" I was lost. Orion paid for my ticket? That was way too much money for him to spend on me.

It's fine Tahlia. It was his choice.

There were two sides of me, one saying that he couldn't do that, it was too much, but the other side of me realizing how much he cared for me, that he truly had my back. He had said multiple times I deserved to go on the trip, and he'd make sure I was there, and he did.

"I wouldn't have said anything if I knew you didn't know." Sophia admitted. "But he did it out of the kindness of his heart. He wanted you here."

I mulled over that information for the rest of our time in the spa. It was kind, so incredibly kind, but was it okay? We were ... sleeping together? I wasn't even sure what to label our relationship, and he'd paid for me to come on this trip. I just didn't know what to think.

I had to talk to him.

Orion and I had agreed to meet at the Sunset Bar at the back of the ship, an hour or so after the spa with Sophia. The bar was bustling with people, live music and laughter filling the space. I could still hear the sound of cocktails being shaken over it as the ship rocked gently on the water. I didn't get dressed up, just went wearing the dress I'd had on all day and ordered an espresso martini while I waited for him.

I had so many mixed emotions about everything. It had been a long couple of days. I needed a vacation. I wasn't sure what to say to Orion, if I should say anything at all. He either didn't want me to know or hadn't had the chance to tell me. It was unlikely he was trying to hide anything from me, that wasn't the kind of person he was. He probably just didn't think to tell me; he was too kind for his own good.

I decided I was going to ask about it, though. I couldn't sit on it. I needed to know for sure why he did it. For no reason other than it was going to drive me mad.

"Hey." Arms snaked around my waist and a kiss was planted on my cheek. I turned to see Orion sliding into the seat next to me, a smile on his face. He was dressed much more casually than normal, in shorts, a t-shirt, and flip-flops. Somehow, it was hotter than his usual suit.

"Hi ... you." Orion's eyebrows drew together in confusion. It was obvious that he knew something was up.

"What's wrong?" He ordered a beer and took a swig as he waited for me to explain. I wasn't even sure what to say. It felt weird, especially in this super open place.

"Maybe we can go somewhere else to talk about this?" I suggested. His face dropped as he nodded. Shit, I was scaring him. We took our drinks and made our way out onto some chairs near where we'd kissed for the first time, only yesterday. I paused, stuck for what to say. I couldn't think of the best way to ask my question, not wanting it to come out wrong.

"You're worrying me, Tahlia, what's going on?"

I took a deep breath, trying to calm myself. "Why did you pay for my ticket?" After saying the question, it sounded like such a small thing to accidentally freak him out over, but to me, it felt big. Money wasn't something that I just had, which I should have thought about before quitting. I was such an idiot.

"Oh." He smiled. "Did Sophia tell you?" I nodded. Orion took my drink and his, placing them on a table before taking my hands in his. "You deserved to be on this trip more than anyone. I knew you likely said you couldn't come because you couldn't afford it. Considering my ticket was paid for, and I have money, I wanted to make sure you could come. I didn't want to be here without you."

"But, I can't pay you back." My head dropped, feeling embarrassed at that thought.

"Oh Tahls." He tilted my chin up, so I was looking him in the eyes. "You don't need to pay me back. It was a gift. If it makes you feel any better, it was barely a dent in my bank account."

I laughed. How much money did this guy have? More than I'd probably ever had in my life.

"Are we good?"

I nodded as a smile took over my face. "Good, you scared me. Here I was thinking you were going to say last night was a mistake."

There was genuine worry on his face. I pulled his hands to my mouth and kissed his knuckles. "Never." Orion pulled me onto his lap and brought my mouth to his, his breath fresh, kind of fruity like he'd chewed some gum, but also mixed in with the smell of his beer. It was so intensely intimate, I wanted to bottle it. All my previous thoughts of everything disappeared, and all I could think about was this. This moment. His mouth on mine, the way I could feel his want for me in his shorts, the way his hands felt on mine.

"I can't do what I want to you out here," he mumbled against my lips.

It was like we blinked, and we were back in my room, the condoms on the nightstand from last night, my clothes still all over the floor, the bed unmade. It was like we'd never left.

I couldn't wait for him to do it, and pulled my dress off, leaving me in a matching set. I didn't usually wear matching underwear—it seemed too much for everyday—but his comment last night and then the desire on his face when he saw what I had on made me want to see what his reaction would be if I actually did have a matching set on.

"Do you like it?" I teased.

"And you got matching nails." He admired me, not touching me, but fuck it felt like he was, the way his eyes raked over my body. "I love it."

Orion joined me, striping down to his boxers, which looked like they were struggling to hold his cock in. I licked my lips, remembering what it felt like to taste him.

"I don't think so." Orion shook his head, drawing my attention back to his face. "It's my turn to taste you, don't you think?"

My mouth went dry as a blush took over my neck and face. My stomach tightened at his words, my panties already soaked.

"Sure thing." I puffed out. How could I say no to that?

He took his time, kissing me, sucking my neck, stripping my bra and thong off. Everywhere he touched felt like it was on fire, goosebumps covering my body. I'd never felt like this before during sex. Sex with Orion was a whole different ball game.

I touched him through his boxers, wanting desperately to rip them off, but Orion didn't let me. He laid down on the bed and waited.

I went to grab his boxers again when he stopped me. "I said I wanted to taste you. Come and sit on my face, baby."

Oh, shit.

I stumbled but quickly complied, a little bit worried I would suffocate him, but by the way he made me give him all my weight, he clearly didn't care. As soon as his tongue touched my clit, I was teetering on the edge. My body bowed in response to his touch, my head resting on the wall to help keep me upright as I gripped his hair to hold him in place. My mind went hazy the closer I came to finishing, and whimpers took over my body, my head flying back as I came from one final swipe of his tongue. I was sure I was going to be getting a call from guest services with a noise complaint real soon but, legs like Jell-O, I found I didn't care.

Orion wriggled out from underneath me, and I heard him grab a condom. I turned to watch as he swiped it on quickly, then reached forward and grabbed my hips, pulling them back towards him with a grin to put me onto my hands and knees in the center of the bed. I couldn't help the moan of anticipation as, his hands on my ass, he lined up and pushed into me with one steady motion.

It somehow felt more intense than last night. He kissed my shoulder as he pumped in and out of me, my heart melting at the sweet sentiment. I knew he was close, but I didn't want it to end like that.

I pushed Orion onto his back and straddled him, his eyes widening with curiosity as I took over. He didn't say anything, just smiled at me—a happy, almost drunk smile. We were chest to chest as I moved up and down, our eyes never straying from each other. We came together, our chests heaving as we kissed, sitting there in that moment, enjoying whatever it was this was becoming.

Chapter Thirty-Two

Orion

FARING A BREAKFAST BUFFET with a five-year-old was no easy feat, but Tahlia looked like she was having the time of her life. Grace was enamored by her, loving her from the minute I introduced them.

Sophia was having a sleep in and insisted I had breakfast with Tahlia and Grace. She didn't even blink an eye about them meeting before she fell right back asleep.

Tahlia followed closely behind Grace, helping her pile pancakes onto her plate, drowning them in syrup. It warmed my heart to watch. I was grateful for Tahlia doing that with her, it gave me a few minutes to type out an email.

I was officially submitting my resignation—without notice. I was sure John was expecting it, he might even be excited, but I didn't care.

"I shouldn't have been surprised by the show John put on." I looked up and found Leslie standing next to my table, a plate filled with food in one hand and a coffee in the other.

I shook my head, trying not to laugh at the memory of John the other night. As embarrassing as it was for Florida Airlines, as I finished typing out my resignation, I couldn't find it in me to care. "Are you meeting someone?" I asked.

"Yeah, you." Leslie sat down with no further warning.

"Please." I chuckled.

"Are you eating alone?" Leslie took a long sip of his coffee as he got comfortable in his seat. It was busy that morning at breakfast, children running around everywhere, waiters coming and collecting the dirty dishes the minute people were leaving, other staff singing.

"No, my daughter and Tahlia are getting food." I nodded over to where Tahlia was getting Grace a glass of juice. Leslie didn't say anything in response and started to dig into his crispy bacon and eggs.

"Just so you know," I began, feeling like I needed to have Leslie understand that I was nothing like John and wasn't putting up with his shit anymore. "That was the last straw. I'm leaving Florida Airlines. You actually interrupted me resigning."

Leslie's fork stopped midair, his eyes wide. "Good, I'm glad to hear. Do you have a plan?"

He continued to eat while I decided whether I wanted to tell him or not. We were friends and had been for a long time, so I didn't need to be worried about him telling people or trying to ruin it for me. He wasn't anything like John, and neither was I.

"I'm starting my own company with a friend." I explained a bit further on what plans Henry and I had. I didn't realize how excited I was about the actual work until I was talking to someone about it.

"If that's the case, I may be reaching out to you—especially now that this merger isn't going ahead."

"I'm glad to hear it." We shook hands and Leslie got up, taking his food over to eat with his family. It wasn't long until Tahlia and Grace were back, Grace telling me all about the different food in the buffet. I eventually went and got some breakfast of my own to fill up on before the fun day we were spending together.

I didn't expect Grace's energy to last all day, but she was unstoppable. We had been on the slides, had done bumper cars, even ice skating, and she was still filled with energy.

A movie was playing in the theater shortly that Grace wanted to watch—I was just hoping she wouldn't still be bouncing off the walls afterward. It had to be the syrup and juice she'd had with breakfast.

Tahlia looked like she was getting as tired as I was, chasing after her. Sophia joined us after lunch, even though I had said she was welcome to have the whole day to herself.

We grabbed some pizza and drinks from the pizza place, then made our way into the theater. Grace picked our seats and chose to sit between Sophia and I, leaving Tahlia on my other side.

There weren't many people in the theater, considering the size of it, but I wasn't surprised because of how nice the weather was. *Frozen* started playing—yes, of course it had to be *Frozen*—and Grace's eyes were glued to the screen.

All of the kids in the theater were giggling and making a ruckus, but Grace didn't seem to care, and neither did Tahlia.

I leaned over to her, my lips so close to her ear I felt her shiver. "You don't have to stay and watch this, you know."

She nodded before turning back to the screen, having no intention of leaving. Her soft hand found mine, and we intertwined our fingers, staying like that the rest of the movie. Sophia definitely looked over and wiggled her eyebrows at me a couple of times, but I ignored it, wanting to enjoy the moment.

I hadn't even noticed, distracted by Tahlia's hand in mine, that Grace had fallen asleep halfway through the movie. Even though it was *Frozen*, I wasn't surprised given how much running and playing she had been doing.

We all still stayed until the end, when Grace woke up, rubbing her eyes, a little bit sad that she missed most of the movie.

As we were walking out, I checked my phone and found a message from Leslie from an hour ago.

Leslie: Have dinner with Andre and I tonight?

Tahlia didn't love the idea of having dinner with people from Air Mexicana, even though she knew Leslie was lovely. She didn't know Andre and, well, neither did I really. But if Leslie had him work that close with him, I had no doubt that he was similar to Leslie.

I gave her a few outs to not come, but she walked in with me, our arms brushing as we made our way over to greet Leslie and Andre, who were already seated.

We were having dinner in one of the exclusive restaurants on the ship. It was an Italian restaurant with dim lighting that was much more intimate than the standard dining rooms. The tables all had red tablecloths, wine glasses ready to be filled, and overflowing baskets of bread waiting to be devoured.

"Orion, Tahlia." Leslie pulled me into a hug and then Tahlia as we arrived at the table, a wide smile on his face. "Tahlia, I'm not sure you have officially met Andre—he is our COO."

"Nice to meet you." Andre shook both of our hands. We obviously weren't friendly enough yet for hugs, but with Leslie here buying what I was sure would be a very expensive bottle of wine, we would all become close friends soon enough.

I pulled out Tahlia's chair. She seemed genuinely confused until I gestured for her to sit. Leslie chuckled from the other side of the table. "No one is used to a bit of chivalry these days."

I placed my napkin on my lap, with Tahlia copying me as the waiter came and poured the red Leslie had ordered into our glasses.

We all looked at the menu, deciding what to order. We ordered copious amounts of garlic bread for the table, Tahlia ordered a vodka penne, and I ordered the carbonara.

"I assume neither of you had anything to do with that disaster of a night." Andre smiled.

Tahlia shook her head as I explained. "Not that specific presentation, no. It was Tahlia's slide deck they used, but as I'm sure you could tell, they had nothing to do with organizing the merger."

"That much was obvious." Andre took a sip of his wine. "I was honestly a bit disappointed that you weren't presenting, Orion. Especially considering your relationship with Leslie—it just made sense."

Our garlic bread was delivered to the table, smelling fucking delicious. We all immediately dug in. "I would have been happy to present, had the opportunity been offered. I would have actually preferred Tahlia did, but that wasn't an option, unfortunately."

Tahlia looked like a deer caught in headlights at the mention of her, a piece of garlic bread halfway to her mouth, her eyes wide.

"So, Tahlia." Andre turned his attention to her. "I hear you were the one to come up with this whole trip idea."

Tahlia visibly swallowed and took a big drink of her water before responding. "Yeah, but I don't know if I want to take credit for it now that it went to shit." She seemed to realize what she said as soon as it came out of her mouth, but Andre and Leslie just laughed. I knew they'd both like her.

"How long have you been with Florida Airlines?" Leslie asked.

"Four months." She looked at me before continuing, seeming to gather some courage. "But I won't be returning." She relaxed after that, a smile blooming on her face after getting it out. I wasn't sure why she was so nervous, but it was kind of cute.

"And you hadn't done a similar role in the past?" She shook her head as Andre and Leslie looked at each other. They were impressed.

"Poor Tahlia. I asked her to accompany me to dinner, not to an interrogation." I laughed, knowing that she probably wanted a break from all the questions. "I believe you asked me here for a reason?"

Our mains were delivered, leaving everyone to mull over what I said. I had a pretty good idea of why Leslie wanted me to have dinner with them, but I hadn't told them I was bringing Tahlia. I was curious about their thoughts of her. I could tell they were impressed, and I knew Leslie liked her.

"I wanted to see what you could do for us, Orion," Andre answered. I was interested in Andre's and Leslie's relationship. It was nothing like John's and mine. They seemed to work together, make decisions together, ask for each other's opinions. I wondered what that was like.

John and I, I was sure, were an anomaly between CEO and COO. Sure, people didn't always get along, but for the CEO to sabotage the work I did for the company we both worked for was surely unheard of. I couldn't imagine Andre and Leslie being like that.

I was sure that Leslie was prepping Andre to take over from him some day. Andre didn't need to be here, but Leslie wanted him, I assumed because he respected his opinion. I respected the hell out of Leslie for the way he handled business.

"Just because this merger failed, it doesn't mean we don't want to improve. We never really loved this idea of a merger, as you would know, but how could you work with us to make us better? I want your ideas," Andre explained further.

I knew these were the sort of questions I was going to be asked, but I still took my time to think before answering. "My first suggestion would be to rebrand." Tahlia was nodding along beside me, like she agreed wholeheartedly with what I was suggesting.

"What do you think, Tahlia?" Leslie asked, seeming to notice what I had.

She seemed taken aback, but quickly pulled her thoughts together. "I agree with Orion. Rebranding would really lift your company up and modernize it. Air Mexicana, while a beautiful name, feels ... outdated. I believe there would be so much you could do even just by changing your name, logo ..."

I don't know how she read my mind, but she did. Tahlia had barely been in the business for six months, but here she was, providing the kinds of ideas some people never even thought of. Or if they did, they certainly didn't have the guts to suggest a total rebrand to a company as well-established as Air Mexicana.

I continued by asking them some deeper questions about their internal systems and workflows, listing off some broad ideas they could implement based on the information they gave me.

"I'm impressed." Andre smiled at us both.

The rest of the dinner went smoothly. We talked a bit more business, had a lot more wine, and overall just chatted and had fun together.

It was obvious how impressed with Tahlia they were, specifically when she came up with all those ideas for their rebrand. We had kept bouncing off each other, giving them more ideas, some of which they pushed back on, but there was no way I wasn't going to be working with them very soon.

A thought was niggling at the back of my head for the rest of the dinner. I couldn't do this without Tahlia—I didn't want to.

Half of the ideas she'd come up with, I would have never thought of. I needed someone who had fresh eyes, who had worked in the business, even if it was for a short period of time, and who knew me. We worked so well together—the thought of us not working together anymore was something I didn't even want to think about.

She had quit Florida Airlines without a backup plan. Maybe she could work with Henry and me? She would fit right in—I knew she and Henry would hit it off. It would just work.

I had to talk to Henry about this quickly and offer her a job before she found another one. But she couldn't just be my assistant, definitely not. I'd get someone else for that at some point, maybe. Maybe she could be our operations manager?

I laughed internally, thinking that Tahlia could basically be our small company's COO.

As I walked back to my room after saying goodnight to Tahlia at hers, I texted Henry that he needed to call me. He, of course, thought I was calling to talk about me—Sophia had clearly spoken to him—but as soon as I suggested Tahlia join us, he was one hundred percent on board.

Chapter Thirty-Three

Tahlia

Quitting Florida Airlines was the best decision I ever made. The month since the cruise had flown by, and I was the happiest I had been in a long time. Orion ended up offering me a job with him in his new venture. I was skeptical about accepting it at first, especially since our relationship was so new, but I was loving it.

There was a knock at the apartment door.

I waved Jeremy away and said, "I'll get it." I opened it to find Sophia, a bottle of wine in one hand, a book in the other. She had her hair in her signature knot and a massive smile on her face.

"Come in!" I pulled her in for a hug and led her to the lounge room where everyone was.

It was a book club evening. These had become my favorite time of the month. I had easily fallen into the group, no longer feeling like an outsider. They had made the move to Florida so much easier, and I couldn't be more grateful.

When I mentioned the book club to Sophia a few weeks ago, not long after we had gotten off the ship, I could see it in her eyes that she wanted to join. I told her she was coming to the next one and, well, here she was.

She had opened up to me that being a single mom meant that it wasn't always the easiest to make friends. The only real opportunities she got were at daycare drop off and pick up and when she went to parents' groups, which she didn't feel like she really fit into.

But I was so glad she did come. Since Orion worked for himself now, he could have Grace.

"Everyone," I called out as we entered the space. Everyone was in their regular seats. Since we hosted book club fairly often, even though we tried to rotate it around, everyone had no issues claiming their unassigned-assigned seats. "This is Sophia, Sophia this is Ashton, Jeremy, Liam, Suzie, and September." There was a range of mumbled "hi's", "hello's", "welcome's", and the exchanging of pronouns. Sophia situated herself on the couch next to Ashton, with September on her right sitting on a new beanbag we got them on the floor.

"Food should be here soon!" Jeremy shouted over all the noise. Book club had slowly become less about books and more about food. We still always brought books and talked about them in some capacity, but we had lately been having takeout or cooking big meals to go with it. It was like a casual dinner party every month. I loved it. "Tahls, can you help me in the kitchen?" I followed Jeremy to the kitchen and started collecting plates and cutlery.

"I feel like we never have time just the two of us anymore." Jeremy pouted. "This new boyfriend and friend of yours, stealing you away from me."

I pulled Jeremy into a tight hug. "You know you'll always be my number one—don't tell Claire." There was a mumbled "obviously" into my shirt before he pulled away.

"How are things going, anyway? With the new job with the new boyfriend?"

It felt weird calling him my boyfriend. Not just because Orion was my boyfriend—which still blew my mind sometimes—but because the word felt so ... young. I knew that I was young and Orion was older than me, that didn't bother me at all. But it felt weird calling him my boyfriend. I don't know, I was probably just overthinking it.

"It's been great, we are working on so many cool projects, but not too many. It's honestly been better than I could have imagined."

"And Orion? Your boss? Your boyfriend?" Jeremy crossed his arms over his chest, one teasing eyebrow raised. "If he isn't treating you right, babe, just let me know." Before I could respond, Jeremy continued. "Jokes aside, I am so happy for you, Tahls. You are just so much happier, thriving, living your best life. I'm so proud of you."

I couldn't respond, my throat tight, my heart warm. "I love you, Jeremy."

"I know."

I couldn't help the laugh that bubbled out. I wanted to ask him about him and Ashton. Things had been weird between them for a while, and I was worried. I didn't know Ashton that well, but I had no idea why he was with a guy like Steve.

But the food was almost here, and I didn't want to spoil Jeremy's mood, so I pulled him in for another hug instead before we carried the plates into the lounge, setting them down right before the pizza arrived.

We usually went for Chinese, or Indian, but pizza was voted for tonight. I wasn't complaining—I loved pizza.

I sat down next to Suzie and Liam, seeing Sophia deep in a conversation with September, grabbed some pizza and wine, and just enjoyed being around all these people that made Florida feel like home.

After we had gotten off the ship, before Orion had even offered me a job, Andre and Leslie reached out officially to start working with him. Air Mexicana was his first official client and everything had been going smoothly.

We were currently in a meeting with Andre and a few others, going over the suggested changes, and potential new business names. Leslie wasn't at this one due to a time conflict, but he trusted Andre to handle it.

I was trying to take notes on what was being said in this meeting, but my head was bursting with ideas. I'd never thought I'd be someone with so many ideas, but it was kind of cool. I quickly jotted them down before continuing to listen to what Andre was saying in this meeting. We ended up going slightly overtime, but everyone seemed to be happy to continue. I looked at the time as we were winding up—it was getting close to when we had to leave, but we weren't late yet. I didn't say anything, figuring Orion would handle it.

I was right. Barely a minute later, Orion checked his watch and looked at me.

"Sorry guys, but we need to run," Orion said when there was a short gap in the discussion. "Gracie has a dance recital."

"No worries." Andre smiled on the screen of the video chat. "You both have a great time. We can't wait to see some pictures."

"I will have plenty." Orion smiled as he packed up. "I'll set up another meeting so we can continue this. Have a great afternoon." We said our goodbyes.

Not only had I been happier since leaving Florida Airlines, Orion was obviously so happy. He saw Grace so much more, had her spend the night every week, and we had so much time to spend together outside of work.

We got in the car and drove over to where the recital was being held. "You excited?" I took his hand in mine.

"Of course." He was such a girl dad, so smitten with her. He would do anything for her. He reached into the back seat and grabbed the bouquet of flowers he'd bought for her. "I think it might be time for me to buy a house, move out of the apartment," he said casually.

I was surprised, not because of what he was suggesting, but because it was right before Grace's recital, so out of the blue. "Oh?"

"The apartment is nice, just not right, though." I nodded, understanding what he meant. I loved his apartment, from the very first time I saw it, but it was just not him. At least not the person he was now. "Will you come look at houses with me?"

"Definitely."

He leaned over the console and kissed me deeply before pulling back.

We met Sophia just outside, who embraced both of us tightly. Making our way in, we found that Henry had already got there and saved us front-row seats. Uncle Hen Hen, as I'd heard him be called, really loved that girl too.

Grace had got lucky with the people she had in her corner growing up.

We didn't have to wait long until the show started. There were so many dances, some older kids, some the same age as Grace, but I didn't have to worry about knowing when Grace was on because Orion made sure of it.

"That's my girl." I wasn't even sure he knew he had said it, his eyes locked on her. Sophia and Henry weren't much different, but I got it. She was special, that kid, twirling around in her tutu, waving at her mom and dad—which I was pretty sure she wasn't supposed to be doing.

Orion didn't take his eyes off her the entire time, looking completely happy, relaxed and just in love with his life. And, for the first time in a while, I was in love with mine.

Sad that Tahlia and Orion's story has come to an end?

Head to www.authorjoannerose.com/bonuschaptersignup or scan the QR code below for a bonus chapter:

Acknowledgements

This book started out as one character, moving across the country to restart her life. It then turned into two, eventually more, and then a draft. A draft I knew wasn't the final version but a finished draft nonetheless. It then morphed into the final book you have just read, but it didn't get there with just my own efforts. There was endless work from so many that I will forever be grateful for.

I have to start by thanking my husband, Alex. For being my biggest cheerleader, reading random chapters and providing feedback even though it was entirely out of context, and encouraging me to continue when I wanted to delete the document and just give up on my dream. There is no way this book or my dream of becoming a published author would have happened without his never-ending support.

Thank you to my family for also cheering me on, asking consistently when they could read my book (which is still a terrifying thought, even though they have probably already read it by now), being the first to subscribe to my newsletter, and even being beta readers, providing some much-needed feedback on the book.

On that note, the beta readers—this book wouldn't be what it is without their feedback. Some new characters were born, chapters written, and changes made to make this book be the best it could be, and I couldn't be more grateful. A special thank you to Lucy for suggesting 'Catching Feelings' for the title.

Cass, my friend, I thank her for being the first to read this book before it went through editing, providing valued feedback on what I knew was a very rough draft. But I also need to thank her for being a great sounding board, advice provider, cheerleader, and author friend who knew the feelings of writing and rewriting. Having another author to talk to throughout this process has made me feel seen and less alone in what can be a very isolating industry.

Finally, to the team at Author's Own Publishing, for helping me bring this book to life. Having a team to help me publish my first book has been a help I never thought I would have. I have learned so many skills and the process of publishing, which I know I would have fumbled through without their help.

About the Author

Joanne Rose is a contemporary romance author from Canberra, Australia with a love for stories with tropes such as enemies to lovers, he falls first, and slow burn. When Joanne is not writing or reading, she can be found snuggling with her cat Catniss, crocheting and watching her favorite shows.

To keep up to date on Joanne's future works, visit her website and Instagram:
authorjoannerose.com
Instagram: authorjoannerose

Check out her books and leave a review!

Scan to review on
Goodreads

Scan to review on
The StoryGraph